RUDE AWAKENING

This time when she woke, her eyes flew immediately to the lamp by her bed. It had gone out. And yet, an eerie glow was filling the room.

Margaret squeezed her eyes shut and began to pray. "Please, dear God, make it go away, and I will never be disrespectful again and I will always obey, and I will not think terrible thoughts, and I will—"

"Who the devil are you?" a harsh voice rang out. "I have a deuce of a headache, and I'm in no mood for games tonight. Nor do I need a whore, so I'll thank you to leave my room now, or I'll boot you out on your pretty arse."

"*Whore?* Why you . . . you insolent scoundrel! You impudent . . . whatever you are!" Carefully holding the blanket to her chin to preserve her modesty, she glared at him.

What are you doing? shrieked a small, panic-stricken corner of her brain. This was a *ghost,* for heaven's sake! Not for the first time in her life, she had allowed her temper to draw her into an untenable situation. Pride kept her chin up and her eyes fastened to his, but her mouth trembled as she waited in dread for him to punish her impudence with some sort of supernatural retribution.

His gaze fell to her mouth . . .

Ghostly Enchantment

✂ANGIE RAY✂

HarperPaperbacks
A Division of HarperCollinsPublishers

This is a work of fiction. The characters, incidents, and
dialogues are products of the author's imagination and are not
to be construed as real. Any resemblance to actual events or
persons, living or dead, is entirely coincidental.

HarperPaperbacks *A Division of* HarperCollins*Publishers*
10 East 53rd Street, New York, N.Y. 10022

Cover illustration by Jeff Barson

First printing: March 1994

Printed in the United States of America

HarperPaperbacks, HarperMonogram, and colophon are
trademarks of HarperCollins*Publishers*

❖ 10 9 8 7 6 5 4 3 2 1

In memory of my father, William A. Scharf,
and with eternal thanks to:
Sandy Chvostal, Colleen Adams, Judy Barton,
Barbara Benedict, and most especially,
my husband, Ken.

Prologue

London, July, 1769

   Soon, very soon, the trial would be over.
Holwell would be found guilty of murder, and then
he would hang.

   Roger Carew, Earl Mortimer, knew what the hanging would be like, for he had attended many.

   His favorite part was when the hangman placed
the noose around the prisoner's neck. The crowd
always hushed at that point. Then came the loud
clacking of the trapdoor and the roar of approval
from the mob. Sometimes—if he was close enough
and the people quietened—he could hear the creak of
the rope and the raw, gasping breaths of the prisoner.
In his mind's eye, Mortimer pictured Holwell hanging
like that, death sucking the last discordant notes of
life from his flailing, twitching body.

   Mortimer smiled.

   A sharp elbow poking him in the ribs distracted
him from his pleasant vision and knocked his wig

askew. With an oath on his lips, he turned to castigate the dolt, only to realize that the long line of lords was moving forward. Quickly he adjusted his powdered wig before following the others into the courtroom.

Beating mercilessly through three high arched windows, the sun heated the small, airless room to an almost unbearable degree. The lords, in their heavy black robes, perspired profusely as they filed into the long rows of benches. Soon the mingled scents of sweat, powder, and cologne thickened the air, making breathing an unpleasant chore. But Mortimer didn't mind, he had waited for this day a long time.

Baron Robeson, appointed Lord High Steward for the occasion, took his place high above the row of judges, facing the lords. His square, heavy jaw dipped toward the Clerk of the Crown, who stepped forward and began reciting the proclamations.

Mortimer managed to maintain a suitably solemn expression while the clerk spoke, but inside he gloated. Although Holwell had put up a lively defense, the preponderance of evidence was against him. Numerous witnesses had told of the loud and frequent arguments between Holwell and Alicia; and yesterday, a maid had testified that she heard Holwell threaten to murder Alicia the night before she died. Mortimer permitted himself a small smile. The trial was going extremely well.

"Is it your lordships' pleasure that the judges have leave to be covered?"

As Lord Robeson spoke, Mortimer quickly composed his features. He answered in a sober voice along with the other lords.

"Aye, aye."

The judges donned their hats and the Clerk of the Crown arose. "Sergeant-at-Arms, make proclamation for the Lieutenant of the Tower to bring his prisoner to the bar."

Mortimer leaned forward. Craning his neck, he lifted a hand to shield his eyes from the windows' glare. He did not want to miss the moment when Holwell would slink into the courtroom. He wanted to see Holwell's face. Would his expression be frightened? Hopeless? One thing was certain. After yesterday's testimony, Holwell would definitely not be smiling.

Just thinking about Holwell smiling made Mortimer's eye start to twitch. How he hated that smile! Whenever Holwell smiled, he tilted his head back and stared down his nose. Somehow, the arrogant angle of his chin, the mocking gleam in his eyes, always made Mortimer feel the way he had many years ago when a whore had laughed at his inadequate performance. That smile made him feel as if Holwell *knew* about the whore's laughter.

Today, though, Holwell would not be smiling, and that would be one small payment for what Mortimer had suffered at Holwell's hands: the defeats, the humiliation, and most of all, the loss of Alicia and Caroline.

"Oyez, oyez, oyez!" the Sergeant-at-Arms announced, pounding his staff on the wooden floor. "Lieutenant of the Tower, bring forth Lord Holwell, your prisoner, to the bar, pursuant to the order of the House of Lords."

Unconsciously, Mortimer leaned forward, twisting the ornate ruby ring on his finger.

The door opened and Phillip Eglinton, Viscount Holwell, entered the courtroom.

Under the bright auburn flag of his hair, Holwell's gray gaze met Mortimer's. Heavy, dark brows arched, and slowly—almost casually—Holwell flicked his thumb across his nose. Then he tilted his head back and smiled.

Mortimer stilled for a moment in utter disbelief before fury raged through his veins. Damn Holwell for a mocking devil! Bending his head forward, he struggled to control his anger. He forced himself to think of his careful planning, of his clever use of the secret he had discovered—the secret of which Holwell knew nothing. Likely Holwell expected to be acquitted or, at the very worst, heavily fined. He would soon discover his mistake and he would hang.

But even this pleasant thought failed to cheer Mortimer. Settling back in his seat, he tried to regain the sense of satisfaction he had felt earlier. It eluded him. Instead, he felt a niggling unease.

The Eglintons had been an irritant to his family for as long as he could remember. His earliest memories were of his father, and his father's father, cursing the Eglinton name. It was ridiculous, and yet he could not shake off the growing apprehension, a foreboding almost, that somehow, somewhere, another Eglinton spawn would come to torment him and his family; that in life and even in death, as always, the Eglintons would triumph.

He had to do more than just eliminate Holwell. He had to do something else. Something to thwart the arrogant Eglinton seed, wherever it dwelled, for all eternity . . .

1

Berkshire, July, 1847

Miss Margaret Westbourne sat silently next to Bernard Denbeigh, Lord Barnett, on the horsehair sofa. She spread her green silk skirts into a perfect half-circle, straightened her spine to a perfect vertical, and clasped her hands together loosely in her lap so that her arms formed a perfect oval. She knew she looked like a perfect lady, because her mother had made her practice the effect in front of the mirror until she got it exactly right. Holding herself rigidly, she waited.

Silence filled the room.

Did Bernard appreciate the graceful pose? Margaret wondered. She decided to risk a peek from the corner of her eye. Much to her chagrin, he was not even looking at her. He was staring down at his watch, turning it in the palm of his hand, studying first the shiny gold bottom, then the intricately carved initial on the lid. She could not quite make out the letter, but from the way Bernard looked at it, she supposed it must be very interesting.

His fingernail pressed against the catch and the lid flew open with a slight click. He stared at the clock-face for what seemed like a long time.

Perhaps he was watching the minutes of his life tick away, thought Margaret.

He closed the lid and she heard a small snap. He began to play with the catch, clicking it open, and snapping it shut. *Click, snap. Click, snap.* Apparently he was fascinated by the way the lid flew open every time he depressed the small metal catch . . . *click* . . . and by the way the lid fitted so neatly against the face . . . *snap. Click, snap. Click, snap.*

The sound stopped suddenly as something caught his eye. Pulling out a handkerchief, he wiped a spot from the case with meticulous care. He tilted the watch in the light, checking the shine. Satisfied that the gold had no further tarnish to dull its luster, he put the watch and the handkerchief back in their respective pockets, inhaled deeply, and turned toward her. For a brief moment his eyes met hers; then his gaze skittered off to a point behind her.

"Miss Westbourne, thank you for allowing me to call today," he began. "I came because I, ah, er, that is, I had a talk with your father yesterday."

He swallowed convulsively a few times, the noise plainly audible in the silent room. Manfully, he continued.

"A most interesting conversation. Most enlightening. We spoke on many topics. Estate matters. Sheep. Horses. Breeding. And . . . and I don't know precisely how it came up, but Mr. Westbourne observed that it was time I thought about marriage. Which is absolutely true. Absolutely. The Barnett title is a proud one. If I don't marry and produce an heir . . . well, the name and title will die out. I don't quite know why I have been so negligent of my duty. He—your father, that is—mentioned that old agreement he and my father made. Mr. Westbourne said, er, that is, he gave me to understand that you have considered yourself betrothed to me all this time. I was completely unaware of this."

Margaret's lips tightened, but she did not say anything. What could she say? That she had been completely unaware of it also?

"After the . . . er, the . . . er, misunderstanding with my father, I had thought the arrangement was completely void. I was very surprised. I . . . I must confess, I had some reservations about the situation. I hope you understand my hesitation. I do not like to go against my father's wishes, even now that he is dead. If he were alive, then of course I would not be making this proposal. Unless he could have been persuaded to change his mind. And naturally, I would have made every effort . . . but . . . but since he is dead, I wish to do the right thing, the honorable thing. So, in spite of some doubt on my part—only because of the way my father felt about you, you understand—Mr. Westbourne convinced me that it was my duty . . . I mean, I decided that a marriage between us would be a very sensible thing."

Bernard's eyes flickered to her face. With conscious effort, she forced a smile to her lips. His gaze quickly returned to that point behind her.

Her smile faded.

Truly, what did it matter if her father had applied a little pressure, appealing to Bernard's gentlemanly instincts? A woman on the verge of spinsterhood could not afford to be particular—especially a woman who was not quite acceptable socially, besides being too tall, with plain brown hair, and unremarkable blue eyes. The important thing was that he was actually asking her to marry him. What did it matter if romance was decidedly lacking in his proposal? She was certainly not looking for Prince Charming to come along and sweep her off her feet.

Fortunately for her.

Discreetly, Margaret studied her suitor. Under drooping lids, eyes of indeterminate color stared fixedly at the wall behind her. His habit of tucking his chin back as far as possible emphasized the slight beakishness of his nose, and tailoring could not disguise the forward slope of his shoulders.

Bernard was certainly no Prince Charming.

"You would be a viscountess," continued Bernard, still not meeting her eyes. "And mistress of your own household. And . . . and one day, Motcomb House and Barnett Manor would be united. My father greatly desired this, before . . . before the 'incident.' He often said that Motcomb House was the best property in the area, and he wished that he had been able to come up with the purchase price when it was for sale all those years ago. But that is really not relevant, so, er, let's see, oh, yes, I . . . I have the greatest respect for you, Miss Westbourne. I admire your virtue, and your maturity, and . . . and . . . and . . ." His throat worked as he struggled to formulate the words. "And your dowry will be put to good use," he gasped. Pulling out his handkerchief again, he wiped his forehead.

Margaret kept her lips parted, but her smile felt suspiciously like a grimace. Although she concentrated on unclenching her teeth and relaxing her neck muscles, she did not think she was particularly successful. It actually didn't matter though, since he still wasn't looking at her.

"I . . . I think we will suit very well," Bernard finished. "What do you say, Miss Westbourne?" He pulled out his watch and started playing with the catch again.

Margaret hesitated. Not because she was thinking of refusing. Certainly not. Bernard was her chance and she meant to seize it—him—with both hands. She would finally be accepted again. By everyone. No one would dare snub the Viscountess Barnett. She would no longer be an outcast, a social pariah because of that scene she had made. . . .

Click, snap.

It was only that accepting Bernard's offer was much more difficult than she had thought it would be. A tiny rebellious part of her that she had thought died long ago, was trying to make itself heard. But she wouldn't listen—she couldn't. Because she couldn't bear for her life to continue as it had for the last eight years. . .

Click, snap. Click, snap.

This sick feeling in her stomach was merely nerves—it would soon pass. It was time to forget her silly dreams. Dreams she couldn't even explain or understand. Dreams that could never be found and could never come true . . .

Click, snap. Click, snap. Click, SNAP!

Margaret jumped.

"Miss Westbourne! May I have your answer?" A disapproving frown pulled the corners of Bernard's mouth down, and Margaret felt a flare of defensive anger. He had waited eight years to remind her of the marriage contract, he could wait a few seconds for her answer.

But her anger fizzled quickly. She must forget the past and think of her future; and there was only one thing to say. Tugging discreetly at her bodice, she straightened her already straight back, and looked him straight in the eye. "Yes, Lord Barnett, I will marry you."

Her parents were waiting in the blue drawing room. Mr. Westbourne looked up from a ledger book, his hazel eyes bright with expectancy. Mrs. Westbourne's needle paused over her embroidery hoop, an eager smile on her narrow, aristocratic face.

Bernard spoke first. "Miss Westbourne has agreed to make me the happiest of men," he said in a colorless voice.

"Ha!" Her father jumped to his feet. For a moment, Margaret thought he would dance a jig. Instead he rushed forward and clapped Bernard on the back. The force of the blow caused her new fiancé to stagger.

"Ha!" exclaimed Mr. Westbourne again, beaming with delight. "It's about time. Congratulations, my boy. Thought you'd never get around to it. Margaret ain't getting any younger, you know. She's already twenty-three, aren't you, Margaret? Yes, we were beginning to think she was going to be an old maid, ha, ha." He turned to her and held out his arms.

Reluctantly, she allowed herself to be clasped in his burly embrace. He pressed her face against his coarse black hair, and hugged tightly, almost squeezing the breath out of her. "Good girl," he whispered. After one more mighty squeeze, he released her and turned back to his future son-in-law.

"You're a lucky man, Barnett. My daughter will make you an excellent wife. You're getting a fine bargain. I shouldn't have had to up the ante, by gad, no, I shouldn't."

Up the ante? Exactly how reluctant had Bernard been? Margaret wondered. She felt like a bit of rubbish her father had to pay the dustman to take away.

"Well, never mind. I don't. The money is well spent if it makes Margaret happy. My little girl engaged! Barnett, this calls for a drink." He pulled the younger man over to the sideboard where fortuitously a bottle of champagne waited. After pouring the liquor, he passed the glasses around.

"To the union of Motcomb House and Barnett Manor," Mr. Westbourne declared, raising his glass briefly before swallowing the champagne. Margaret's chest was still too tight to drink anything, so she pretended to sip hers. Bernard gulped his down—rather desperately, she thought. The two men headed back to the bottle, leaving Margaret and her mother in relative privacy.

"Darling, how wonderful!" Mrs. Westbourne rose on tiptoe to kiss her daughter's cheek. "At last I'll be able to hold up my head again." She sipped her champagne daintily. "It hasn't been easy these last eight years. People are slow to forgive the kind of behavior you exhibited. But not even Lady Creevy will be able to criticize you now, not when you will outrank her. Besides, who is she to condemn, when Lord Barnett himself has obviously forgiven you? I must call on her this afternoon to tell her the news. You've done well, dear."

Feeling vaguely uneasy, Margaret tugged at her bodice where the wool pads of her "bust improver" were chafing. It was rare that her mother approved of anything she did. Gaining Mrs. Westbourne's approbation usually meant doing something Margaret didn't want to do.

Her mother nodded in satisfaction. "I am so happy for you. Lord Barnett is such a good man, you won't even notice his nose after a while. It is a pity he's not a shade taller, though. He's barely an inch or two taller than you, isn't he? Not that his appearance matters, so long as you are happy. You are happy, aren't you dear?"

"Of course, Mama."

"Of course you are. He's such a nice boy. I'm very fond of him, although I used to think he was a trifle spiritless. But now I see I was mistaken." She drank the last of her champagne and moved toward the sideboard where the bottle rested.

Margaret looked away from her mother and over at the men, who stood some distance away. She could hear her father talking about tearing down fences and consolidating flocks.

"What a great day it will be, when the two estates are one," boomed Mr. Westbourne. "I only wish your father could be here today."

Her fiancé looked down at his glass. "As do I, sir."

"When is the wedding to be?" Mrs. Westbourne inquired, returning from the sideboard.

"I thought perhaps October," said Bernard.

"Oh, no," Margaret said involuntarily. All eyes turned to her and she swallowed hard.

"That's less than two months away," she stammered. "Not nearly enough time for all the preparations. There is so much to be done. The wedding dress, the trousseau . . ." Her voice died away.

"Margaret's right," Mrs. Westbourne said. "We don't want this to be a paltry affair. Lady Creevy will not be able to sneer at the smallest detail. November will be much better."

It was a small reprieve, but a reprieve nonetheless.

"Hmmm," grumbled Mr. Westbourne. "I don't see what takes almost three months to prepare." He looked suspiciously at his daughter. "But I suppose if that's what you want, we can wait."

In her relief, Margaret smiled radiantly. Mr. Westbourne blinked, then returned the smile, his whole face softening perceptibly. "Whatever you want, Meggy, that's fine with me. You're a good girl." He hugged her again, and this time, Margaret hugged him back, clinging to him for a long moment.

Bernard coughed, and spoke hesitantly. "If I might make a request? I am sure my aunt, Miss Leticia Chetwynd, would like to meet my future wife. Would it be possible for Miss Westbourne to come with me to visit her? My sister and her husband will be there also."

Margaret's heart sank. The idea of visiting with Bernard and a houseful of his relatives was not appealing.

"Miss Chetwynd?" Mr. Westbourne frowned. "I seem to recall your father mentioning her. Didn't you live with her for a while when you were a boy?"

"After my mother died, until I was ten," said Bernard. "In later years, my father and she did not get along. She is a trifle . . . eccentric. Fortunately, they did not have to see each other very often since she lives in Durham."

"Durham? Where is that?" Geography was not Mrs. Westbourne's long suit.

"It's north of Yorkshire, Mrs. Westbourne."

"North of Yorkshire!" Her tone was as shocked as if Bernard had said St. Petersburg. "Heavens, that is quite a distance. Margaret will have to have a chaperon." She seemed to wilt a little. "I wish that I could accompany her, but my health is so delicate."

Mr. Westbourne patted her hand. "My dear, you mustn't think of taking such an arduous journey."

"I fear you are right, Mr. Westbourne," said his dutiful wife. "Perhaps Cousin Winifred could accompany her."

"She won't want to leave her garden," Margaret predicted, hoping to somehow avoid the visit.

"Nonsense. Once you're there, Miss Chetwynd will be sufficient chaperon and Cousin Winifred may return."

"I would like to leave in one week, if possible," said Bernard.

"I will send a message to Cousin Winifred right away. Excuse me, please." Mrs. Westbourne left to write her letter and Bernard picked up his hat and gloves.

"I will make the preparations, then." He bowed to Margaret. "Good day, Miss Westbourne. Until next week." With a nod to her father, he strode hurriedly from the room.

Mr. Westbourne smiled beatifically after him. "My little Margaret—engaged!" he said joyfully.

Cousin Winifred spent much of the journey complaining about the noisy, smelly train, and her crotchets increased when they arrived in Durham and found no carriage waiting. Standing in the heat while Lord Barnett hired a vehicle caused the bunion on her big toe to ache and her faded blond curls to droop.

When she first saw Durnock Castle, however, Cousin Winifred was considerably cheered. "How romantic!" she exclaimed, sticking her head out the window. "Your aunt is very fortunate to live in such a place, Lord Barnett."

The central rectangular building stood between two eight-sided towers, all built of gray stone, with slitlike windows. In front, the huge arch where carriages had once passed had been completely walled in except for the doorway. There were even two gargoyles on either side of the arch to glare at arriving guests. As Margaret climbed down from the carriage and walked up the steps, the sense of oppression that had plagued her all week lightened.

Cousin Winifred is right, she thought. It is romantic.

The massive oak door opened with a shrill creak and a solemn-faced butler bowed them into the castle. After the heat outside, the huge flagstoned hall felt pleasantly cool to Margaret. In the dim light, she noticed a faded red-and-gold banner hanging on one wall and an old suit of armor lurking in a dark corner under the staircase.

"Where is my aunt, Gibbons?" Bernard asked, handing his hat and gloves to the butler.

"In the west parlor, my lord. Shall I announce you?"

"No, we will go ahead. Thank you, Gibbons."

They trekked across the hall to a door, which Bernard opened, revealing an eight-sided room. On a delicate rosewood sofa sat a tiny old woman, wearing an enormous gray wig. She looked up with a startled expression. Seeing the small group standing in the doorway, she rose to her feet, a jar clutched to her bony chest.

"Who are you? What do you want?" she asked in a quavering voice.

"Aunt Letty, it is I, Bernard," said Bernard, moving forward to kiss her cheek.

"Bernard?" She peered nearsightedly at his face. "Is it truly you? What are you doing here?"

"I brought Miss Westbourne to meet you." He took the jar from her unresisting grasp and placed it on an ivory-inlaid table. "The lady I am going to marry."

"Marry!"

"Yes. Remember I wrote you a letter?"

"Oh. Oh, yes. It must have slipped my mind. My dear girl, how wonderful to meet you." With surprising grace, the old woman walked over and embraced Cousin Winifred. Bernard pulled her away and redirected her to Margaret.

"My dear girl," she said again, unfazed. She hugged Margaret warmly, causing her wig to slip a little to one side.

Margaret, feeling sharp, brittle bones, hugged her back gently.

"I am so happy for you and Bernard." The old woman smiled up at Margaret, a thousand wrinkles splaying out over her face.

She must be ninety years old, at least, Margaret thought. "Thank you, Miss Chetwynd."

"No, no. You must call me Aunt Letty. And I shall call you . . . what is your first name, dear?"

"Margaret," Bernard supplied.

"Margaret," repeated Aunt Letty, nodding and smiling. "And who is this other lady?"

"This is my cousin, Miss Winifred Driscoll." Margaret's reply was a trifle distracted. She had noticed a large hole in Aunt Letty's wig. It looked as though moths, or perhaps mice, had feasted upon it.

"Delighted, Miss Driscoll," said Aunt Letty. "But come, sit down, please." She sat back down on the sofa, next to the little table where the jar was. There were only two hoop-backed chairs in the room, so Margaret sat down next to Aunt Letty on the sofa.

The butler came in with a tea tray and Aunt Letty asked Margaret to pour. "My hands are not so steady as they once were," she explained.

"Certainly," Margaret replied, glad for something with which to occupy herself.

"What a surprise this is," said Aunt Letty, accepting her cup with a hand that shook slightly. "Bernard, you should have told me you were going to ask Margaret to marry you."

"I wrote you," he said again.

"Did you? Never mind. My dear, let me look at you." Aunt Letty leaned over closer to Margaret, almost spilling tea in her lap. Margaret gave an uncertain smile. "Ah, yes, how pretty you are. Bernard, you didn't tell me how pretty she is." She looked accusingly at Bernard. He hunched his shoulders and didn't reply. With a shake of her head, Aunt Letty lifted Margaret's hand and patted it with skeletal fingers. "I suppose I shouldn't complain just because Bernard omitted a few details. Actually, he has told me so much about you, I feel as though I know you."

Her cup halfway to her lips, Margaret paused.

"Aunt Letty—" Bernard clanked his cup down, causing some of the liquid to slosh over the edge. "Could we go up to our rooms? We must change for dinner."

"Oh, are you staying?" the old woman asked. Then she laughed. "Of course you are, how silly of me." She rang the bell and the butler appeared.

"Gibbons, do you think you could prepare three rooms?"

"The housekeeper is already attending to it, Miss Chetwynd. They should be ready in a few more minutes."

"Thank you, Gibbons. Let's see, am I forgetting anything else?"

"Shall I inform Cook there will be three more for dinner?"

"Oh, yes, of course. How clever of you, Gibbons." Aunt Letty stared fondly after the butler's departing figure. "I don't know what I would do without Gibbons. He is such a dear man." She picked up a biscuit and popped it into her mouth. "Tell me, Miss Driscoll, was your journey comfortable?"

"It was very pleasant," replied Cousin Winifred. With considerable relish, she went on to list in detail all the discomforts she had suffered. Margaret's attention wandered.

The room was an odd mismatch of baroque, Georgian, and Regency styles. There was little in the way of ornamentation; no knickknacks on the gilded tables, or porcelain displayed on the blue-and-cream-striped wallpaper. There were only the tea things and Aunt Letty's jar—which could not be considered decoration, Margaret decided. She peered at the jar, trying to identify the object inside. It looked like a lumpy ball of dirty linen.

"Cecilia and Geoffrey and Jeremy haven't arrived yet?" Bernard asked. "I thought they were due last week."

"They were delayed, I believe," said Aunt Letty. "I am certain they will be here any day now."

"Who is Jeremy?" Margaret asked.

"Jeremy is my nephew."

Margaret stared at her fiancé in amazement. "I didn't know you had a nephew."

Bernard shrugged.

She supposed she shouldn't be so surprised, Margaret thought. After all, their families had barely spoken in the last eight years. It just seemed strange that Bernard had become an uncle and she hadn't known.

"You naughty boy, Bernard," said Aunt Letty. "Imagine not telling your fiancée about your nephew. Never mind, dear," she said to Margaret. "You will meet Jeremy soon. And you can meet the rest of the family after dinner."

Margaret stared at Bernard. He had pulled out his watch and was fiddling with the catch. Exactly how many unknown relatives did he have? "The rest of the family?"

"Of course! Didn't Bernard even tell you about Phillip?"

"Aunt Letty . . ." *Click, snap.*

"Oh, hush, Bernard. I can't believe you haven't told this dear child about my uncle Phillip."

"Your *uncle*?" Margaret tried to hide her amazement. Evidently longevity was a family trait.

"Phillip Eglinton is no relation of ours." *Click, snap.* "He was just married to Aunt Letty's sister."

"My sister, Mary. She was his first wife. I only called him Uncle because he was so much older than I," explained Aunt Letty. "And we were very close. He left me this house."

Margaret could not make sense of this strange statement. "I don't understand. If he left you this house, then isn't he . . ."

"Dead? Oh, yes. My goodness, for years and years." Aunt Letty smiled fondly at Margaret's confused face.

"He is a ghost now," she said blithely.

2

"*A ghost?*" *Margaret echoed,* setting down her cup.

"A ghost!" exclaimed Cousin Winifred, clasping her hands together. "How terribly exciting!"

"Now, Aunt Letty, you know you've never actually seen him," Bernard said weakly.

"No, but I often feel his presence, and sometimes he whispers to me—"

Gibbons entered at that moment, cutting Aunt Letty off in midsentence. "Dinner is almost ready, Miss Chetwynd."

Bernard made a noise that sounded suspiciously like a sigh of relief and returned his watch to his pocket.

"However," the butler continued, "the carriage with the ladies' luggage has not arrived."

"Oh, dear. Margaret, Miss Driscoll, shall I put dinner back or would you prefer to dine now?"

Margaret's stomach rumbled, evidence of how long it had been since luncheon. "I wouldn't want your dinner to be spoiled," she said politely. "Perhaps if we could wash up a bit?"

Gibbons escorted Margaret and Miss Driscoll to a small anteroom and provided a basin of water and towels. As the two women washed their hands and faces, Cousin Winifred remarked, "This seems like a very pleasant place. How fortunate that your mother convinced me it was my duty to come! Do you think Miss Chetwynd will tell us more about the ghost at dinner?"

"Really, Cousin Winifred, the ghost is only an elderly woman's fancy."

"Oh, do you think so?" Looking disappointed, she dried her hands. Then she brightened and said, "I don't know, Margaret. The moment I saw the castle, I felt a sense of foreboding. Exactly like Drusilla in *The Specter of the Black Forest.* Little shivers went up and down my spine—"

"It must have been a breeze," Margaret interrupted. "Come, the others will be waiting."

After gathering in the parlor, everyone proceeded to the dining room. Aunt Letty sat down at the head of a long refectory table and set the jar next to her plate, patting it fondly. After everyone else was seated, she nodded to the butler, causing her wig to slip sideways a bit. Nonchalantly, she raised a hand and straightened it.

The butler brought in the first course. Margaret could smell the enticing aroma of potato leek soup. She inhaled deeply, her mouth starting to water. Heavens, she was hungry! She scooped up a spoonful of the creamy soup and sighed with pleasure as she tasted it.

"This is excellent soup," remarked Bernard. His voice echoed a bit in the huge oak-paneled room.

"We grew the potatoes right here," Aunt Letty said proudly. "I keep meaning to tell Jenkins to plant some more. Although it is so warm, I'm afraid it may affect them. I don't remember ever having such a hot summer. I do hope the heat doesn't bother you, Miss Driscoll."

"It's very pleasant in here," Cousin Winifred said.

Aunt Letty nodded. "The house never truly gets warm. Which is perhaps fortunate since I think spirits don't like warm places."

Bernard choked a little on his soup. Margaret, seeing him flush, realized how embarrassed he must be. Although Aunt Letty was sweet, he must feel her wandering wits reflected poorly on him. Margaret felt a twinge of unladylike glee before politely feigning deafness while she finished the rest of her soup.

"How very odd," said Cousin Winifred. "I wonder why they don't like warm places?"

"Perhaps it reminds them of their probable destination," said Aunt Letty.

Bernard's face looked like a ripe tomato. "Aunt Letty—"

"Not that Phillip needs to worry," the old woman continued, oblivious. She nodded at a footman to take the soup bowls away. "His spirit roams within these walls, unable to rest in peace because of the terrible injustice done him."

"Oh, the poor man," said Cousin Winifred as the butler brought in the second course. "An injustice, you say?"

The second course was frilled potatoes. Still trying to ignore the old woman's eccentric conversation, Margaret took a helping.

Aunt Letty heaped them on her plate. "Yes. He was accused of murdering his wife. His second wife, that is. Not my sister."

"How awful!" smiled Cousin Winifred.

"Yes. I'm sure the accusation was false. Dear Phillip would never have done such a thing."

Cousin Winifred took a bite of potatoes. "I would think a jury would agree with you, Miss Chetwynd."

"No, they didn't. Phillip was hanged. Over seventy-eight years ago."

"Aunt Letty, why don't you tell us what has been happening in the village?" Bernard said a trifle desperately. He had not touched his potatoes, Margaret noticed.

Aunt Letty was agreeable to this suggestion, and while she recited the births and deaths that had occurred in the last several months, the butler brought in the next course. Roasted potatoes.

"Gibbons, bring in the dessert, also," ordered Aunt Letty.

The potato pudding arrived forthwith.

The meal was soon finished, everyone except Aunt Letty picking at the last two dishes. When Aunt Letty had taken her last bite of potato pudding, she gave a blissful sigh. "What a delicious dinner. Gibbons, be sure to tell Cook."

"Yes, Miss Chetwynd," he said impassively.

"Now, if everyone is done, it's time for Margaret to meet my family. Especially Phillip." Aunt Letty stood and picked up her jar. "Miss Driscoll, you are welcome to come if you like."

"I think I will forgo the port and join you," said Bernard, rising also.

Aunt Letty herded them all along to the picture gallery, much to Margaret's relief. She had half-expected Aunt Letty would take them to the family graveyard. The gallery was a long, narrow hall lined with full-length portraits. Immediately in front of them, a rather dashing-looking gentleman wearing a powdered wig stood next to a pretty, dark-haired woman with a delicate face and smiling eyes.

So this was Phillip, thought Margaret. He certainly did not look violent. His face was kind, and his blue eyes gentle. "I think you are right, Aunt Letty. I don't believe he murdered his wife. See how carefully and tenderly he holds her arm?"

"Oh, that's not Phillip," said Aunt Letty. "That's Phillip's father, the first viscount. He was something of a rake until he fell in love with Jeanne, a French-woman, and married her. They were very happy." She pointed to a portrait behind them. "There, that is Phillip."

Everyone turned. Margaret caught her breath.

"Phillip Eglinton, second Viscount Holwell." Aunt Letty sighed worshipfully, clasping the ever-present jar to her bosom.

He was not at all handsome, thought Margaret, her spine unconsciously stiffening. In fact, he looked wickedly dissolute. Deeply hooded eyes stared cyni-cally down a long, aquiline nose at the small group. One corner of his mouth curled in a sardonic smile, both repelling and inviting. Dark red hair, almost the same hue as the ruby ring he wore, was pulled back in a simple queue, somehow adding to his air of dissipa-tion. And although he was dressed for hunting, in a loose-fitting shooting coat and a belt with a pouch on it, something about the way his fingers stroked the gun in his arms made her think it wasn't game he was after.

He looked as if he deserved hanging, thought Margaret, her skin prickling with dislike.

"Isn't he divine?" asked Aunt Letty.

"Oh, yes," simpered Cousin Winifred, much to Margaret's disgust. "So *virile.*"

Margaret felt compelled to make some remark. "Very interesting technique. Who is the artist?"

"Unfortunately, I do not know," said Aunt Letty.

"Aunt Letty, could we please move on?" Bernard, his foot tapping, was not even looking at the portrait. Obviously he, like Margaret, thought there was noth-ing remarkable about Phillip.

Aunt Letty's brows arched in surprise and she peered at Bernard's face. "How you have changed,

Bernard! You used to sit here for hours when you were a child, staring at Phillip."

Bernard flushed. "Simply a normal interest in dead people. Er, I mean in history. Nothing unusual in that."

"But Bernard, don't you remember you used to hear him whispering too? Why, one night you even said—"

"Nonsense," he growled, growing redder. "It's late, Aunt Letty, and we're all tired."

"Oh, dear, how thoughtless of me. You must all be longing for your beds after your journey. Come along. We will save the rest for another time."

Margaret took one final peek at Phillip. He seemed to be staring at her, his gaze mocking and seductive all at once. Hastily she averted her eyes. I must be tired, she thought, following Aunt Letty out of the gallery.

Bernard escorted her to her room. He lingered a moment, his eyes intent on her face, but when she met his gaze, he looked away. "Good night," he mumbled before hurrying down the long corridor.

Her hand on the brass doorknob, Margaret watched him until he turned the corner. With a deep sigh, she turned the knob and entered her room, only to stop abruptly, staring at the sight in front of her. She blinked her eyes a few times, but to no avail. The astonishing bed remained.

It was fashioned after the Chinese style, with a pagoda canopy and yellow silk coverlet. Bed curtains, from the same bright material, were tied back with gold tassels. Red lacquer bedposts contrasted dramatically.

Tearing her gaze away, Margaret looked at the rest of the room. To the left of the bed was a green and gold japanned dressing table with a mirror on folding hinges, while on the other side was a matching escritoire. The fireplace, on the right wall, was flanked by two windows and two red lacquer chairs with yellow cushions. The yellow cushions were repeated on a padded settee at the foot of the bed.

Margaret had never in her life seen such a garish room. It flaunted every rule of Victorian good taste. It was too bright, too gaudy, too *much* for words.

She loved it.

A smile curving her lips, she moved forward to trail a finger along the smooth silk bedcover and trace the intricately carved dragon in the headboard. She could almost imagine she was in China, or some other far-off, exotic place.

Had Aunt Letty decorated the room? Very likely. Margaret tugged on the bellpull, her smile widening. Bernard's aunt might have a few cobwebs in her attic, but Margaret liked her very much. She only hoped the "ghost" would not "whisper" to the old woman within earshot of her. She would not know what to do if Aunt Letty started carrying on a conversation with some unseen person.

Her maid, Yvette, came in answer to Margaret's summons and helped her change into a nightgown. After Yvette left, Margaret sat down on the bed, sinking into the soft, inviting mattress. She lay back with a blissful sigh.

A painting on a panel on the underside of the pagoda canopy caught her eye. The trim of the roof cast deep shadows, concealing the edges of the painting. In the center, where the light was unobstructed, she could see a Chinese man, with a long moustache, sleeping peacefully.

She wouldn't mind following his example, she thought, her eyes closing.

She wanted to mull over the impressions she had received that evening, but the bed was very soft, a rushlight provided a comforting glow, and the thick walls shut out all noise. Sleep stole over her. Too tired to fight it, she soon fell into a deep slumber.

It was very late when something woke her. Groggily she lifted her eyelids and saw a flickering light.

3

Margaret was suddenly wide awake. Her heart began to pound. The hair on her arms stood up straight as shivers tingled up and down her spine. The source of the light seemed to be somewhere behind her, but she was too frightened to turn and look. She lay on her side, very still, not even breathing, so as not to reveal her wakefulness. Her hearing grew more acute as she listened for a sound, any sound, that might provide a clue to the intruder's identity.

The smell of tobacco, rich and sweet, filled her nostrils.

She kept her eyes half-closed, but through her lashes, she could see that the light appeared to be moving. Her shoulders tensed. She sensed something coming closer, closer, closer. . .

Taking a deep breath, she rolled over and croaked, "Who's there?"

The light vanished, leaving the room in impenetrable darkness.

Margaret lay motionless again. Her eyes were wide

open, staring into the dark, trying to see. She could hear nothing except the loud thumping of her heart. An interminable length of time passed, but nothing happened. Everything was perfectly still.

Gradually, she became aware that the rushlight had gone out, and the room was freezing cold. Reaching down, she pulled up the extra blanket at the foot of the bed and huddled under the covers, shivering.

She closed her eyes, but all of her senses remained extraordinarily heightened. She heard a board creak. Her eyes flew open, the small noise pounding against her eardrums like a cannonball, but the room was dark. She shut her eyes again.

It was a long time before she finally fell asleep.

In the clear light of morning, Margaret told herself it had been a dream. Heaven knew, listening to Aunt Letty ramble on about ghosts was enough to give anyone nightmares. And that dinner! Four courses of potatoes would cause indigestion in any person and disturb their sleep. The idea that someone had been in her room was absurd.

"Absolutely absurd," she murmured to herself as she went down to breakfast. Bernard looked up from the newspaper when she entered the morning room.

"Good morning," he said.

"Did you come to my room last night?" she blurted out.

"Miss Westbourne!" He thrust the newspaper aside, his eyes wide with shock. "Certainly not!"

She bit her lip. Her question had not been worded very well. "I beg your pardon, Lord Barnett. I thought I heard something last night, and I thought perhaps Aunt Letty was ill." A lame excuse, but it was the best she could come up with at the moment. She turned to fill her plate from the sideboard. Her stomach churned a little as fried potatoes and leftover potato pudding met her gaze. She opted for bread and butter.

"Aunt Letty is fine," said Bernard. "Even if she weren't, I would have sent your maid to inform you."

"Of course," Margaret murmured, taking her seat. "Please forgive my thoughtless question."

Picking up his knife and fork, Bernard began to dice a piece of leftover potato on his plate. "I would never jeopardize your reputation by doing something so reprehensible as entering your bedchamber. I want no breath of scandal attached to your name."

She gripped the butter knife tightly for a moment. Then, she buttered her bread and calmly bit into it. His high moral standards were very . . . admirable, she told herself. Certainly he could not respect a woman who allowed him into her room when they were not married. Why, he would in all probability break off their engagement if she showed such loose morals as to allow him in. That was the way of the world, and certainly she agreed with him.

"I believe, as do you, in the strict observance of society's rules." A deep flush suffusing his face, he repeated, "I would never do anything so reprehensible as entering a lady's bedchamber."

Margaret opened her mouth to ask what he planned to do when they were married, then changed her mind and took a bite of bread and butter instead. She did not want to cause him apoplexy, she thought as she chewed a bit more fiercely than usual.

After demolishing the potato, Bernard pulled out his watch and started playing with the catch. Margaret found herself chewing in time to the click, snap, and consciously had to stop herself. He stared at the wall, not speaking until she finished her tea.

He cleared his throat. "If you are done, would you like to see the gardens? The parterre garden is very pleasant."

She stifled the impulse to say no. She needed some fresh air—maybe it would clear away the lingering cobwebs in her brain.

The parterre garden was indeed a pleasant place. Underfoot, wild thyme grew between paving stones, and as they walked, some of the plants were crushed, releasing a tangy fragrance. She inhaled deeply, enjoying the energizing scent. She could almost forget about potatoes and strange lights and marriage. . . .

Four paths led to a sundial in the garden's center. Margaret paused to look at it. The small lines in heavy cast metal did not make any sense to her. She could not tell what hour it was. "How long did you live here?"

"Five years. When my mother died, my father had no idea what to do with a five-year-old child, so he sent me to Aunt Letty. Until I started school. After that, as you know, I spent summers at Barnett Manor."

Margaret nodded absently, remembering that first time she had found him sitting forlornly at the border between their two properties. She had been only eight, three years younger than he, but even at that age she had thought he seemed lost and lonely. There were few children in the area, none at all that the old viscount had approved of as playmates for his only son. Even Margaret, with her father's merchant background, had not been welcomed by the snobbish Lord Barnett. It wasn't until her grandmother died, leaving Margaret a tidy fortune, that the old Lord Barnett had changed his mind. He had even gone so far as to approach her father about arranging a match between the two families. Her father had been ecstatic.

"I hope you weren't frightened by Aunt Letty's talk of ghosts."

"Certainly not." Margaret pushed aside the memory of last night. That had been a dream. "I don't believe in ghosts."

"I didn't mean to question your good sense," Bernard assured her hastily. "I have no doubts about that."

"Thank you." She tried to squash the feeling that she had just been insulted. "Is she your father's aunt?"

"Actually, she is my great-grandmother's cousin."

"Good heavens."

"Yes, she is quite old. Ninety-one, in fact." He paused for a long moment.

"Miss Westbourne . . ." Bernard coughed, and Margaret turned toward him, but he was looking down at the sundial. "Miss Westbourne, I think perhaps it would be acceptable . . . it would not be improper . . . for us to call each other by our Christian names. Only when we are alone, naturally."

Margaret was glad to comply. Privately, she considered the dropping of formality long overdue. She had not liked it when, upon his return to Berkshire, he had started calling her "Miss Westbourne." In spite of everything that had happened, she still thought of him as Bernard, and using the title was irksome. Besides, "Lord Barnett" always made her think of his father. "If you wish, Bernard."

He frowned when she immediately called him by his first name. Now what? she wondered. He seemed uncomfortable, as if he thought she had been forward.

Again, she felt a twinge of anger. What did he want from her?

"Oh, there is Jenkins, Aunt Letty's gardener. I wonder if Aunt Letty ever remembered to tell him to plant more potatoes? Perhaps it would be a good idea for me to ask him. Would you excuse me for a minute?"

"Certainly, Bernard." It would give her a chance to control her temper. "I will go on ahead."

He still hadn't caught up with her by the time she reached the front door with its glaring gargoyles. Probably he didn't want to, Margaret thought. Making a face at the stone beasts, she entered the castle and started up the stairs, only to be stopped by Gibbons.

"Miss Chetwynd would like to see you in the parlor," he said. "She has a guest."

"Oh, I must change, then."

"No, there is no need. She wants to see you *right away.*"

Margaret hesitated, but the butler's voice was strangely insistent. Reluctantly, she walked toward the parlor. As she approached she could hear voices within.

"I cannot wait much longer," an unpleasant voice said.

"Please, Mortimer, I'm sure my luck will turn soon."

Hearing Aunt Letty's quavering tones, Margaret stopped, her hand on the doorknob.

"I just need a little more time. I will come next time, and—"

Feeling uncomfortable at her inadvertent eavesdropping, Margaret pushed the door open. Aunt Letty and the man she had called Mortimer both turned, their expressions startled. Aunt Letty was clutching her jar to her chest, as though it were a talisman that could ward off evil.

Margaret disliked Mortimer on sight. He had oily-looking blond hair and a thin moustache on his upper lip. He wore rings on all his fingers on both hands, including one large ruby in an ornate gold setting. When he spoke, his voice was as oily as his hair.

"Well, well, and who might you be?" he leered.

Margaret stiffened at his rudeness, and Aunt Letty hastily made the introductions. "Miss Westbourne, may I present Lord Mortimer, a neighbor of mine. Mortimer, this is Miss Margaret Westbourne, my nephew's fiancée."

Mortimer paused in the act of bowing over Margaret's hand. A look of astonishment passed over his face. "Your nephew? Do you mean Barnett?" When Aunt Letty nodded, he burst into loud laughter.

Her distaste increasing by the second, Margaret pulled her hand away.

"Ah, forgive me, Miss Westbourne," he said, wiping his eyes. "It's only that Barnett and I are old friends."

"Indeed?" Margaret's frozen reply was echoed by another voice. Turning, she saw Bernard standing in the doorway, a look of dislike hardening his usually bland expression.

"Bernie!" Mortimer strode forward to grasp Bernard's hand. "Congratulations, old boy. I hope you didn't trip over your feet when you proposed."

Bernard's frown deepened and Mortimer laughed again. "Bernie's always been the clumsiest fellow," he said to Margaret.

"I hate to rush you on your way," Bernard said, his voice cold. "But we are leaving for church soon."

Mortimer's eyes narrowed, but his thin lips did not lose their smile. "I will go, then. We will have to talk over old times another day. Perhaps next week. Your aunt was just inviting me to dinner Monday next, weren't you, Letty?" His cold eyes bore into Aunt Letty.

"Yes, of course," stammered the old woman.

"Until next week, then. Good day to you all. Miss Westbourne, it's been a true pleasure." His loud laughter echoed through the room as he departed.

Bernard's neck was stiff as he glared after Mortimer. "Aunt Letty, how could you invite that knave here?" he demanded through gritted teeth.

"Now, Bernard." Nervously, Aunt Letty reached up to tug a curl on her wig. "He is our nearest neighbor. And it's about time I returned his hospitality. I often go to the little parties he has every month."

Bernard stared at her. "How can you, of all people, associate with that blackguard?"

"Oh, Bernard, don't be angry with me!" Large tears welled up in Aunt Letty's eyes and her face crumpled. "It's only that there's not much to do around here, especially at my age, and Mortimer does have the most amusing parties. Everyone goes, and oh, I do so love a good game of cards."

"Here, now, don't cry, Aunt Letty." Hastily, Bernard pulled a handkerchief from his pocket and thrust it at her. "Naturally you may invite whomever you like here. It is your house, after all."

"Oh, thank you, Bernard." Aunt Letty's tears dried up magically. "I won't ask him here again while you're visiting. Now, I must go change for church."

"Wait," Margaret said. "Didn't you want to see me?"

Aunt Letty frowned. "I don't think so, dear."

"But Gibbons said . . ." Margaret's voice drifted off as she realized what had happened.

Aunt Letty appeared to understand also. "Dear Gibbons, he is like a mother hen. So protective. He disapproves of Mortimer, you see."

Bernard frowned after Aunt Letty. Then, with an abrupt bow to Margaret, he left the room also, still frowning.

*   *   *

At dinner, Margaret was dismayed to see course after course of potatoes again. Yet even that torture paled in comparison to listening to Cousin Winifred read aloud afterward.

She had chosen *The Ghost of Trevellyan Castle*. With moans and squeaks and dramatic voices that would have done an actress proud, she related the adventures of poor Belinda and the evil spirit haunting her ancestral home.

Margaret really didn't want to listen. She was too tired. Which wasn't surprising since she hadn't slept well last night. The sensible thing to do would be to excuse herself and go to bed. But the more she heard about the Trevellyan ghost, the more reluctant she grew.

Not because she believed this silly ghost business, she told herself, as Cousin Winifred started a new chapter. Last night had merely been a particularly realistic dream. She was completely certain of that. She was not frightened at all. Well, maybe just a teeny-tiny bit . . .

Her eyes closed for an instant, then fluttered open. As Cousin Winifred's voice droned on, Margaret's eyelids grew heavier and heavier. A few times she nodded off, and was awakened by her head falling sideways.

Aunt Letty finally noticed.

"Margaret, dear child! Take yourself off to bed, or you will be asleep on the sofa."

Margaret roused herself and looked blearily around the room. The fog cleared a little when she noticed Bernard staring at her strangely.

"Very well. I am tired," she said, trying not to yawn.

Bernard rose to his feet. "I will escort you."

"No, no, that's not necessary. Good night, everyone."

But as she walked up the stairs she began to wish she had accepted Bernard's offer. It wouldn't have hurt to ask him to check the room for her. Only he probably would have given her another lecture about the observance of society's rules or something.

Her steps slowed and her fatigue dissipated as she approached her room. No one is in there, she told herself sternly. Absolutely no one.

Her hand on the doorknob, she hesitated. Leaning forward, she rested her ear against the smooth panel, listening intently.

How foolish she was. She couldn't hear a thing. All was quiet; completely, absolutely si—

Wait! What was that? It sounded like . . . like a footstep! Inside her room!

Heart racing, she threw open the door with a crash.

Yvette jumped and turned around, her hand covering her rounded bosom. "Lord, miss, what a fright you gave me," she exclaimed.

"Sorry, Yvette." Margaret glanced around the room. It looked perfectly normal, yet instead of calming her, somehow it made her more nervous.

She stood tensely, her eyes darting as Yvette helped her into the white cotton nightgown.

"Good night, miss." Yvette left, leaving Margaret alone.

She placed the lamp on the table by the bed. Deciding to leave it lit, she pulled the blanket up to her ears and closed her eyes.

For a few minutes, her senses remained alert. But she truly was very tired. Gradually, her body relaxed, and before long she drifted off to sleep.

This time when she woke, her eyes flew immediately to the lamp by her bed. It had gone out. And yet, an eerie glow was filling the room.

Margaret squeezed her eyes shut and once again smelled the rich aroma of tobacco. She began to pray. "Please, dear God, please make it go away, and I will never be disrespectful again and I will always obey and I will not think terrible thoughts and I will—"

"Who the devil are you?" a harsh voice rang out.

4

Margaret opened her eyes a tiny fraction.

A hazy figure was standing by her bed, glaring down at her.

She squeaked and closed her eyes tightly.

"Dammit all," the voice roared. "What are you doing here?"

Timidly, she raised her eyelids a notch. The apparition was still there. She opened her eyes a little wider, and gradually the figure took on definition. She could see the tapping foot, the arms akimbo, the sensuous lips frowning at her, the haughty aquiline nose, and the deeply hooded eyes which were flashing with ill-disguised impatience. He was not wearing the loose hunting clothes he had worn in the portrait; instead he wore a form-fitting dark blue-green coat, with a light buff-colored waistcoat and knee breeches, which made his shoulders look broader, his arms and legs more powerful. His hair was different, too, she saw. It was cropped close to his head. But there could be no doubt.

It was Phillip Eglinton, second Viscount Holwell—a ghost.

He looked like a real person, except that he was bathed in an unearthly glow, and she rather thought that he was hovering above the ground. She shut her eyes. This could not be happening.

"Damnation, are you deaf or just a lackwit?"

"I . . . I'll thank you not to swear, sir," Margaret croaked inanely, her fingers clutching at the blanket. Then gathering up her courage, "And I'll thank you to leave my room at once."

"Your audacity is most entertaining, sweeting," he said. He didn't look entertained. His eyes were cold and indifferent. "But I have a deuce of a headache and I'm in no mood for games tonight. Nor do I need a whore, so I'll thank you to leave my room now, or I'll boot you out on your pretty arse."

Whore? She sat up straight, the word ringing in her ears, anger drowning out some of her fright. "Why you . . . you insolent scoundrel! You impudent . . . whatever you are," she said, less than eloquently. Carefully holding the blanket to her chin to preserve her modesty, she glared at him.

He frowned fiercely, but Margaret, quivering and sputtering, refused to look away. His heavy dark brows lowered, but she only angled her chin higher. He muttered an ugly oath; she pursed her lips.

What are you doing? shrieked a small, panic-stricken corner of her brain. This was a ghost, for heaven's sake! Not for the first time in her life, she had allowed her temper to draw her into an untenable situation. Pride kept her chin up and her eyes fastened to his, but her mouth trembled as she waited in dread for him to punish her impudence with some sort of supernatural retribution.

His gaze fell to her mouth.

When he glanced up again, there was a spark of laughter lighting his eyes. The harsh lines in his face softened and his stance eased. He looked positively amused.

"My dear girl, I am only a man, and though by rights I can call myself a gentleman, 'tis not often I try to make that claim. Especially when there's a woman in my bed." His gaze swept over her unbound hair and a different light entered his eyes. His lips curved sensuously and his voice grew husky. "Perhaps I am in the mood for love after all, sweeting. How can I refuse such an exquisite invitation?"

Margaret felt a blush creeping up into her face. He smiled wickedly and moved—floated?—closer. He loomed by the side of the bed, large, male, threatening. Margaret's mouth went dry, her skin prickled.

"It's devilishly cold in here, my dear. What do you say I ring for a fire and a bottle of brandy?" He leaned over her, his face drawing nearer. She pressed herself back against the pillows, watching him with wide mesmerized eyes. He was so close, she could see the fine texture of his skin. A barely discernible shadow of stubble on his chin made him look more rakish, more dangerous than ever.

She closed her eyes once more. "You are a figment of my imagination," she said sternly. "A dream. When I open my eyes you will be gone. I do not believe in ghosts."

Margaret opened her eyes and stared into the ghost's smiling eyes.

"I am glad to hear it, my dear. I don't believe in 'em either."

"But—" Was she insane? "You are a ghost."

"What the devil is the matter with you, girl?" He drew back from her, his smile fading. "Are you in truth deranged? Of course I am not a ghost." He looked tired suddenly, his hand rising to rub wearily at his forehead. "At least—"

He broke off, his brow creasing. Slowly he lowered his hand and stared at the glowing palm. He held up his other hand and turned them both this way and that, flexing and spreading his long slender fingers, as if trying to find the source of the light.

Dropping his hands, he stared hard at Margaret. "Who are you and why are you in my room?" he asked again, his voice deadly, all traces of amusement gone.

She quailed a little under his look. "I am Margaret Westbourne, and I am sorry, I didn't know this was your room. I would think Aunt Letty has your room. I'll gladly move if that is your wish."

For the first time he looked around, his gaze lingering on the bed's pagoda canopy and the japanned dressing table. His hand passed across his eyes. "Forgive me. I don't know how I made such a mistake. I see now this is not my room. But this is Durnock Castle, is it not?"

"Oh, yes."

"Then why are you here, Miss Westbourne? I don't remember inviting you."

"You didn't. Bernard did. Lord Barnett, that is. My fiancé. He brought me to meet Aunt Letty. Durnock Castle belongs to her now."

"That is impossible. I own this castle."

"Perhaps you should discuss this with Aunt Letty," Margaret said uneasily. "I know she would like to see you, since she was so fond of you when you were alive."

"When I was . . . hell and the devil! Are you trying to say I am . . ." His voice trailed off as he held up his hand again, staring at it. "What year is this?" he asked in a strange voice.

"Eighteen forty-seven," she whispered.

His features froze into a mask of shock. The glow around him flared, a pure bright white, then rippled in ever-increasing waves. His form wavered and dissipated, the light fading and shrinking into one tiny spark. It hung suspended in the air for a second more, then vanished, leaving the room in cold, dark silence.

Her heart thudding, Margaret sat quietly for several long minutes. She reached out and groped for the candle on her bedside table and lit it with shaking hands. Lying down, she turned on her side so she could stare at the spot where he had stood. She pinched herself hard and felt the sharp sting of pain. She was awake. Wide, wide awake.

She closed her eyes, her brain a mad jumble. Only one thought was clear and no explanation, no excuse could serve to deny it.

She had just been visited by a ghost!

5

Bright sunlight illuminated Margaret's room the next morning, making such notions as ghosts seem incredible. Last night had a fantastical quality to it that defied belief. Perhaps it had been a dream after all, insisted her rational side.

But in her heart, she knew it had been no dream. Phillip had been too real, too vital. Lying on her side, her cheek against the pillow, she looked over at the spot where he had appeared. She could recall every movement, every expression, every word, as clearly as if he stood beside her now. She could remember his barely constrained impatience, his cold anger, and his flirtatious smile.

He had been incredibly crude. Certainly she could never have imagined such a disgusting dialogue. Telling her he did not need a whore! Obviously she was no such thing. He should have known immediately that she wasn't that kind of woman. Such a female would have smiled at him. She would probably have drawn back the blanket, and held out a hand to him, so he could climb in beside her and . . .

Margaret could feel her blood rushing through her veins. From indignation, of course.

Sitting up, she rang for her maid. "Yvette," she said when the girl made her appearance. "I am feeling a trifle indisposed this morning. I will take my breakfast here."

While she ate, it occurred to her that perhaps someone was playing a practical joke on her. Hurriedly she finished her meal and started searching the room for evidence of the ghost's presence. Evidence that would point to a human presence. Crouching down, she carefully inspected the green carpet for wax drippings or cigar ashes or anything else that would show that someone had been in her room.

She found nothing.

Perhaps there was a secret passage. She examined the wallpaper, with its pattern of leafy green trees, for cracks. She knocked on panels, pressed knobs, and checked the fireplace for loose bricks. She did not find anything, but she made a mental note to ask Aunt Letty if such a passage existed.

When she had exhausted all the possibilities, she sat down at the dressing table, propping her elbows on its surface with her chin in her hands. In her mind, she relived the entire scene, recalling every word the ghost had said.

How hateful he had been, she thought. And yet, there had also been something compelling about him. Some force that made him seem very much alive, very magnetic, very attractive . . .

Dear heaven, she was deranged. Her corset must be too tight and lack of oxygen was affecting her brain. She was sighing over a ghost! It was obviously a mistake to stay in this room and let her fancies run wild.

She rose abruptly from the dressing table. She needed some rational company. She would go downstairs and seek out . . . well, not Aunt Letty or Cousin Winifred. Bernard, perhaps. Yes. She could count on him to be sensible at all times. Perhaps she would even tell him about the ghost. He might be skeptical at first, but he would believe her. Besides, she was bursting with the need to tell *someone*.

After dressing in a cerise print muslin gown and a lace cap, she went downstairs. She found Bernard in the study, a small room off the much grander library. He sat in an armchair, reading, his forest green coat clashing with the bottle green velvet upholstery. Laying the slim volume aside, he rose to his feet. "Margaret, are you feeling better?"

"Yes, Bernard." She sat down opposite him and tried to think of a way to introduce the subject of Phillip. She didn't want to blurt out something foolish the way she had yesterday. Her gaze fell on the book he had placed on the table. "What are you reading?" she finally asked.

"The Metamorphosis Insectorum Surinamensium," he replied. "Although old, it contains some excellent studies of insects."

"Oh. How . . . interesting." She detested insects, but Bernard had always liked them, she remembered.

"I enjoy reading something educational. I don't care for the gothic novels that Miss Driscoll favors."

"Nor do I." Margaret was glad to agree with him for once. "I prefer travel books." Travel books had been her greatest pleasure the last several years. "I am reading one about the Sandwich Islands."

He frowned. "I wouldn't think travel books were appropriate reading material for an unmarried woman."

"But they are very interesting. The different cultures are fascinating. Why, in the book I am reading, it tells how the natives stand up on pieces of wood and sail over the waves."

"What nonsense. The author must have made it up."

"No, I'm sure he didn't. He was a missionary, and I doubt a man of the cloth would lie."

"Nevertheless, it sounds highly unlikely."

"Yes, but wouldn't it be wonderful to go to such a place? And to see such sights?"

"Traveling is not so romantic as it sounds, Margaret. You know I spent the last seven years in India. It was often dirty, ugly, and smelly. You will be much happier at Barnett Manor, in our own little village with our good friends and neighbors. Don't you agree?"

"Yes, Bernard." Of course, he was right. She didn't know why she felt so disappointed. She didn't truly want to go haring off to the Sandwich Islands; she wanted to settle at Barnett Manor and enjoy watching Lady Creevy and the rest of the village eat humble pie.

But perhaps it wasn't such a good idea to tell Bernard about Phillip. Although she had once confided everything to him, that had been a long time ago. Everything had changed now.

She became aware of a tightness in her chest. Her corset was definitely too tight. In fact, it was so tight, it was practically suffocating her. She sucked in her breath, trying to ease the restriction.

Margaret was glad when a commotion out in the hall provided a distraction. She heard a clear voice call out, "Aunt Letty! Aunt Letty! Hello!"

Margaret looked at Bernard.

"My sister," he explained. Then he added, "She's never been one for formality."

He rose to his feet and together they went out in the hall. A plump woman with dark shiny hair stood there, directing the servants with the luggage in between calls for Aunt Letty.

"Hello, Cecilia."

"Bernard! What are you doing here?"

"I brought my fiancée to meet my family."

"Your fiancée! Good heavens! Geoffrey! Geoffrey!" she yelled out the door. "Come here! Bernard is engaged!"

A tall, slim man with a crutch under one arm entered the house. As he moved forward, Margaret could see that his right leg was missing from the knee down. She swallowed a little and looked up into his face. He had cold green eyes, and deep lines grooved his forehead.

"Miss Margaret Westbourne, my fiancée," said Bernard briefly. "Mrs. Cecilia Barstow, my sister, and Mr. Geoffrey Barstow, her husband."

"What a pleasure to meet you," said Cecilia, giving her a warm hug. Geoffrey nodded.

"Bernard, why didn't you to write us?" continued Cecilia.

"I did. To Aunt Letty, that is. I believe she forgot."

"Oh, dear. But never mind. This is so exciting. It's time you married."

Before he could reply, a streak of arms and legs flashed by Margaret and skidded to a halt in front of Bernard.

"Look, Uncle Bernard, a twitchbell!" the boy exclaimed.

"Jeremy Barstow," scolded his mother. "Mind your manners! Make your bow and say hello to the lady your uncle is going to marry."

Jeremy complied, the excitement dying out of his face. He was a thin, wiry boy, seven or eight years of age, with his mother's dark hair and eyes, but without her vivacity. He did not respond to Margaret's tentative smile.

"Why don't you show me your twitchbell now?" Bernard said.

Margaret glanced at him in surprise. Somehow she

had not expected him to take much interest in his nephew.

Jeremy opened his fist to reveal an earwig on his palm. It immediately tried to escape and he closed his hand again.

"An excellent specimen," said Bernard. *"Forficula auricularia* if I'm not mistaken."

"Fascinating," Margaret murmured. Of course he would be interested in an insect.

Still not smiling, Jeremy was about to escape when he caught sight of Aunt Letty coming down the stairs. Margaret stared. The gray wig was gone.

"Aunt Letty! Aunt Letty!" Jeremy shouted, his small intense face brightening a little, although he still didn't smile. "I have a twitchbell!"

"Do you, dear? How wonderful. Cecilia and Geoffrey, I'm so glad you're back."

Aunt Letty was close enough now that Margaret could see thin, spiky black and white hair that barely covered her scalp. Where was the wig?

"Aunt Letty, could I put it in your jar and keep it?" asked Jeremy.

Aunt Letty drew back, hugging the jar. "Certainly not!"

"Come, let's not stand here," said Cecilia. "Let's all go in the parlor. Although, come to think of it, we'll need more chairs. Gibbons!" she bellowed.

Gibbons silently appeared. "Yes, Mrs. Barstow?"

"Please bring a few more chairs into the parlor and have a servant take our luggage up. Oh, and bring in some tea, also."

"I will join you in a minute," said Aunt Letty. "There's something I need to discuss with Cook."

"Can't it wait?" asked Cecilia.

"Er, no, my dear. I'll only be a minute."

Cecilia's eyes narrowed. "Aunt Letty, you haven't been up to your old tricks, have you?"

Aunt Letty fingered a straggly curl. "Why, whatever do you mean, dear?"

"I mean potatoes, that's what."

"Oh, well . . ."

"Miss Westbourne, have you been eating potatoes for every course at dinner?"

Aunt Letty threw a pleading look at Margaret.

"Why, ah, let's see . . ."

"Never mind, I know it's true. I can see I'm going to have to have a word with Cook."

"Now, Cecilia, don't get upset. It wasn't Cook's fault. I thought it was time for her to have a little visit to her family. The poor woman hadn't seen them in over six months. Naturally I had to hire someone else temporarily while she was gone. And could I help it if she likes to make potatoes? I meant to say something, but it kept slipping my mind. I will do it now, though."

"I'll go with you, Aunt Letty," said Jeremy. "Maybe Cook will have some tarts. I'm very nearly starving."

With a guileless smile, Aunt Letty slipped away, Jeremy in tow.

"Honestly, that boy. And as for Aunt Letty, she is impossible." Cecilia shook her head, then looked around at the others. Her bright gaze rested on her husband's face for a moment. "Darling, would you like me to see if your room is ready, yet?"

Geoffrey shook his head. After only the barest hesitation, Cecilia nodded, then smiled at Margaret and led the way to the parlor. The ladies sat on the sofa, while the gentlemen took the chairs.

"I suppose she has been wearing that awful wig, too," continued Cecilia. "I specifically forbade her to wear it when we found the nest of mice in it, but she has only grown more sly. Would you believe she puts it on when she goes to bed?" Cecilia shook her head. "I hope Bernard warned you about Aunt Letty, Miss Westbourne, before he asked you to marry him."

"He did say she was eccentric." She glanced at Bernard who was talking to Geoffrey, paying no attention to his sister. She heard him mention White-hall, and saw Geoffrey nod his head.

"Eccentric! Ha! That doesn't begin to describe Aunt Letty. I daresay you've noticed that jar she carries around?"

"Why, yes. I've been wondering what is in it."

"A religious relic of some sort, I believe. That sort of thing was very popular in the last century, you know. Tricksters sold items supposedly belonging to saints, claiming they had magical powers. Knowing Aunt Letty, it's probably a potato from St. Patrick's garden." Cecilia sighed. "Did she tell you about Phillip's ghost, too?"

Margaret averted her gaze and swallowed. "A bit."

The other woman rolled her eyes. "All that non-sense about him whispering to her? You poor girl. You've truly gotten the full benefit of Aunt Letty's eccentricities. Ghosts! What will she come up with next? I hope she won't put you off marrying Bernard."

"Oh, no. That is, she is very sweet."

"It's good you think so, because Bernard dotes on her. He visits her frequently. We visit as often as we can, too. She needs a keeper."

"How nice." Margaret couldn't think of anything else to say. "You live with your husband's parents?"

"Yes, in Cumberland. Ever since Geoffrey lost his leg and had to leave the army."

Margaret glanced at Geoffrey and saw that he had heard his wife's words. A bleak look crossed his face.

The door opened and the butler came in with the tea tray. Three more servants followed behind with chairs. Hard on their heels came Aunt Letty and Cousin Winifred.

Introductions were made and refreshments passed

around. Cecilia kept up a lively patter of talk, managing within a few minutes to get everyone on a first-name basis, even Bernard. "Don't be so stuffy," she told him when he tried to protest the informality.

In contrast to his wife's gregariousness, Geoffrey seemed almost morose. He contributed very little to the conversation; whenever Margaret happened to glance at him, he would be staring broodingly into the fire. There was something rather intimidating about him, she thought. Although why she would think so, when she had successfully dealt with a ghost, was beyond her.

Thinking of Phillip made Margaret lose track of the conversation around her. As she remembered how she had talked back to him, she felt almost faint. Where had she found the courage to speak as she had? She was fortunate he hadn't struck her down with a lightning bolt or something. But somehow, in spite of his loud words and threatening pose, she must have sensed that he would not harm her. Perhaps because of the gleam of laughter she had glimpsed in his eyes; or the weariness she had heard in his voice; or even the confusion in his expression when he stared at his glowing hand.

Would he appear again tonight?

The thought hovered in the back of her mind all through the delicious dinner—not a single potato!—and afterward, when everyone sat in the back parlor and Cecilia told stories of Jeremy's antics. When the group finally broke up, it was close to midnight.

Margaret walked slowly to her room, pausing at the door.

"Good night, Margaret," Cousin Winifred whispered as she slipped into the neighboring room.

"Good night," Margaret murmured, her mind barely aware of the other woman. Inside her own room, the beat of her pulse quickened.

Would he appear again tonight?

Her nightgown was lying on the bed, and as Yvette started to undo the long row of buttons on her dress, Margaret remembered how he had stood beside the bed, leaning over her, watching her with that dark gaze. She shivered. Would he come tonight? Or was he perhaps already here, waiting for the maid to go, watching as Yvette . . .

Margaret pulled away from the maid, clutching the neckline of her dress together.

"Wait, Yvette. I would like a dressing screen, please."

The maid stared at her as if she had gone mad. "A screen? Now?"

"Yes, now."

"Are you feeling all right, miss?"

"Yes, yes, I'm fine. Please go find a screen. There must be one somewhere in this house."

There was, and half an hour later, two footmen carried it in and placed it in the middle of the floor. The mythological scene painted on the screen didn't match the room's decor, but Margaret didn't care.

"Over in that corner, please."

After the footmen left, she stepped behind the screen and looked over the top at the place where Phillip had stood last night. Satisfied, she beckoned Yvette to come behind the screen.

The maid rolled her eyes a bit, but kept silent, much to Margaret's relief.

After Yvette left, Margaret quickly climbed under the concealing covers, debating whether or not to leave the lamp lit. It had gone out last time he appeared, she recalled. Had he extinguished it, or had it gone out by itself? Perhaps he would not come if there was a light in the room. But then she would not know if he truly had been a figment of her imagination.

Making up her mind, she leaned over and blew out the lamp. Light still filled the room, and she blew again before she realized that the lamp was not lit.

He was there.

6

Phillip stared down at the woman, Margaret Westbourne. With her thick, golden brown hair cascading about her shoulders, she looked remarkably beautiful. *If* he were in the mood to appreciate it, which he wasn't. She was staring back, her brilliant blue eyes wide with a look of half fright, half fascination. He supposed it was a natural expression for someone seeing a ghost, but he certainly did not care to have it directed at him.

But then, he did not particularly care for being a ghost.

He could scarce believe it even now; he had meant to think on it, after leaving her presence, but in some strange way time seemed to have passed without his being aware of it. As if he had been in a deep, dreamless sleep. Or as if he were only alive to this woman.

"So, Miss Westbourne," he said coldly, folding his arms across his chest. "I am forced to believe you are correct. I am a ghost."

"I am naturally delighted that you do not doubt my veracity," she said, her voice equally cold. "Will you please leave now? It isn't proper for you to be here."

She tilted her chin in the impudent manner he had noticed before, but this time he felt no amusement, only anger and confusion. He wanted some answers. Now.

"Virtuously said," he sneered. "I would willingly relieve you of my company, but first we must clear up one small matter. Why am I here?"

"How should I know?" she said, her voice rising. "You are the one who keeps coming here and scaring me half to death."

She did not look scared. The single row of lace on the prim cotton nightgown covering her breasts fluttered a bit with her rapid breathing, but it was clearly from indignation, not fear. "You must know something since it is to you that I appear. Did you summon me with black magic?"

"Certainly not! I know nothing about you! Appear to Aunt Letty or Bernard if you have any questions."

He frowned, considering her suggestion. "I don't think I can," he said slowly. "Appear to someone else, that is."

"Why not?" she asked crossly.

Stroking his chin thoughtfully, he tried to pin down the source of his feeling. He could feel the connection his mind made to hers. There was an openness, a reaching, that he sensed he could not find elsewhere. "There is something about you. Your mind is extraordinarily receptive."

"It most certainly is not! My mind is completely closed. I mean, I don't even believe in ghosts! I just want you to go away!"

"I don't think I can," he said again. "There is something I must do." What was it? The answer hovered barely beyond his consciousness, teasing and flirting like any woman. He struggled to capture it, but it flitted away, much to his frustration. "Dammit, I can't seem to remember, but there has to be a reason I am here."

"You are probably here to atone for your sins," she snapped. "Or perhaps to avoid your just reward in the afterlife."

"Hell, you mean?" In spite of his frustration, his lips twitched with laughter. By God, the vixen had a sharp tongue to her. Didn't she know it was dangerous to look at a man like that, her lips all pursed up, inviting any red-blooded male to kiss away the primness? He was tempted to take that invitation, only . . .

"Very likely this is hell. What could be worse than being in a woman's bedroom and not being able to do anything about it?"

He watched with interest the way she stiffened, the very picture of offended propriety.

"I am certain God will mete out a more fitting punishment."

"What more fitting? Most of my sins involved a woman's bed."

"I think the Lord will want to punish you for the small matter of murdering your wife."

Phillip's amusement died a rapid death. "Murdering my wife! Do you mean Alicia? What absolute rot!"

He began to stride about the room, hands clasped behind his back, a deep frown on his face. This was too much. What the devil was going on? Could God truly be punishing him, as the girl suggested? Perhaps he had done a few things God did not approve of, but he'd never murdered his wife.

He stopped once more by her bed. She watched him with wary eyes, which for some reason made him angrier than ever. "How do you know this? You said you know nothing about me."

"I only know the little that Aunt Letty told me."

"Who is this Letty?"

"Leticia Chetwynd. Your first wife's sister, I believe."

"Letty!" He smiled, a picture of a mischievous, elfin face flashing into his mind. "Little Letty! She's still alive?"

"Very much so."

"So, what did she have to say?"

"She said you were accused of murdering your second wife and hanged for it seventy-eight years ago."

He stilled, staring off into the darkest corner of the room, half-remembered emotions surging through him. His hand rose to his throat, partly in horror, partly in denial. Jumbled puzzle-piece memories swirled in his brain, defying his attempts to connect them into a comprehensible picture. He concentrated harder, forcing the pieces to align themselves, forcing them to come together, even though part of him didn't want to see, didn't want to know. Slowly, the picture took on shape, came into focus. . .

Something caught his eye and the picture shattered. Cursing silently, he stared into the dark corner, trying to determine what he had seen. Nothing moved. The corner was dark, still. He stared harder, but the dark only grew blacker, more still.

Deep tremors coursed down his spine. Something was in the corner. He couldn't put a name to it, but it was dark and cold. And it was waiting. He felt himself grow dim, his thoughts blur. The cold darkness crept toward him.

With all his will, he focused on Margaret's heart-shaped face, fighting against the insidious darkness. "I don't quite remember what happened." He forced the words from his mouth, and the darkness receded, leaving him feeling weak and dizzy. Collapsing into one of the red-lacquered chairs, he muttered, "God, I need a drink."

He glanced around the room, but no bottle stood on any of the ornate tables. He groaned. "You must help me."

"Help you get a drink?"

"No, no. Help me clear my name. That must be why I am here."

Margaret fingered one of the gold tassels tying back the yellow bed curtains. "How can I do that?"

"Talk to Letty. Perhaps she will know how to go about it."

Margaret's better sense told her to say no, to tell him to go away and never come back. Surely he could resolve this problem himself, without her help. There was no need for her to get involved. Besides, for all she knew, he might actually have killed his wife. Although Aunt Letty had said he was unjustly accused, Margaret didn't quite believe an innocent man could be convicted of murder. "Do you remember anything?"

His brow furrowed, and he gazed into the far corner, a distant look in his eyes. "I seem to remember something about my trial. I could swear I was convicted by a ghost. And I remember people staring at me."

His hand went to his throat again, his fingers stretching across his neck, rubbing the skin. "Their faces were avid, yet indifferent. They cheered."

Her fingers grew still on the tassel. A shiver crept up her spine. She waited to see if he would say more, but he didn't. Silently, he continued to stare into the corner, as if seeing another place, another time. She watched him, trying to read his expression, but his face was remote.

Except for his eyes. The pupils of his eyes were dilated, making them look almost completely black. Black with . . .

Fear?

She heard herself speak.

"I will help you," she said.

7

She must be insane.

Staring into the mirror while Yvette dressed her hair, the realization came to Margaret. How else to explain her impulsive agreement to help Phillip? Dear heaven, how else to explain that she even *saw* Phillip?

Margaret picked up a crystal perfume bottle and twisted the lid back and forth, her eyes still fixed blindly on the mirror. She should have told him to go away. How shocked everyone would be if they knew a man had visited her in her room at night—even if he was a ghost.

A ghost!

An obnoxious ghost. She didn't like him one bit. Certainly he had deserved whatever happened to him.

But that look on his face . . .

She shuddered, her fingers rising to her own throat for a moment before returning to twist the perfume cap even more convulsively. What exactly had he remembered? Pain? Agony? Fear?

"Miss . . . Miss!" Yvette shrieked as perfume

spilled out across the polished surface, filling the room with a heavy rose scent.

Margaret jumped up. "Oh, dear. I'm sorry, Yvette."

"Hmmph, what a mess," the maid grumbled. "I'm sure his lordship must be waiting for you downstairs, Miss Margaret. Maybe you'd better go on down."

But belowstairs, Bernard was nowhere in sight. Geoffrey, Cecilia, and Jeremy were the only ones in the morning room when Margaret entered. Geoffrey had a black frown on his face and Cecilia's chin trembled. She looked relieved to see Margaret. After exchanging greetings, Margaret filled her plate and sat down next to Jeremy who was finishing off the remains of his poached eggs.

"Papa, could we go fishing?" he asked.

Before Geoffrey could reply, Cecilia spoke. "Your father had a bad night, Jeremy. He will need to rest today."

Jeremy nodded, making no protest, but seeing his drooping mouth, Cecilia added, "Perhaps you may dine at table tonight if Aunt Letty gives permission."

"Gives permission for what?" asked Aunt Letty, entering the room.

"For Jeremy to dine with us tonight, if Margaret doesn't mind," said Cecilia. Margaret shook her head.

"What a delightful idea," Aunt Letty said. "I'll look forward to your company, young sir."

"Thank you, Aunt Letty." Jeremy quietly excused himself, and slouched out of the room.

Cecilia looked after him, a worried expression on her face. "I don't know what's the matter with that child."

"Why, whatever do you mean?" Aunt Letty's sparse eyebrows rose in surprise. "He's a sweet boy. He reminds me of Phillip." Eschewing food, she poured herself a cup of tea and sat down. She proceeded, in between sips, to describe in detail Phillip's many charms until Cecilia finally protested, "Please, Aunt Letty! You're giving me indigestion."

Aunt Letty's brow crinkled in worry. "Is something wrong with the food?"

Cecilia shook her head, whether in answer to the question or in exasperation, Margaret wasn't sure.

"Margaret, where is Bernard?" Cecilia asked, changing the subject.

"I don't know." An idea occurred to Margaret. "Aunt Letty, would you show me the rest of the picture gallery while I'm waiting for him?"

Aunt Letty's wrinkles quivered with the force of her smile. "Of course, dear child."

As Margaret followed the old woman from the room, she heard Cecilia say, "I just don't think it's a good idea, Geoffrey." The closing door muffled Geoffrey's reply.

Margaret forgot the incident when Aunt Letty pointed out the portrait of Phillip's first wife. She had a narrow, sallow face, and wore a dark dress with a high neck and long sleeves. She sat stiffly on a hard, uncomfortable-looking chair.

"Poor Mary," said Aunt Letty, looking up at her sister's unsmiling face. "She was so plain. But she had a huge dowry, and the Eglinton family needed to marry money. Phillip came courting and he was so dashing, so brave, so handsome. How I adored him. When he and my sister married, I visited them often, and he always had a gift and a compliment for me. I was ever so jealous of my sister. I wished I could have married him, but alas, I was only six. But when my mother died in a carriage accident, I went to live with them. He taught me how to ride and to dance, and even to handle a rapier. How charming he was! All the ladies adored him. Whenever we had company for dinner, I would watch from the landing as all the women flirted with him and stood close to him and dropped their fans and all manner of silly things. Especially that Alicia." Aunt Letty moved to the next painting.

Margaret looked at the portrait of Phillip's second wife. Her hair curled in blond ringlets down her back, her lips and eyes smiled knowingly, and she wore some sort of gauzy drapery that Margaret supposed was meant to be a dress. The diaphanous material slipped off one shoulder, low over her right breast, as if she were undressing. In the background, a sylvan glade waited invitingly.

"Phillip married to please himself the second time," Aunt Letty said unnecessarily. "How I hated her! She already had Lord Mortimer—the first earl, I mean—on a string, but she was never satisfied. My sister died in childbirth and that was all that harpy needed. She started lurking about—coming to the house alone, or running into Phillip when he was out riding. She came over every day to 'console' Phillip and never left him alone for a minute. He married her a year later." Aunt Letty glared at Alicia's painted face. "The trollop."

Margaret choked a little and Aunt Letty smiled innocently at her.

"Are you all right, dear? You should be careful. I had a cousin who suffered a coughing spell like that and choked to death before anyone knew what happened."

"Yes, Aunt Letty," Margaret said, recovering. "What happened after Phillip married Alicia?"

Aunt Letty's eyes grew bright with malice. "Phillip said I could still live with them. *She* didn't like that, of course. She didn't like me, even though I was *ever* so sweet to her. Every time her hem came undone or she found a lizard in her dressing table drawer or pepper got in her perfume, she blamed me. She was a very untrusting person. They argued over that and they argued over other things, too. One night I heard a great ruckus and I sneaked out on the landing. Phillip and Alicia were below, dripping wet. There was a fearful storm that night, and they must have been out in it. Alicia screamed that she hated him, that he was cold and mean; he shouted back that she was a greedy slut."

Aunt Letty shook her head with vigorous satisfaction.

"The next day, Alicia was feverish. I can't say I was surprised. She stayed in her bed and I certainly didn't visit her, but I heard the servants whispering about her mad ravings. The next night Phillip pushed her down the stairs and I don't blame him a bit. She deserved it."

Dear heaven, he *had* murdered his wife, thought Margaret, reaching out to the wall to steady herself. A *murderer* had been in her room last night. And yet— "But Aunt Letty, I thought you said he was *unjustly* accused."

"Certainly he was. Giving someone a little nudge is hardly the same thing as murder." Aunt Letty smiled ingenuously at Margaret.

Margaret smiled back weakly. Was the old woman completely amoral? "Aunt Letty, couldn't it have been an accident?"

"I don't think so. Alicia was carrying on with Lord Mortimer. Phillip must have found out." Aunt Letty's brow furrowed in confusion. "I simply don't understand what she saw in the earl. He was a greasy sort. Much like the current Lord Mortimer. Poor boy. How unfortunate that he so closely resembles his grandfather. Not that I hold his looks against him. He can be very understanding at times. And I do enjoy his card parties."

"But Aunt Letty, what makes you think—?"

The door swung open, stopping her in midsentence. Bernard stood there, frowning, chin folded against his neck, arms crossed. "There you are, Margaret. I have been looking for you. Would you like to go for a ride?"

Margaret hesitated. She had not found out anything to help Phillip yet, and the conversation with Aunt Letty was becoming very interesting. "I don't know, Bernard. Aunt Letty is telling me about Phillip."

"Nonsense, child. Run along. I remember what it is like to be young and in love. I wouldn't dream of keeping you from Bernard's side." Aunt Letty smiled benevolently.

Bernard held out his elbow. With a brittle smile, Margaret placed her fingers on his sleeve, barely touching the fabric.

As soon as they were out of earshot, Bernard said, "Margaret, I wish you wouldn't encourage Aunt Letty to talk about Phillip. I am afraid she is losing her grip on reality."

"I am sorry, Bernard," she said dutifully, trying not to grit her teeth.

She rode out with him and after a while he forgot his displeasure enough to deliver a highly technical discourse on the anatomy of the common housefly.

Had she truly moped that whole summer when she was twelve because he had gone to visit a friend instead of coming home? She knew she had, because she remembered her mother had given her a nasty strengthening fomentation that tasted like tree bark, but listening to Bernard now, she could scarcely credit it.

As Bernard explained the difference between upper and lower mandibles, Margaret's thoughts wandered to Phillip. Could he truly be a murderer? She didn't want to believe it. If only she could have talked to Aunt Letty a bit longer! Perhaps when she returned to the house she would be able to corner the old woman again.

Unfortunately, Margaret had no such opportunity any time that afternoon, and after dinner Bernard suggested a game of cards, to which Aunt Letty enthusiastically agreed. In the parlor, her hopes of getting the old woman by herself effectively destroyed, Margaret picked up a book and started turning the pages.

"Margaret, do you wish to play?" Bernard asked.

"No, thank you. I'm not much of a cardplayer," Margaret said. She didn't want to get tied up in a game that could very possibly go on until all hours of the night. "This book is fascinating."

The others began playing, and Margaret pretended to read while she mulled over what Aunt Letty had told her today. Not much. If only Bernard hadn't interrupted!

Perhaps it wouldn't matter. Perhaps Phillip would not appear tonight.

Although she would think he would want to find out what she had discovered.

But truly, she wished he would stay away. She never wanted to see the rudesby again. He was unbelievably insolent and arrogant and—

She looked at the clock. Half-past eight. It was still light outside. Could she possibly retire so early?

She turned another page in the book and tried to concentrate on the words in front of her. It was some sort of deadly dull poem. She flipped back a few pages to see the title. "'Ode to Prince Albert,'" she read.

The clock struck the quarter hour.

"I do believe I'll retire." Margaret yawned. "I am most extraordinarily tired."

Upstairs, her pace quickened as she approached

her room. With lightning speed, she changed behind the screen, almost popping the buttons off her dress in her haste. She was about to dismiss Yvette, when she remembered something.

"Yvette, would you bring a decanter of brandy and a glass here?"

Yvette tottered a few steps. "Brandy, miss?"

"Yes, brandy. Please hurry."

Muttering under her breath, the maid hurried away. After she returned with the brandy, Margaret dismissed her, and turned her attention to the lamp on her dressing table.

Should she leave the lamp lit or blow it out? Better to leave it lit. She felt safer when she had some control over the light. It was too creepy to have lights suddenly appearing and disappearing. With a nod, she picked up the lamp, placed it on her nightstand, and climbed into bed.

Should she be sitting up or lying down when he came? Sitting up was definitely more proper, she decided. She shoved the pillows up against the dragon on the headboard and wiggled into an upright position. She tucked the yellow silk blanket up under her arms, making sure it completely covered her chest, folded her hands in her lap, and waited.

And waited.

As the minutes stretched into hours, irritation replaced her anticipation. Where was he? She punched the pillows a few times, feeling foolish. Perhaps she ought to lie down, instead of sitting there as if she were expecting him. He might think she was waiting for him. Better to lie down.

Pushing the pillows down, she lay down and closed her eyes. She sniffed. She could still smell the rose perfume she had spilled this morning, but nothing else. Where was he?

It was impossible to keep her eyes shut. She

opened them and stared up at the underside of the pagoda canopy. The light from the lamp cast a different angle of light, and something caught her eye.

For the first time, she saw a painted cloud near the edge of the canopy. Grabbing the lamp and holding it up, she rose to her knees to see better. She saw that the sleeping Chinese man was surrounded by puffy white clouds, each with a scene painted in the middle. The first cloud showed the Chinese man standing on a ship, fighting off a hoard of pirates. The next showed him listening to a man playing a flute. In another he was surrounded by laughing children and in another he and a woman were—

Margaret gasped and lowered the lamp, but it was too late, the picture had imprinted itself on her brain. A man and woman in a strange position. Naked.

She was shocked. Did Aunt Letty know about this . . . this indecent picture? Thinking of the sweet old lady, Margaret decided she must be unaware. How embarrassed she would be if Margaret told her.

Perhaps she shouldn't mention it. And perhaps she should look again—merely to make sure she hadn't been mistaken.

No, she wasn't mistaken. The man appeared to be joined at the hip with the woman and his hand rested against her breast. A strange tingle lodged low in Margaret's stomach. What did it feel like? she wondered. What did it feel like to be so intimate, so—

"Good evening, Margaret."

Margaret jumped, almost setting the bed on fire. A blush suffused her entire body. Clanking the lamp down, she scrambled under the blanket, glaring at Phillip. Had he noticed what she was looking at? "I wish you would knock or something!"

"Forgive my impatience."

In spite of their politeness, his words were a trifle brusque. Conversely, Margaret breathed a little easier. Apparently he had seen nothing out of the ordinary.

"Being a ghost is very tiresome," he continued. He stood by her bed, his stance casual, but a tension radiated from him. The glow around him shone very brightly, highlighting his broad shoulders and muscular thighs. "I want to rest in peace or go wherever I am supposed to go."

"I wouldn't be so eager to arrive at my destination if I were you," Margaret said grumpily, shoving the pillows back up for the second time.

Phillip looked at her sharply. "What have you discovered?"

"Aunt Letty said she believes Alicia and Lord Mortimer were having an affair, which you discovered. You argued with Alicia, and the next night pushed her down the stairs."

"Mortimer," he said slowly. "I do seem to remember something about him. There was a storm. I remember a swordfight in the rain. I left him there in the mud and dragged Alicia home."

Phillip passed a hand across his brow. "How she screamed at me. I can almost hear her shrieking in that perforating voice of hers. I very nearly strangled her right then."

Margaret inhaled sharply.

Looking up, he saw her expression. He continued testily, "But I didn't—I wouldn't. She caught pneumonia, and I believe she was delirious when she fell down the stairs. The idea that I pushed her is ridiculous."

The breath eased out of Margaret. "Then why did the jury convict you?"

"Because . . ." His black brows drew together and

he frowned at a gold tassel. "Hell and the devil, I can't remember." He raked his fingers through his short auburn hair. "What did Letty say?"

"I didn't get a chance to ask her about the trial."

He stared at her. "You didn't get a chance? Why the devil not?"

"It's not easy to ask questions about a ghost," Margaret said defensively. "Aunt Letty tends to ramble. She went on and on about how handsome you were and how charming and how the ladies adored you."

Phillip started to grin. "Dear Letty. She always was remarkably astute."

"The way she talks, I'm surprised you haven't been nominated for sainthood," Margaret said sourly, disliking his smugness.

"Oh, I would never qualify for sainthood. . . . "

Margaret disliked the leer on his face even more.

" . . . I have too much of a fondness for the ladies. Women are so soft and pretty and wondrously sweet in bed." The glow around him softened, became less harsh as he smiled down at her.

She could feel her color rising. Her heartbeat trotted at an uncomfortable rhythm. "Really sir, this conversation is most improper."

He laughed wickedly and sat down on the bed. The pace of her heart increased to a canter. He leaned toward her, the cold air around him raising goose bumps on her arms. Hastily, she scooted away. He laughed again, and she pressed up against a bedpost, aware that now there was a very different look to him—a sleepy, languorous look that spoke of forbidden things.

"So prim, Margaret? What do you think I will do to you?" His voice was as warm and smooth and seductive as hot chocolate.

"I . . . nothing . . . that is . . ."

The light around him pulsed and shimmered.

Mesmerizing gray eyes gazed into hers, and her heart positively galloped.

What *would* he do to her?

8

Phillip rose abruptly to his feet. He stood with his back to her for several long moments. When he turned, she shrank a little from his hard expression.

He must have sensed her confusion, because his face softened and he smiled a little as he said, "Don't worry, Miss Westbourne. Your virtue is safe with me. Even if I wished it, I could not touch you."

"You couldn't? Why not?"

"I'm not sure. I just have this sense that I cannot touch you."

"Oh." Her heart slowed to a plodding walk. "One of the rules of being a ghost, I suppose."

"Yes, I suppose so." His gaze lingered on her hair before he turned away again.

An odd disappointment filled her. Not that she wanted him to touch her, it was merely that she was . . . curious. It was perfectly natural to be curious about a ghost. She watched him bend down in front of the mirror on her dressing table. No reflection looked back. How strange. Did it bother him? she wondered. "Phillip," she said tentatively. "What is it like?"

"What?"

"Being a ghost."

"Oh." He walked over and put his hand through the wall, then pulled it out. He stared at the intact wall and his undamaged hand, then repeated the process. "It is not much different from being alive. I feel cold, though. Colder than I've ever been, but it doesn't come from the outside, it comes from within."

He stared over at the corner as if he could see something there by the wardrobe. Margaret followed his gaze, but the light didn't extend that far and all she could see was darkness.

"I feel everything I did when I was alive. Almost everything," he amended, pulling out his hand and wiggling his fingers. "But it all seems very far away, out of reach, as if a great distance separated me from you." He looked at her for a moment, his expression unfathomable. Then he turned and continued his hand game. "Also, as you are aware, my memory is rather foggy. It seems as though everything happened a long time ago."

"Seventy-eight years is rather a long time."

"Yes, but I don't remember anything in between. It is very peculiar."

"Nothing at all?"

"No. Wait. Yes, I do remember something. A dream, I think. I know Mortimer was in it, and a man who looked like Mortimer, but that's all."

"How odd. Nothing else?"

"I vaguely remember a voice whispering to me."

"Aunt Letty?"

"Probably." He prowled restlessly around the room, inspecting the dressing screen, the carved red bedposts. When he saw the crystal decanter on the escritoire, he stopped, his face lighting up. "Brandy, by God!"

He flashed her a look of burning gratitude and

turned toward the small desk. He reached for the decanter, but his hand passed right through the glass. He swore, and tried once more, but it was no use. Bending over the bottle, he sniffed. With a groan, he collapsed on the chair, dropping his head between his hands. "Damnation, I can't even smell it!"

His distress made her wish she hadn't asked for the brandy. It hadn't occurred to her that he wouldn't be able to drink. What a strange, terrible existence he had, living in an in-between world, unable to remember his own past. How bleak. How lonely.

Huddling under the blanket, she remembered that time in her own past when she had been so alone, when she felt invisible to the rest of the world. She had sworn never to endure that loneliness again. Marrying Bernard ensured that she wouldn't. But Phillip could not resolve his loneliness so easily. If she could help him, he might go on to a better place, but if she couldn't—

A sigh from Phillip interrupted her anxious thoughts. He raised his head, and as he met her eyes a whisper of a smile curved his lips. "Being a specter is more difficult than I thought it would be." His gaze flickered to the brandy. "This must be further punishment for my sins."

How could he joke? But then again, what else could he do? Wail and moan like a more traditional ghost?

Sudden determination filled her. "Cousin Winifred— who chaperoned me on the train—is leaving tomorrow. I'm driving to the train station with her to see her off. Aunt Letty is coming, too, and on the way back I will question her again. Don't worry, Phillip," she said earnestly. "We will find a way to clear your name."

He studied her for a long moment. Then he smiled, not flirtatiously, but warmly, in a way that made her heart flutter. "You're an unusual woman, Margaret Westbourne."

"Because I want to help you? Anyone would do the same," she said, forgetting how her common sense had tried to dissuade her from doing so.

"No, not so much that," he replied. "Because you didn't run, screaming hysterically, from the room. Even now, you sit calmly talking to a ghost as if one had visited you every day of your life."

Margaret blushed. Her behavior was shocking. But if she were absolutely truthful with herself, she would have to admit that she rather enjoyed being visited by a ghost. Especially one who had apparently lived an exciting life. Her own existence these past few years had been painfully uneventful, boring even. Until now.

But of course, she couldn't tell him that. "Hysteria would serve little purpose," she said, pursing her lips.

His dark eyes gleamed for a moment. Still smiling, he saluted, then disappeared.

Startled, she waited a few minutes to see if he would come back. When he didn't, she blew out the lamp and went to sleep, a smile on her face.

The next day at the train station, Cousin Winifred thanked Aunt Letty. "I've enjoyed my visit to your home. Now Margaret is settled, I must get back to my cottage."

"You're welcome to stay," said Aunt Letty.

"Oh, thank you, Miss Chetwynd. But I am most anxious about my garden. I fear my herbs may not be able to tolerate this warm weather."

The day was indeed stifling. Standing on the platform, the sun beating down on them, Margaret wished she had chosen a different dress to wear. The long-sleeved, high-necked cloth of her carriage dress was sweltering hot.

"I instructed a neighbor's girl to water them," Cousin Winifred continued, "but I am not certain she is reliable. I will return, though, when it is time for Margaret to come home."

With a flurry of hugs and waves, Cousin Winifred boarded the train, and Margaret and Aunt Letty started back for Durnock Castle.

Now was the time.

"Aunt Letty," Margaret began tentatively. "I wanted to ask you something about Phillip."

"Ah, poor Phillip," the old woman sighed. "How restless he was. He always seemed to be searching for something, but I don't believe he ever found it. Did I tell you how charming he was?"

"Yes—"

"After my sister died, he courted my cousin Caroline for a while. She told me how he serenaded her one night; and another time he whisked her away from a ball, so they could—"

"Aunt Letty," Margaret interrupted ruthlessly, "don't you think Phillip might wish to go to his heavenly reward instead of being trapped here on earth?"

"Very likely. I would miss him, though."

"Yes, but don't you think we should try to help him?" Deciding subtlety was wasted on the older woman, Margaret came straight to the point. "I think he haunts the castle because he wants us to prove he didn't murder Alicia."

"You think so, dear? You may be correct, but I don't see how we could prove such a thing."

"Who saw Phillip push Alicia?" asked Margaret.

"No one."

"No one? Then how could he be convicted?"

"I don't know, dear," Aunt Letty sighed. "If only he had never married that horrible woman."

Margaret mulled over this new information. Why would a jury convict Phillip, a nobleman, of murder without any concrete evidence? It didn't make sense.

She was still puzzling over this when they drove up to Durnock Castle.

Cecilia greeted them at the door. "Margaret," she said gaily, "since we are going to be sisters, we must become better acquainted. Would you like to go riding with me? I can have Cook prepare a picnic lunch for us if you like."

"I would enjoy that, Cecilia," Margaret said as Aunt Letty flitted away. She felt frustrated. The older woman was right. How could anyone prove Phillip was innocent after all this time?

After agreeing to meet at the stables in thirty minutes, she went to change while Cecilia talked to the cook.

Margaret managed to change in half that time. As she wandered out toward the stables, it occurred to her that she could try asking Cecilia about Phillip. Aunt Letty had probably inundated her with stories throughout her childhood, and perhaps Margaret could learn something that would help. Feeling more cheerful, she was busy formulating her questions when she felt something solid plop on her head. Startled, she stopped and looked down at the ground. An apple core lay there. Looking up, she saw Jeremy stretched out on a branch, taking a large bite from another apple. When he saw her watching him, he stared at her solemnly.

"Sorry, Miss Westbourne, I didn't notice you."

Margaret immediately gained the impression that not only had he noticed her, but that he had also taken careful aim.

She opened her mouth to rebuke him when a new voice intruded.

"Jeremy, you will apologize to Miss Westbourne at once," Geoffrey ordered his son sharply.

Jeremy, a look of dismay on his face, tumbled off

the branch and scrambled to his feet to face his father.

"Beg pardon, Miss Westbourne. Didn't mean anything."

Margaret nodded.

"Jeremy, I would like to speak to you inside the stables."

Margaret bit her lip as she watched the two enter the stables. She had not wanted Jeremy to get a whipping.

She heard the whistling and smacking sound of a switch being applied before the door opened and Jeremy came out rubbing his posterior. Geoffrey followed. Margaret stood awkwardly, watching them, not knowing what to say.

"Cecilia and I are going riding," she finally said to Geoffrey. "Would you and Jeremy like to come along?"

"No, no, no!" a new voice intruded. Margaret turned to see Cecilia striding down the path, a bright smile on her face. "Forgive me, Margaret, but I have been looking forward to having some time alone with you. You cannot want these hulking men along."

Cecilia directed her gaze at Jeremy. "You should be attending your studies, young man." Glad to escape, the boy ran off and Cecilia turned to her husband. "Geoffrey, I'm so glad I found you. Aunt Letty is looking for someone to play backgammon. I already told Margaret I would ride with her, so I was wondering if you would mind?" Cecilia smiled pleadingly at her husband.

Geoffrey stiffened a little, but his voice was mild. "Of course, darling." With a slightly awkward bow to Margaret, he stumped off toward the house.

Cecilia frowned after him. Then with a shake of her head, she said to Margaret, "I apologize for cutting you off like that, but he's not supposed to ride."

"Oh! I'm sorry. I had no idea."

"It's not your fault. Actually, I was afraid he might accept. Every so often, a reckless humor overtakes him. I have to watch him constantly. Did Bernard tell you about the position he found for Geoffrey in London?"

"No," Margaret said.

"It's with the Board of Trade. When Bernard heard about an opening for a clerk, he thought of Geoffrey."

"It sounds perfect for your husband!"

Cecilia shook her head. "I don't think he will accept. After we discussed it, he realized there would be too many drawbacks to living in London. Besides, he's not certain he's ready for the stress of a regular post."

"I see," Margaret said, although she was surprised by the other woman's assessment. Geoffrey seemed very healthy to her. "How did he lose his leg?"

"His horse fell on him in a battle. His entire leg was crushed and the lower portion had to be amputated. He had to leave the army. It's been a difficult adjustment. For the longest time, Geoffrey was restless. He had nothing to occupy him, you see. When Jeremy came, it was a blessing. He pulled Geoffrey out of his megrims."

"He seems like a very nice boy," Margaret said politely.

Cecilia laughed. "I don't know if I would describe him as 'nice.' A 'handful' would be more appropriate. I only wish we could cure him of his atrocious habit of practical jokes." She frowned for a moment. "Although, actually, he hasn't played one for the last few months. He's changed. He didn't used to be so sullen. I don't know what's the matter with him."

Cecilia sighed. Then, with a bright smile she said, "Why on earth are we standing here? Come along, let's not waste any more of this glorious day."

*   *   *

Glorious or not, Margaret was very hot when they returned later that afternoon. They had ridden over much of the extensive castle grounds, past an ornamental lake, through an oak spinney, and down to the river Tees. Although she had enjoyed herself, unfortunately she had learned nothing about Phillip. When she delicately asked about him, Cecilia had only laughed and said she never paid attention to Aunt Letty's nonsense. Instead, Cecilia spoke of her experiences in Burma and Africa, and for a while Margaret had forgotten about Phillip.

She went up to her room to change. While Yvette unbuttoned her dress, Margaret was lost in a pleasant daydream of hot blue skies, emerald green forests, and tall purple mountains. What would it be like to visit such a place? she wondered dreamily. She was about to pull down the bodice, when she felt a sudden draft of cool air on her skin. She froze for a moment before twisting her head around. Phillip, leaning against one of the red bedposts, was watching her lazily.

With a squeal, Margaret grabbed the neck of her dress and ran behind the screen. "What are you doing here?" she asked in a shrill voice.

Yvette's brow creased. "Helping you change, miss."

Straightening, Phillip walked forward a few steps. He inspected the scene of Diana bathing, painted on one of the screen's panels, before looking up to grin unrepentantly at her. "I wanted to speak with you."

"Couldn't you wait?"

"I thought you wanted to change," Yvette said in bewildered tones.

"I'm glad I didn't. My impatience is greatly rewarded." His glinting eyes dropped to her shoulders, barely visible above the screen.

Margaret opened her mouth to make a blistering

reply, but fortunately caught sight of her maid's confused face. Biting her lip, she glared at him instead.

Phillip laughed, but then rubbed his arms, shivering. "Damn, it's cold in here. Tell your maid to light a fire."

Margaret hesitated, but she wanted to be able to talk to Phillip without worrying about the maid, so she said, "Yvette, would you please get some wood for the fire?"

Yvette stared at her as if she were a bedlamite. "Gibbons said today's the hottest day in a decade."

"It's a bit chilly in here," Margaret said weakly. "Please, Yvette."

With a shake of her head, the maid left.

Behind the protection of the screen, Margaret glared again at Phillip. "I didn't know you could appear during the day."

"Nor did I. It takes a considerable amount of concentration. I should do so more often; being a ghost has a few unexpected benefits." His eyes dropped again and for one terrible moment, Margaret thought he could see right through the screen.

"You can't see through the screen, can you?" she stammered.

He smiled a devilish grin, and she almost fainted, until, much to her relief, he shook his head. "Alas, no. But you need not be so modest, Margaret. I am a phantasm. A spirit cares nothing for clothes. Your state of dress—or undress—is a matter of complete indifference to me."

"Then you won't care if I stay behind the screen."

He grinned at this sally before continuing with spurious sincerity. "Truly, you ought not be concerned. Clothes are meaningless to a ghost. In fact, I'm surprised I even appear to be wearing any. Do you think I can take them off?"

He lifted a hand to his cravat and Margaret

screeched, "Don't you dare!"

His hand hovered near the neckcloth. "Surely you're willing to sacrifice your modesty for the advancement of scientific knowledge?"

Her eyes flickered over him, and a picture of the naked man painted over her bed flashed into her brain. For one insane moment, she was tempted to agree and advance not only scientific knowledge, but her *personal* knowledge. Her gaze rose to his, and seeing the wicked sparkle in his eyes, she regained control of her wits. She frowned fiercely.

He sighed. "I suppose not. Women are so cruel, so selfish."

"Oh, do be quiet." She was beginning to feel foolish, hiding behind the screen, and his outrageous teasing was not helping. "Why are you here?"

"I am eager to know what you have discovered."

"Oh." Margaret lowered her gaze and traced a finger along the burled edge of the screen. "It's very strange, Phillip."

"What is?"

"Aunt Letty says no one was present when you . . . I mean, when Alicia fell down the stairs. She doesn't think we can prove you are innocent."

It was Phillip's turn to glare. "There has to be a way. What did she say about the trial?"

"I didn't ask about the trial."

"You didn't? Why the hell not?"

"I didn't think of it. I'm sorry." She felt ridiculously guilty for her failure. "I'll ask tonight, I promise." She sighed. "It is too bad you can't talk to Aunt Letty directly. Are you certain you cannot appear to her?"

"Yes." He paused, a thought occurring to him. "Although perhaps I can appear when you ask the questions. Then I can steer you in the right direction. And just hearing her may prompt my memory." He gave a decisive nod. "I will try for dinner tonight."

This did not sound so good. His mocking presence would be difficult to handle with everyone else present—especially Bernard. "I don't know, Phillip. The whole family will be there. It will not be easy to question Aunt Letty."

He looked at her consideringly. "You mentioned you are betrothed. Your fiancé will be present, I take it?"

"Bernard? Of course. As well as his sister, her husband, and their son. You see how difficult it would be to ask questions?"

"Not at all," he said coolly. "In fact, I find I'm curious to meet everyone. Especially Bernard."

Margaret hesitated. She could not really refuse; he would probably come anyway. Nodding reluctantly, she was aware of an uneasy feeling that she would not enjoy her meal tonight.

9

Margaret was halfway through her onion soup when she looked up and saw Phillip leaning against the sideboard behind Geoffrey. Nervously she glanced around the table, not quite able to believe that no one else could see him. He was fainter, his auburn hair not so bright, the blue-green of his coat darker. But although his image wasn't quite as distinct, he was still plainly visible—at least to her. Everyone else was eating and conversing, oblivious to his presence.

"Dear heaven, what is that you're eating? It looks delicious," he said, inhaling deeply. "I can almost smell it." He gazed with rapt attention as she lifted a spoonful to her mouth.

With all the pathos of a starving dog, he watched her swallow. "I'm famished," he said. "Do you realize it's been over seventy-eight years since I had a meal?"

"Men," she muttered. All they thought of were their wretched stomachs. They never paid attention to important things, like the special care a woman sometimes takes with her appearance.

Perhaps he noticed her displeasure because suddenly he turned on the full force of his smile and said, "But where are my manners? Good evening, Miss Westbourne." His eyes roved over her appreciatively. "How lovely you look this evening. That dress is vastly becoming."

Some of her displeasure dissipated. She knew it was. The neckline was cut low, showing off her arms and shoulders. The tight fit of the bodice emphasized her slim figure and the rose hue lent a touch of color to her cheeks. She had worried a bit about the absence of her bust improver, but the wool pads were too uncomfortable in this hot weather.

She had selected the dress with care. Not because she wanted to impress Phillip, but because . . . well, because she wanted to look nice for Bernard. Still, she was glad Phillip had noticed. Bernard certainly hadn't, she thought with a glare at her unsuspecting fiancé.

"What a treat to see you dressed so fine. It's rare that I get to see you in such a dress. In fact, now that I think on it, it's rare I see you in any dress at all."

"Are you all right, Margaret dear?" Aunt Letty asked, peering down from the end of the table. "You look flushed."

"I'm fine, Aunt Letty. It's a bit warm in here."

"Good God, is this little Letty?" Phillip exclaimed. "She looks about a hundred years old."

Aunt Letty's spoon stopped in midair and she cocked her head, as if listening. Margaret held her breath. Could the old woman truly hear Phillip "whispering"? Would Phillip be able to talk to her directly after all? But Aunt Letty said nothing and after a moment, resumed eating her soup.

Plainly she had sensed something, though. Margaret

looked at Phillip and raised a brow, but he did not see. He was staring transfixed at Aunt Letty.

"How odd to think this old woman is the girl I once knew." He crouched down beside her, his hand going out as if to stroke her hair before he caught himself. "She was the sweetest child," he murmured. "Although she made Alicia's life hell." He smiled a little, but his eyes were sad. "She was like a daughter to me. I wish I could have seen her grow up. Did she ever marry? Have children?"

He looked at Margaret and she shook her head slightly, a small lump in her throat.

"I had a most enjoyable afternoon shopping, Margaret," said Cecilia. "You should have come with me."

Phillip shook off his abstraction and rose to his feet. He glanced around the table, his gaze lingering on Geoffrey. "The gloomy-looking fellow is your betrothed? How did he lose his leg?"

"Your immoderate ardor for fashion will cloud your mind with malignant emotions if you don't take care, Cecilia," said Bernard. "Vanity can often lead one down the path of folly. Don't you agree, Margaret?"

"Who is this braying jackass?" Phillip looked down his nose, a fist on his hip.

"Yes, Bernard," Margaret said stiffly, not sure if she were more annoyed with Bernard or Phillip. "Although one must have a care for one's appearance, also."

"Bernard? Surely this cannot be your betrothed?" Phillip gazed in disbelief. Bernard was hunched over his bowl, his chin tucked even farther back than usual as he spooned soup into his mouth.

Phillip swung around to face Margaret again. "Why the devil have you betrothed yourself to such a damned looby?"

Margaret gripped her spoon, all traces of sympathy for him evaporating in a rush of anger. How dare he call her fiancé names? And how dare he judge Bernard so quickly, so unfairly? Perhaps Bernard had acquired a slightly stuffy manner, but he was still her fiancé.

She never should have agreed to let Phillip come. She should have known that he would take delight in goading her. He had almost succeeded, too, because she was nearly overwhelmed by a childish desire to fling a spoonful of soup at him. Controlling the impulse, she set her spoon down. It clanked loudly against her bowl.

"Finished, dear? Gibbons, the next course, please."

The servants brought in a game pie and a boiled leg of mutton with capers while Margaret glared a furious reprimand at Phillip.

"It's a good thing I am already dead," he observed. "Or that look surely would have sent me to my grave."

Margaret sniffed, his humor in no way mollifying her, and her frustration at being unable to give him a tongue lashing building. She glared at him again for good measure, but Phillip had caught sight of the steaming platters of food. In a trancelike stupor, he followed the footmen around the table as they served the pie and mutton.

He'll be drooling like an infant in a moment, she thought with disgust.

She could feel the cold air behind her when he stopped at her side. A quick peek revealed that he was staring down at her plate, his face pale and yearning.

She made a point of taking a large bite of mutton. "Aunt Letty, this is divine," she said with a sigh of pleasure. Actually, it was as tough as rope. She had to chew an awfully long time before she managed to swallow. Spearing another piece, she casually waved her fork under Phillip's nose. "You must compliment Cook."

"Margaret—" Phillip's voice was low and hoarse. "Have pity on a dead man."

Sudden righteousness straightened Margaret's spine. Phillip was too arrogant by half. A little suffering would be good for his soul, she thought piously. Obviously, he had had things too much his own way when he was alive. She continued to eat her dinner with considerable and exaggerated relish.

"You're a cruel woman, Margaret Westbourne."

A thread of amusement had entered his voice. Discreetly, she turned her head. She had his full attention now, and there was laughter in the eyes that met hers. Then his gaze dropped to her low-cut bodice.

When he looked up, for a brief moment, she glimpsed a similar—but different—raw yearning.

Quickly she turned back to her plate and stared down at her game pie.

"This is prime, Aunt Letty," Jeremy said, his mouth full.

"You oughtn't use slang in front of the ladies," Bernard said.

"Pardon," muttered Jeremy.

Phillip snorted. "Is he always so pompous?"

Margaret compressed her lips.

"Never mind. Ask Aunt Letty about the trial."

She remained stubbornly silent.

Phillip sighed. "Very well. Forgive my impertinence. I won't say any more about your beloved Bernard. Now please ask about the trial."

Margaret turned her nose up at this sorry excuse for an apology. She was tempted to ignore him altogether, but she was curious about the trial too. After a few minutes, she couldn't resist any longer and eased into the subject. "Aunt Letty

showed me the portraits of Phillip's two wives,"
she said casually.

"Ah." Cecilia leaned forward a bit. "What did you
think of Alicia?"

"Er . . ."

"Amazing a man could make such a fool of himself
over that tart, isn't it? I wonder if Phillip had any
brains except for you-know-where," observed Cecilia.

Margaret, after one glance at Phillip's indignant
face, said in a loud voice, "You must be right, Cecilia.
How else could a man get himself hanged for murdering his wife?"

"Yes, you would think he would have made sure
there were no witnesses," said Geoffrey.

Aunt Letty's indignation almost matched Phillip's.
"You know nothing about it! There were no witnesses. Phillip was not such a fool."

"Thank you—I think," Phillip muttered.

"The trial was rigged or something, I'm sure."

"Were you at the trial, Aunt Letty?" Margaret
asked.

"No, I wasn't allowed in at the indictment or the
trial in London. The hanging was public, however, so
of course I went to that."

Bernard's fork clattered against his plate.

"What was it like?" Jeremy asked with ghoulish
interest.

"Really, Aunt Letty, I don't think this is appropriate—"

"Nonsense, Bernard." Cecilia took a sip of wine
and licked her lips. "I've never heard about this and I
want to know, too."

"It was terrible," said Aunt Letty, waving at a servant to take her plate. "I was only thirteen and I cried
and cried, even though everyone else was quite
merry. It was rather like a fair, actually. People were
selling all sorts of things and jostling each other, and
laughing. Even when a man set up a puppet show

right next to me, I could not be cheered. Punch and another puppet fought a duel, then Punch murdered Judy and thought he was ever so clever. But at the trial, Judy's ghost appeared and pointed her finger at Punch and said, 'He killed me!' Punch got hanged and thinking of poor Phillip I was quite consumed with grief."

Margaret looked at Phillip, but his expression was unreadable. An odd ache lodged itself in her heart.

The dessert course arrived, and Aunt Letty paused long enough to accept a serving of trifle. She took a huge bite, managing to get whipped cream all around her mouth. She carefully wiped away all traces before continuing.

"The cart came soon after that. How tall and brave he stood! He never cowered, not even when that horrible crowd started throwing all manner of nasty things at him. Then they hanged him, and his face turned a nasty purple color—"

"Aunt Letty," Bernard interrupted. His face was much the same color as Phillip's must have been. "I must ask you to refrain from sullying Margaret's ears with such unpleasant reminiscences."

Phillip's expression changed from coolness to contempt.

" 'Refrain from sullying Margaret's ears'?" snorted Phillip, looking down his long aquiline nose as if Bernard were one of Jeremy's earwigs. "Can you truly intend to marry this poor excuse for a man?"

The insult was an effective antidote for the ache in her heart. "He's worth ten of you!" she hissed, infuriated past bearing by Phillip's derogatory tone.

"What's that, Margaret? I didn't quite hear you," said Bernard.

"You should think of your children, Margaret. What if they inherit that chin?"

"Be quiet!" cried Margaret.

Bernard drew himself up in affront.

"My dear, are you feeling well?" asked Cecilia.

"Perhaps she is overwrought," Bernard said stiffly.

"Has he taken you to bed yet?" asked Phillip.

"Certainly not!"

"Gad, does the man have blood in his veins? No wonder you're so tight-lipped and tight-ar—"

"Oh, you poor dear," said Aunt Letty. "Perhaps I should not have talked about the hanging after all. It really was most unpleasant. Especially when that awful woman stood up and cursed poor Phillip."

Margaret and Phillip both grew still.

"He was cursed, Aunt Letty?" asked Cecilia. "By whom?"

"An old hag. Phillip was hanging there, his neck all twisted, and the horrible creature stood up and cried, 'A curse on you, Phillip Eglinton!' The crowd grew silent, all the cheering stopped, and she spoke in a voice that could be heard by all. It was terribly eerie, I assure you."

Margaret leaned forward, her body tense. "But what did she say? What was the curse, Aunt Letty?"

The old woman recited it without hesitation. "'Thee and thine, thy wishes will go wanting; thee and thine will falter and fail; thee and thine will diminish and die.' The hag looked so triumphant when she finished I wanted to slap her. I was very glad when the crowd fell upon her and dragged her away, crying, 'Witch! Witch!' I believe they threw her in the Thames and she drowned." Aunt Letty pushed the remains of her trifle around on her plate. "But I think the curse came true."

Tears began to pour down Aunt Letty's cheeks. "There weren't many Eglintons, and most of them have died out or lost their fortunes." She sniffled noisily. "My life was ruined, too. I never married."

Cecilia reached over and clasped Aunt Letty's hand. "You aren't truly related to Phillip. Surely the curse wouldn't affect you."

"I think it did, b-be-because Phillip and I were so close. And when I was nineteen I had a beau, Mr. Gillingham. I loved him ever so much, but we fought over something stupid and he went away and married someone else and I never saw him again. I never gave my heart to another, and now I am just a l-l-lonely old woman."

Her face awash with tears, Letty left the room. An appalled silence settled over the table.

Phillip, his voice harsh, said, "Margaret, please go after her, tell her I'm sorry. It's all my fault—"

Bernard stood up to follow Aunt Letty, and Margaret quickly rose to her feet. "Bernard, let me go." He looked at her doubtfully, and Margaret said, "Please."

"Very well. But let me know if she wants to talk to me."

With a nod, Margaret left the room.

Margaret found the old woman in the parlor. She was sitting on the sofa, cradling her jar in her arms, and crying with the noisy abandon of a child. Margaret's heart went out to her.

"Please don't cry." Sitting next to the weeping woman, Margaret put an arm around her, struggling to find words of comfort. She could feel Aunt Letty's thin bones shaking. "Please don't cry."

"I'm sorry, my dear. It's only that I'm so-so-so *old*," Aunt Letty bawled. "Everyone I know is dead and everything is so different now."

Just like Phillip, Margaret thought, an ache in her throat. Poor Aunt Letty. Poor Phillip. "Surely things haven't changed all that much."

"They have, too. The clothes are different. I can't even wear my wig!"

"Perhaps I can convince Cecilia to allow you to wear it if your maid will take care of it and make sure no mice get into it."

Aunt Letty sniffled. "The food is different. I hate it! All those fancy sauces instead of plain meat and potatoes. And I can't even eat meat because it hurts my teeth!"

"Perhaps we can talk to Cook. I don't see any reason why she can't prepare potatoes in addition to the usual courses."

"The people are different. They're cold and stiff. When I was young, everyone was so alive! We shouted and argued and loved with passion. With real feeling."

"Everyone here loves you. That has not changed."

The flow of tears ebbed a little. Aunt Letty pulled out a handkerchief and blew her nose loudly. "There. How silly I am. I still have a few pleasures left to me . . . playing cards and my family. I don't usually allow the heavy burden of being under a curse to weigh me down."

Aunt Letty's wrinkled, tear-streaked face was so pitiful, Margaret could hardly bear it. "At least you can still talk to Phillip," she said, trying to sound cheerful.

"That's true." The tears stopped. "What a good girl you are, Margaret. I am glad you are marrying Bernard. He has become so solemn and serious. You will be good for him—make him happy. He used to write me long letters about you."

"He did?" Margaret could barely conceal her amazement.

"Oh, yes. About the wonderful games you would make up and how you pretended you were crusaders or explorers or pirates."

Margaret smiled a little. "Why, yes. We did have some good times." How long ago those days seemed now, overshadowed by the events that followed. Bernard had ceased being her friend; she doubted he even remembered their games now.

"Yes, until that business with his father. Bernard admired you so much for standing up to George."

"He did? I thought he despised me." The old woman must be mistaken. A pang of remembered hurt assailed her as she thought of how he had stood silently in church that day, not looking at her. In the space of a few minutes, their friendship of eight years had been wiped away.

"Oh, no. He was always a rather quiet boy. His father was a cold man, and often Bernard withdrew into himself. But I know he thought the world of you."

Aunt Letty was definitely confused, thought Margaret. But she didn't want to disillusion the old woman. "I see."

"Dear Margaret, thank you for bearing with me." Pulling out a cambric and lace handkerchief, Aunt Letty dabbed at her cheeks, then wiped off her jar where a few tears had fallen. "You run along now and get some sleep. I will be fine."

Obediently, Margaret rose to her feet. She leaned over and kissed the old woman on the cheek. "Good night, Aunt Letty."

Upstairs, when she opened the door to her room, a blast of cold air greeted her. Phillip paced recklessly about the room. The smell of tobacco was in the air, but it was a pungent, almost bitter smell, not the pleasant aroma she was used to.

"Is she all right?"

"Yes, she's fine. You mustn't blame yourself, Phillip—"

"I remember," he interrupted. His voice harsh and

abrupt, he turned, heavy brows drawn, eyes hollow. "Mortimer accusing me, the trial—what a farce that was!—and the hanging. Dear God, I remember the hanging."

10

Margaret quietly closed the door and leaned back against it, her eyes never leaving him. "Tell me," she said. "From the beginning."

"The beginning?" He laughed bitterly. "That would have to be when I wedded Alicia."

"Why did you marry her?"

"Need you ask? She was amazingly beautiful, with golden curls, lustrous brown eyes, and a figure like a goddess. Half-mad with desire, I married her."

Margaret, feeling slightly envious of the woman who had inspired such an emotion, pushed herself away from the door and sat down on the desk chair. Phillip sprawled into the red lacquer chair by the fireplace.

"It was a moment of rash lust," he confessed, his fingers making a silent drumming motion on the arm of the chair. "She was vain, spoiled, and selfish, and her demands were constant. She wanted to go to London, she wanted gowns and jewels, and most of all, she wanted me by her side every minute of the day. Within three short months, I regretted I'd ever met her."

Frowning, he stared into the blackened fireplace. "Alicia was outraged when I began to return to my old pursuits. She tried several methods to regain my attention. When scolding and throwing temper tantrums failed, she ran away with my old enemy, Roger Carew, Earl Mortimer."

Phillip jumped to his feet and began to pace again. Margaret watched him circle to the other side of the bed, then return. "The feud between Mortimer and me had been simmering for years. At first, it was mostly a matter of rivalry in matters of sport and women, but Mortimer loved Alicia—as much as it was possible for him to love anyone but himself. When I won her away from under his nose, he swore revenge."

Phillip's voice took on a sarcastic edge. "I'm sure it was an easy task for Mortimer to persuade my neglected bride to run away with him." Stopping by the escritoire, he glared down at a loose sheet of paper lying there. "Alicia thoughtfully left a note. I would never allow anyone—especially Mortimer—to steal my wife."

He swatted his hand at one of the gold tassels on the bed, but his hand passed right through it. Gritting his teeth, he continued.

"I rode after them. The night was dark, the moon almost obscured by gathering storm clouds, but I caught them easily enough. When I opened the carriage door, Alicia immediately began to shriek. Ignoring her caterwauling as best I could, I took hold of her arm and told her to come down."

Margaret shivered a little at Phillip's stern expression. She would not have liked to have been in Alicia's shoes that night.

Phillip laughed without humor. "Mortimer was in his element. 'Unhand her or I'll see you in hell,' he threatened me. He always had a taste for melodrama.

Unfortunately, I was in no mood to tolerate his absurdities. 'That wouldn't be a challenge, would it?' I asked. I was cold and tired, itching to thrash that knave, and more than willing to settle the score then and there. Mortimer, after looking at Alicia, accepted. I'm certain she hoped I'd be killed so she'd be free to marry her lover."

Phillip paused, staring into the dark corner by the wardrobe.

"Did you fight him?" Margaret asked.

Phillip tore his gaze away from the corner. "Yes," he said, his voice clipped. "We fought. The postboys held torches, but as Mortimer and I saluted each other with our swords, it began to rain. The torches kept going out. It was the uncanniest duel I've ever fought. All shadow, and flickering torchlight, and glinting steel. The visibility was almost nil. I had to rely heavily on other senses. Singing steel and Mortimer's feral scent were often the only warnings I had of an attack."

Margaret's fingers tightened on the arms of her chair. What he described sounded barbaric and made her feel slightly ill. Why would he risk death or mutilation over such a woman? Or any woman? Thank heaven men nowadays were more civilized, less bloodthirsty.

"Mortimer fought well, with his usual viciousness, but I was always the better swordsman. The duel ended with Mortimer lying in the mud, the tip of my blade at his throat. I left him there and took Alicia home. She cried the whole way. At the house, she turned hysterical, screeching how she hated me and what a cold, inhuman monster I was. She exclaimed that she rued the day she married me."

Phillip shook his head. "Not as much as I rued it. If I'd known what a greedy slut she was, I would have taken a mistress to satisfy my lust and saved myself the trouble of a wife. I said as much to her, and breast heaving, she slapped me, then bolted up the stairs. The next night she was dead."

Margaret leaned forward. "But how, Phillip? You didn't push her did you?"

"Certainly not. She caught a chill, which worsened rapidly. Delirious, she tried to run away again, only to fall down the stairs to her death. I had nothing to do with it."

Relief spread through Margaret. Although she had never truly doubted him, part of her couldn't help but wonder if perhaps—just perhaps—he actually had murdered his wife. Aunt Letty certainly thought he had. "Why did everyone think you did?"

"Mortimer accused me of killing her. In front of half the village, in the graveyard where I had just buried her. I was feeling numb, not with grief—I'd lost all affection for her—but with the waste, when Mortimer hissed, 'You killed her.'"

"Good Lord," Margaret said blankly.

"That was how I felt. I was so unutterably weary, all I could think was why couldn't Mortimer have chosen some other time for a confrontation. I was too tired to deal with his irrational spite right then, so with a humorless laugh, I said, 'You'll have the devil of a time proving it,' then left before Mortimer could say more. I regretted my flippant reply when I was arrested and indicted for murder by the Durham grand jury."

"They indicted you for making an idle remark?"

"Oh, Mortimer planned his revenge well. Using his influence, he packed the jury box with various cousins, second cousins, and cousins-in-law. The indictment was a foregone conclusion. Using his wealth, he bribed enough officials to keep me in prison almost a year until the trial."

"You spent an entire year in prison?" Margaret was appalled. "How did you bear it?"

"It could have been worse. At least, I was wealthy enough to purchase some amenities and obtain certain privileges. For a small fee, the guards allowed the prisoners to visit one another, and at least that alleviated some of the tedium." He grinned bleakly. "I met some interesting characters there. One, a gentleman thief, explained to me how doctoring certain documents could win me a fortune. Another, a Captain Sharp—a card cheat—was so skilled, he could determine what card he had dealt by looking at its reflection in the diamond ring he wore. Yet another, an anarchist, tried to recruit me to his cause—if I were willing to assist in the assassination of the king, he would help me escape."

"Good Lord!" Margaret could not hide her shock.

Phillip's grin widened a little at her horror. "I spent many an amusing hour in his and the others' company, until the trial."

The trial. Margaret rubbed her arms, trying to warm them. "What happened at the trial?"

His smile fading, Phillip took a deep, ireful breath. He didn't think he could find words to explain an event so incomprehensible. "Till the very first day of the trial, I had no doubt I would be found innocent. But when I walked into that courtroom and saw the Lord High Steward, I knew I was in trouble. It was no coincidence that he was there. He had a grudge against me, and Mortimer knew it."

Phillip paused a moment, remembering the endless days of the trial. The memories grew more vivid, and once again he felt the helpless anger that had consumed him.

11

By the time the last day of the trial arrived, Phillip knew he would be found guilty. He didn't quite know how Mortimer would do it—the evidence was appallingly circumstantial—but Phillip had no doubt what the verdict would be. Which was why he made it a point to stride into the ovenlike courtroom as if he hadn't a care in the world.

He approached the bar, made three reverences, and knelt before the Lord High Steward. Rising, he made a show of dusting off his faultlessly cut breeches and immaculate white linen before looking up to see Mortimer's avid gaze.

Phillip wanted to laugh. Did the fool think he would slink into the room, cowering like a dog? An Eglinton would never sink so low. Deliberately, anticipating Mortimer's reaction, Phillip slowly, almost casually, flicked his thumb across his nose. Then he tilted his head back and smiled.

Mortimer's face turned an ugly, dark red. His fists clenched and under the black robe his shoulders shook.

Phillip's smile widened. He enjoyed tweaking Mortimer, although it was a small retribution for the hell he had endured. Soon, though, he would seek full revenge. The trial was almost over; only Mortimer had yet to testify. After today, tomorrow at the latest, he would be free, and then Mortimer would regret his lies.

A small frown knit Phillip's brow. There was one detail that didn't make sense. Surely Mortimer knew that even if found guilty, Phillip would still be set free. Didn't the fool realize what would happen then?

As if sensing Phillip's thoughts, Mortimer looked up. The two men's gazes met and clashed, battling for victory, but even more importantly, battling for the other's defeat.

"Lord Mortimer, please rise."

With one last hate-filled glance at Phillip, Mortimer rose to testify.

"Lord Mortimer, would you please tell the court how you knew Lady Holwell?" asked the Attorney-General.

"Her parents lived on an estate bordering mine. Alicia and I practically grew up together. She was like a sister to me."

Phillip snorted. The Lord High Steward frowned at him, then nodded at the Attorney-General to continue.

"Lord Mortimer, please tell the court the conversation you had with the prisoner on the day of May sixth, 1768."

"It was at Alicia's funeral. I was very upset, and I admit, slightly out of my head with grief. When I accused Lord Holwell of murdering Alicia, I did not actually mean it, you understand. I spoke from anger at her tragic death. But to my surprise he didn't deny it." Mortimer shot a sly look at Phillip, then shook his head in pretended disbelief.

"What *did* Lord Holwell say?"

"He laughed. Like a fiend from hell. Needless to say I was shocked. But worse was to come, for he said, 'You'll have the devil of a time proving it, Mortimer.'"

"What did you do then?"

"I notified the magistrate, and Holwell was arrested and indicted for murder."

"Lord Mortimer, isn't it true that something has occurred since that time, something that proves Lord Holwell's guilt?"

Phillip looked up sharply. He caught a glimpse of the glee in Mortimer's eyes before the blackguard lowered them to his piously clasped hands. What new lie had he invented now? Phillip wondered grimly.

"Lord Mortimer," said the Attorney-General. "Tell the court, if you please, what happened on the evening of May fourth, 1769."

"I had stopped at the vicarage, to discuss some matter with the vicar. Our business done, I wandered over to the graveyard where Alicia is buried. The sight of that cold marble tombstone nearly unmanned me. Fighting tears, I picked a few flowers from the roadside—yellow lilies, they were—then entered through the gate to place them on dear Alicia's grave. No sooner had I done so, than a strange feeling came over me and a voice whispered in my ear. I looked around, but could see no one. The whisper drew out into a horrible groan."

"And then?" prompted the Attorney-General.

"And then I saw it . . . a white wispy form hovering over her grave."

"Lord Mortimer, did the apparition identify itself?"

"Yes." The room grew so quiet, only the scratching of the clerks' pens could be heard. "It said it was Alicia's ghost!"

A low murmur swept the room.

"What else did the apparition say?"

"It said that Alicia's death had been no accident. It said that she had been murdered most foully, murdered by her very own husband, Phillip Eglinton, Viscount Holwell!"

The murmur grew to a roar. The Sergeant-at-Arms pounded his staff. "Order! Order!" he cried.

Phillip stood immobile, disbelief and outrage filling him. He glanced around at the rustling, whispering lords, wondering what they were thinking. Surely they did not believe this cock-and-bull story?

When the noise had subsided, the Solicitor General rose to his feet. "Your lordships," he said in a high, squeaky voice. "This seems highly irregular. May I inquire of the court if there is any basis for allowing testimony from a . . . a phantasm?"

"There is," answered the Attorney-General smoothly. "I draw your attention to the Sergeant Davies murder case of 1749. It was tried before the Edinburgh High Court of Justiciary. Testimony by one Alex McPherson, who claimed to have had conversation with the victim's ghost, was admitted into evidence."

The Lord High Steward took a few minutes to confer with the judges. Their hushed discussion was almost drowned out by the lords whispering behind their hands. Finally, the Lord High Steward called for order and announced the decision. "We will allow it. Proceed."

"Nothing further, your lordship." The Attorney-General bounced triumphantly back to his seat.

The Lord High Steward turned to where Phillip stood frozen in stunned disbelief. "Lord Holwell, do you wish to examine this witness?"

"I do, your lordship." Anger at the farce being played out before him almost overwhelmed Phillip. He knew it would be impossible to prove Mortimer was lying, but by God, he would make certain Mortimer looked like the fool he was. It was an effort to prevent any trace of emotion from showing in his face as he looked down his nose at Mortimer. He stared for several long moments, not speaking.

Sweat rolled down Mortimer's face. His ferretlike eyes darted around the room and he reached a finger up under his wig to scratch.

Phillip pulled out a lace handkerchief and gently waved it like a fan. "A trifle warm, isn't it?" he inquired with spurious courtesy.

Mortimer visibly seethed.

Smiling, Phillip continued to wave the handkerchief. "Now, Lord Mortimer, you have testified that Alicia was like a sister to you, is that correct?"

"Yes," Mortimer said warily.

"And yet on the second of May, 1768, you ran away with her. Forgive me, Lord Mortimer, but exactly what sort of 'brotherly' relationship did you have with your 'sister'?"

A titter swept the room and Mortimer flushed angrily.

"Are you perhaps unaware that incest is illegal?"

The titters magnified.

"I sought only to protect her from your abuse," Mortimer snapped. "Even then, she was frightened for her life."

"I see." Phillip returned the handkerchief to his pocket. "You say that when you first saw Alicia's ghost, she groaned. Could you tell the court what this groan sounded like?"

"Like a long, sighing moan," Mortimer answered readily.

"Could you be more precise?"

Mortimer looked confused. "What do you mean?"

"Would you demonstrate for the court what this moaning sounded like?"

"Well, sort of like this . . . Ooooooh. Ooooooo-ooooooh. Oooooooooooooooh!"

A shout of laughter rang through the room. Chuckles and muffled laughter were plainly heard. The Sergeant-at-Arms pounded his staff, trying to restore order. The laughter was stifled, and for a moment, coughing was heard throughout the room.

When the room was silent, Phillip said, "Thank you, my lord, for that, er, spirited demonstration. Nothing further."

Many of the lords were once again seized by coughing fits. Mortimer, his face red and his fists clenched, sat down. A short while later, the lords left for their deliberations and even as fury wracked him inside, Phillip smiled.

"Her *ghost!*" Phillip pounded his balled fist against the wall, only to have his hand disappear. Startled, he pulled his hand out and glared at it. "Have you ever heard anything so ridiculous?"

"No. Except, that is . . . you are a ghost."

He swung around, facing her fully, his body taut with menacing rage. "What does that have to do with anything? Of all the henwitted . . ." He stopped and took a deep, calming breath, then continued through gritted teeth. "You shouldn't be able to convict a man based on the testimony of a ghost."

Margaret pressed back against the chair, slightly unnerved by his anger. "I'm surprised they would allow it," she agreed hastily. "And the lords found you guilty?"

To her relief, he resumed his pacing, arms behind his back.

"Yes. Mortimer must have used every means possible to win that verdict."

"It must have been a shock when they found you guilty," she said.

"Oh, yes. Even though I expected it, still it was a shock. But not as great as the one I received when Robeson pronounced the sentence."

"Robeson?" she asked. The name sounded vaguely familiar, but Margaret couldn't think why.

"The Lord High Steward on the case. At worst, he should have fined me. That's the usual penalty in a case like this."

"Oh, I see. Murdering a wife is obviously no serious crime."

"Exactly." He appeared oblivious to her sarcasm. "I tried to claim benefit of clergy, but he denied it on the grounds that my father was a Catholic. Then when I asked for trial by combat, he refused, saying my de facto accuser was a ghost and it is impossible to challenge a ghost!" He stopped by the fireplace, staring blindly at the carved mantelpiece. "He relished handing down the sentence. He said that since Alicia was 'so tortured by the horror of her death that she could not rest in peace,' he felt it was his 'duty to levy the severest punishment possible.'"

Margaret rubbed her arms again. The room seemed colder. "Why would he do such a thing?"

Phillip opened his mouth to reply, then bit back the words. He looked at her face for a moment, seeing the innocent curve of her cheek, her guileless eyes.

He shrugged. "I don't know. Likely Mortimer bribed him. He probably even arranged for him to be the Lord High Steward. That cur bribed half the House of Lords, I'll wager."

Margaret shook her head. "So then what happened?"

"I was hanged." Again his hand rose to his throat, his fingers stretching across his neck in gruesome imitation of the noose. He did not remember much of the cart ride. The raucous jests, the stinging missiles pelting him, had barely penetrated his consciousness as he fixedly watched the noose swaying in the breeze. Climbing the stairs, he had approached the knotted hemp until his entire view was framed by the circle of rope. For endless seconds, he had stared through it at the mob below. Avid eyes consumed him, and for a moment, he had almost tried to bolt.

Then, in the crowd, he had seen a gloating, greedy face.

Squaring his shoulders, Phillip had stood quietly as the noose was fitted around his neck, his gaze never leaving Mortimer. As the hangman released the trapdoor, Phillip had tilted his head back and smiled. . . .

The black void loomed, feeding off his pain, dragging at him.

"Phillip!"

Margaret's urgent voice dragged him back from the edge of the void. He looked at her white face. "It was not a pleasant experience," he said tersely.

"I don't imagine it was." The skin on her neck crawled. She swallowed, trying to dispel the sensation. "What about the curse?"

"I don't remember that at all. It must have happened after I, er, lost consciousness. A curse! Of all the nonsensical things." He began to pace again. "Why would anyone curse me?" He stopped abruptly, his fists clenching. "Mortimer," he spat. "I should have known."

"You think Mortimer had something to do with it?"

"I am certain of it. He excelled at exactly that sort of spite and he hated me with all the extreme virulence only a Mortimer is capable of. I have no doubt he paid some witch handsomely to wipe the Eglinton name from the earth."

She watched him pace, his anger actually tangible

in the bright, cold glow surrounding him. "But . . . but do you truly believe in this curse?"

"What else can I believe? Why else would I be here?"

"I don't know," Margaret said slowly. "I don't think I believe in curses."

"You believe in ghosts but not in curses, you foolish woman? You and that doltish Bernard have more in common than I thought."

Margaret stiffened. "Phillip—"

"Don't you understand what this means?" he interrupted impatiently. "I am trapped here." He stopped in front of her. "Just as you will soon be trapped in marriage to Bernard." He laughed, but without humor. "Our fates are very similar, do you realize that, Margaret? Both of us are trapped—forever."

12

Phillip's words haunted Margaret all night and gnawed at her through breakfast. Bernard had to repeat her name twice to gain her attention.

"Margaret! Were you able to reassure Aunt Letty last night?" he asked.

"Not exactly," Margaret replied. "She is very upset about this curse."

"Hmmph. Perhaps I should sit down with her and explain that there is no scientific basis for her fears."

"I don't think she would believe you," Margaret murmured.

"I don't understand why she's never mentioned it before," Bernard muttered. "I will have to think of some way to prove to her . . ." He broke off and said more loudly, "I will talk to Aunt Letty." He paused again, then said, "There is an interesting bridge not too far from here, Wynch Bridge. If you would like to ride out with me, I'll show it to you."

She had an urge to say no, to run away and try to escape. Stifling the foolish impulse, she nodded.

Half an hour later, after changing into a habit of dark green cloth and a matching Spanish hat with a black feather and veil, she met him by the stables. He helped her mount, then they rode in an easterly direction.

The bright August day was already warm. She was sure the linen collar and cravat of her habit were wilting, but the exercise did feel good. She had been spending too much time in her room lately.

They kept to a steady canter, covering the distance quickly. As they rode, they passed workers in the fields, and sheep and cattle grazing. She could hear blackbirds, thrushes, and other unidentifiable birds singing with all their might. Small cottage gardens full of marigolds and foxglove provided bright patches of yellow and purple against the lush green of the rolling hills. The pleasant scene lifted her spirits.

She could hear the roar of a waterfall almost before Wynch Bridge came into view.

Margaret's breath caught when she saw it. A long, narrow bridge, perhaps sixty feet long and two feet wide, was suspended by iron chains over a deep gorge. In a great sheet of foam, the falls rushed over the cliff and crashed onto rocks far below. A mist rose up to cool her heated face.

"How beautiful," she breathed as she dismounted.

"What?" Bernard shouted.

"I said it's beautiful!" she yelled back. The veil of her hat fluttered in her face. Pushing it back, she walked toward the bridge.

He hurried after her. "Wait, Margaret. Where are you going?"

"I wish to go out on the bridge." She continued forward, craning her neck to get a better view of the gorge. A rainbow danced into view, sparkling and glowing. Smiling with pleasure, she had placed a foot on the bridge when Bernard caught her arm and pulled her back.

"Margaret, I'm afraid I cannot allow you to go out on the bridge. It's not safe."

Her pleasure ruined, she stepped back just as two boys brushed past them and ran out on the bridge. They stopped in the middle, laughing, evidently taking much enjoyment from the way it swayed. It did look rather dangerous. Margaret stared longingly. It also looked enjoyable, exciting, thrilling, and for one wild moment she was tempted to ignore Bernard and follow the boys.

"Those lads will be lucky not to break their necks," Bernard muttered, escorting Margaret back to her horse.

Margaret looked at him. When they were both children, they would have been right out there with those boys, trying to make the bridge sway, daring each other to let go of the chains, laughing and shouting. How had Bernard changed so much? How had she?

Trapped.

Later that night, Phillip's words still echoed in her head. She tried to read her favorite book, *Journal of a Residence in the Sandwich Islands,* but she kept imagining Bernard's reaction to some of the natives' more unusual customs. She was frowning down at the page when Phillip appeared.

"Phillip!" Setting the book aside, she smiled up at him.

He couldn't help smiling back a little. Did she know what she did to a man when she smiled like that? He doubted it. Yet the unconsciousness of her invitation made her even more desirable, more enticing. He only wished he could accept it. She was so full of warmth and light. He wanted to feel it. He wanted to feel anything except this damn miserable cold.

He looked into her eyes, and something tugged at his heart. The icy coldness receded a little.

He enjoyed being with her. God, how he enjoyed

being with her. She helped keep the coldness, the darkness, the *loneliness* at bay. He wanted to be close to her—as close as it was possible for a ghost to be.

Glancing about the room, his gaze fell upon the settee. Invitingly, he beckoned. "Come, sit here next to me."

Margaret stared at him. Uncertainly, her gaze moved to the settee, then back to him. There was something different about him, she thought nervously. He seemed friendlier. She didn't want to leave the protection of the concealing covers. To do so seemed so . . . immodest.

"Seeing you in that bed is unbearable torture," he said in a provocative voice.

Margaret jumped from the bed. She grabbed a sea green shawl to cover her nightgown, even though the high-necked white cotton was perfectly respectable.

"You look perfectly respectable," he said, echoing her thoughts. The wicked glint was back in his eyes, although it was softer, gentler, than she had ever seen it. "Very virginal. Bernard is a lucky man."

Margaret blushed, not sure how to respond. "I don't think we should be discussing such things," she said primly.

"What better for a man and woman to discuss?"

"I think we should be discussing this curse."

"Not tonight, sweeting. Tonight, I simply want to enjoy your company. Come, sit down."

She sat on the edge of the settee, her knees pressed together, her arms folded across her chest.

For some reason he looked vastly amused. She tilted her chin.

He chuckled.

Turning her head, she glared at him. Quickly, he composed his face into more serious lines, but she was not deceived. His eyes were still gleaming.

He leaned back, lounging in a disgraceful way

against the back of the settee. "Tell me, why have you betrothed yourself to that dull—I mean, that dashing fellow?"

Margaret looked away and pulled at the lace fringe on her shawl. "Our fathers arranged it years ago."

"Oh, so you've known Barnett a long time."

"Yes. We played together as children. In fact, he was my best friend. He was different then. Often quiet, but not so rigid. He intimidated many of the neighboring children because he was so studious."

"But not you?"

Margaret smiled a little. "No. I was a trifle head-strong, you understand. I did very much as I pleased. And it pleased me to play with Bernard. Although he was quiet, he was always willing to enter into the most outlandish of my games. We would imagine ourselves Hindu royalty or Chinese peasants. The captains of a ship sailing around the world. All sorts of things."

Somehow she had relaxed enough that she was now leaning back against the settee, too. His arm rested just behind her, so close she could feel the coldness radiating from it, so close it was almost an embrace. It should have been uncomfortable. Instead she found she rather enjoyed his proximity.

"So you fell in love and he proposed?"

"Oh, no," Margaret laughed. "We never thought of each other like that. I was in love with a boy named Corbin. He was a perfect idiot, but he had beautiful golden hair and bright blue eyes. As for Bernard, he regarded me like a little sister. No, we didn't fall in love. We were too young, actually. I was fifteen, Bernard eighteen, when we became betrothed. We lived on adjoining estates, so it was a very practical match."

"Then why haven't you married him long since?"

"Something happened the following year." She

paused, remembering the terrible scene. Slowly she continued, choosing her words with care. "The servants gossiped a lot, as servants do, and they weren't always careful about what they said around a sixteen-year-old girl. Anyway, I heard them talking about a maid, whose master had gotten her with child and turned her off without a reference. They went on to enumerate the other girls this same man had seduced and abandoned."

Margaret traced a finger over the settee's velvet upholstery, not looking at Phillip.

"I was horrified, naturally, but I also felt a certain . . . detachment, I suppose. Somehow I assumed this must be going on somewhere else, not in our own little parish. I couldn't believe anyone I knew could be so wicked." She shook her head at her own naïveté.

"So that Sunday, when the vicar denounced Colleen from the pulpit, I was stunned. I knew Colleen, you see. She was a kitchenmaid at Lord Barnett's, and she would often sneak us treats. I realized Bernard's father was the horrible monster who seduced servant girls."

"You must have been very shocked, young as you were," Phillip said gently.

"Yes. Well, actually, I was furious. Not only at what he had done, but at the hypocrisy of the vicar in denouncing Colleen. My temper got the better of me, and I stood up—right there in church—and I said some horrible things to Lord Barnett."

"In church?" Phillip's shoulders began to shake. "I wish I could have been there."

She smiled a little. Looking back, it had been rather funny. The gentlemen turning purple, several ladies swooning, everyone gasping with shock. Unfortunately, the rest of the story wasn't quite as amusing.

"My parents hustled me home, but I remained unrepentant. Next Sunday, we went to church and not a single person spoke to me. I didn't care, but my mother almost had a fit. She confined me to my room for a month. When the month had passed, I thought everyone would have recovered from their anger, but they hadn't."

Phillip stilled, his laughter gone.

"When I went to church, no one spoke to me. When I went into the village, people avoided me. Friends I had played with my entire life weren't allowed to associate with me. I was completely shunned."

"That's ridiculous. Surely people would make some allowance for your age."

"Perhaps they would have, but Lady Creevy was particularly outraged. Everyone followed her lead. At first I tossed my head and said I didn't care, but I did. It was so difficult to pretend, especially when Mama would apologize over and over to Lady Creevy for me." She glanced away from him. "I felt so *alone*."

Anger surged through him at the hurt he saw etched on her delicate features. Why hadn't her parents just stared everyone down? Such a small scandal would have been soon forgotten. "Where was your betrothed during all this?"

"I don't know precisely. He . . . he wouldn't look at me that day in church. I expected . . . that is, I thought he might call the next day, but he never came. Later, I heard he had gone away."

"And your betrothal?" Phillip asked tightly.

"Was assumed broken, although nothing was ever said. Indeed, old Lord Barnett never spoke to anyone in my family again. I didn't see Bernard until years later, right after Lord Barnett died. By then I was at my last prayers. Fortunately, Bernard agreed to honor the marriage contract."

"Your last prayers? I find that difficult to believe.

Didn't you have a season in London? You would have been snapped up there."

Margaret shook her head, smiling sadly. "As luck would have it, Lady Creevy was in town my first season. She spread the tale of my disgrace. I think she hated me, though I never understood why."

"She probably had a couple of whey-faced daughters."

"Why, yes. Five of them. At least, I mean they were very sweet, not at all like their mother. What did they have to do with anything?"

Phillip only shook his head. "And her spite drove all the men away?"

"Almost. I confess, my own foolishness chased away a very likely prospect. My second season, Lord Hugh began paying me particular attention. I was on my very best behavior, you understand. I barely spoke a word and behaved with the utmost propriety. He was equally proper, or at least, so I thought. But one day I saw him in the park with his mistress. And I so forgot myself as to stare. And I kept on staring until, even though he appeared not to see me, he blushed. He never called again."

Phillip was at a loss. He understood Lord Hugh's reaction. One of the most basic rules of society was that a lady should turn a blind eye to men's infidelities. His first wife had understood that; his second hadn't. By far, he'd preferred Mary to Alicia. No man wanted a wife who would raise a fuss over a minor indiscretion or two.

And yet, part of him could almost believe that Margaret would have been worth it—because he sensed that if she cared, a man would never want another woman. . . .

Margaret, watching the play of emotion on his face, wondered what he was thinking. Wanting to lighten the tension, she asked brightly, "What of your childhood? Do you remember it now?"

"Bits and pieces. I recall that I wanted to be a priest."

"A priest?" Margaret stared incredulously at him.

He grinned. "I was only six or seven. I used to sneak away from my tutor and visit the chapel. My nature has always been a bit wild—which I inherited from my parents. Although they loved each other, they were very passionate people. They fought frequently when I was young. Our house was not a peaceful place, and I often escaped to the chapel where it was quiet and restful. The priests fascinated me. They were always calm and serene. I admired that. Father Benedicto was especially kind, and when my tutor quit out of frustration, he took over my lessons."

"Are you a papist, then?" Margaret asked with all the repugnance of a good Anglican.

"No. My father converted shortly after the Rebellion of '45. Politically, he felt it was too costly to be Catholic." Phillip smiled, but it did not quite reach his eyes. "I was devastated. The chapel closed and Father Benedicto had already left when I went to say good-bye. However, I did see Father Clement."

"How sad you did not see Father Benedicto," Margaret said. "At least you were able to say good-bye to Father Clement, though."

"Yes, he told me my family and I would roast in hell for renouncing the true Church, that God's wrath would rain down upon us." Phillip smiled a little at Margaret's patent shock. "Father Clement was very zealous."

"But you were only a child. You must have been frightened to death."

"Certainly not. Eglintons are never frightened." His lips curved.

"I see," she said.

"Do you? Do you really?" His gray eyes were cool and amused. "It's all nonsense, you know."

Margaret looked uncertainly at him. Surely he wasn't saying . . .

"You do believe in God, don't you?"

He laughed. "Oh, yes. For my sins I almost wish I didn't." He laughed again at the confusion on her face. "Perhaps I should let you sleep on that one, Margaret." He smiled down into her eyes.

"Oh, no! Don't go," she said, forgetting his strange words. Then she blushed. Heavens, what was she thinking of? "I mean, I can't sleep."

"Probably that fascinating book you were reading."

"Oh. That is, yes. It is called *A Journal of a Residence in the Sandwich Islands.*"

"The Sandwich Islands? Isn't that in the Pacific?"

"Yes, and it is ever so interesting. The weather is incredibly warm there; the sun shines all the time. Although it rains, too. Strange fruits grow on the trees and the beaches have white, white sand, and the people swim in the ocean. They have canoes, live in huts made out of grass and they wear only a strip of cloth around their hips—"

Margaret's rush of words stopped as her eyes met his. His were very dark.

"I . . . I know that is very shocking."

"You think so? I think it sounds very sensible in such a tropical climate."

"But to be almost naked—"

"Yes." His voice was almost a whisper. "I rather wish we were there now."

Somehow Margaret rose to her feet. He stood up also. Her heart pounded. She clutched the shawl more tightly to her breasts.

"I think I am tired after all," she whispered.

He stared at her, very still.

No one had ever looked at her quite like that. His

eyes flickered with some strange emotion that she did not quite recognize. A sort of wildness. As if he wanted to consume her.

The silence stretched and grew and Margaret thought surely, surely he must hear the pounding of her pulse.

"You are so beautiful, Margaret. Why are you wasting yourself on that spineless idiot?"

"I'm not wasting myself." Margaret hated the tremor in her voice. She wanted to look away from his seductive gaze, but she couldn't. "And I'm not beautiful."

"Of course you are. Don't you know it? Are the men blind nowadays?" His voice grew lower, huskier. "I suppose that frown you so often show frightens them off. But can't they see how soft and smooth your hair is, how the light catches glints of red, like hints of the passion you try so hard to conceal?"

His voice was mesmerizing her. Helplessly, she stared into his eyes.

"And when you smile, your eyes sparkle like the bluest of jewels, like the promise of heaven. And your lips . . ." His voice dropped to a whisper. "How incredibly sweet, they curve so beguilingly, so sensuously. How they beckon, more enticing than any siren song. Margaret, dear Margaret, you are so beautiful and you don't even know it. I wish we were in the Sandwich Islands. I wish I could see all of you."

"Phillip . . ." Surely he could not be asking what she thought. It was too shocking, too forbidden.

"Margaret, please, would you let me see you—just one glimpse of heaven for a man consigned to what surely must be hell."

She wanted to. Dear heaven, she wanted to do what he asked. "Oh, Phillip," Margaret whispered achingly. The planes of his face were taut, his eyelids drooped heavily over darkened eyes, eyes dark with an emotion that should have frightened her, but instead made her ache to be held in his arms.

"Please, Margaret. Please be a little generous. Forget those useless inhibitions of yours."

Somehow, the shawl slipped from her nerveless fingers. Somehow, her fingers were at her throat, unbuttoning her nightgown. Somehow, without conscious thought, she shrugged it off her shoulders, and the concealing white cotton fell in a pool at her feet.

"Ah, Margaret," he breathed. His gaze moved over her pale white skin, over her breasts, traveling down her long white limbs, then returning to her breasts and lingering there. "Can you truly be as soft as you look? Do you know what exquisite torture it is to know I can never find out?"

It wasn't fair for a man to have a voice like that, she thought dazedly. So warm, so resonant, it slipped over her skin like caressing fingers, making her tingle and quiver all over and her breasts and her legs tremble. She felt strange, languid, warm.

"Dear God, you are beautiful. I wish . . . how I wish . . ."

He lifted a hand toward her breast. With agonizing slowness his fingers reached out and she knew she wanted him to touch her. She wanted it more than she'd ever wanted anything in her entire life. Fascinated, she stared at the glowing hand that was scarcely an inch from the peak of her breast. She barely breathed. Her breasts ached with longing. His fingers drew closer. . . .

A sharp stinging raced from her breast, tingling down to the pit of her stomach where it exploded, sending shock waves to her toes, her fingers, and the very ends of her hair.

With a bright, blinding flash of light, he was gone.

13

Margaret woke slowly the next morning. Not so slowly, came the memory of last night. She groaned and pulled the covers over her head, wishing she could disappear as easily as Phillip did.

What had come over her? Had she been insane? Had Phillip worked some ghostly magic on her to make her do what she had done?

Dear God, she had stood before him—a man she had known for only five days—naked as a tree in winter.

She felt as though even her toes were blushing.

What a fuss over nothing, her rebellious side scolded. So a man—correction, a *ghost* of a man—saw you naked. What of it?

Margaret squirmed. It goes against everything I've been taught, she answered silently. To be modest, to be virtuous—

Bah! You've been modest and virtuous your whole life and what has it gotten you? A fiancé who's more interested in insects than you, that's what. Margaret hastily jumped out of bed before any more heretical thoughts could surface.

But when she entered the morning room, it was deserted, and Phillip's seductive words whispered inside her brain as she ate breakfast.

He had called her beautiful. Strange how such meaningless words could mean so much to her. But somehow, coming from his lips, she had known the words were sincere, and somehow they had transformed her so that she had indeed been beautiful for that moment in time. And when he had touched her . . .

Geoffrey pushed the door open with one of his crutches and limped in, glancing around the room. "Have you seen Jeremy?" He was frowning, his forehead creased even more than usual. "We were supposed to go fishing."

"No, I haven't," she said. The way Phillip had looked at her. He had looked . . . hungry. And everything in her had responded to that look. Because she was hungry, too. Hungry for excitement, hungry for a life completely different than the one she had agreed to.

His frown deepening, Geoffrey turned on his crutches and almost bumped into Bernard, who was on point of entering.

Bernard looked duller than ever.

"Margaret!" he said. "There you are. I would like to speak to you."

He paused expectantly.

Then speak, she thought irritably. She wished he would go away. She wanted to relive that moment when a bolt of electricity had leapt from Phillip's fingers and coursed through her body. And she wanted to try to figure out whether Phillip really had touched her or if he had disappeared before his fingers had actually come into contact with the point of her br—

"Margaret? I must speak with you. In the garden, please, so we can be private."

Now what? More complaints? "Yes, Bernard," she managed to murmur politely.

In the garden, he led her to a bench by a clump of deep blue gentians and pink asters. He dusted off the stone seat with his handkerchief before they sat down.

"Ahem." He fixed his gaze on a rosebush some twenty feet in front of them. "I walked by your room last night."

A lengthy pause ensued. Margaret shifted on the hard stone bench and recrossed her ankles. Still Bernard did not continue, so she said, "Oh?"

"I noticed a light under your door." He looked at her then, directly into her eyes. His own were serious and inquiring.

"I was reading," Margaret said glibly, and not untruthfully.

"I heard you talking. And laughing."

"Oh. I, ah, I read aloud to myself sometimes." As soon as the words were out, Margaret blushed at the ridiculousness of her lie. "It was a very amusing book," she said feebly.

Bernard stared at her strangely.

"I see." He continued to stare at her, causing her to fidget. It was very unlike Bernard to look at her for such a long period of time.

"Is something the matter?" she finally asked, when she could bear it no longer.

"Yes. No. That is, you look different."

Dear God, did it show?

"You look, well, prettier."

Margaret gaped at him in astonishment.

"I, that is, of course you have always been pretty. At least, I have always thought so. I mean, I am sure everyone thinks so. I mean . . ."

Laughter bubbled to her lips. His eyes moved to her mouth, and Margaret froze.

Hastily, he stood up. His hands fumbled in his pocket and pulled out his watch. *Click, snap. Click, snap. Click, snap.*

"I had better go find Geoffrey and Jeremy," he mumbled. "We are supposed to go fishing." He turned and stumbled on the paving stones. Regaining his balance, he hurried away.

Margaret remained where she was, her thoughts a jumble.

For a moment, she had almost thought he was going to—no, she must have imagined it. He would never kiss her. It was unthinkable that Bernard would do something so, so *fiancé like*. Perhaps he had seen a freckle by her mouth, or some other blemish, and that was why he had stared so intently. Still, there had been something strange about him. And he had noticed something strange about *her*.

She supposed she shouldn't be surprised. She *felt* strange. Part of her wanted to turn her face up to the sun and dance around the garden. The other part of her was shrieking, Be careful! Don't do anything foolish! Her emotions were at war with her brain and she didn't know what she wanted anymore. She only knew that somehow, Phillip was involved, and if she was sensible, she would turn her back on him and his problems and concentrate on Bernard.

She was tired of being sensible.

A rustling noise interrupted her cogitations. She looked up. A rosebush in the middle of the garden was shaking. Going over to investigate, she found Jeremy, lying on his stomach, grubbing in the dirt.

She had not spoken to him since the apple-core incident two days ago. "Hello, Jeremy," she said tentatively.

He didn't answer for a moment. Then she heard a grudging, "Hello, Miss Westbourne."

He did not move from his position under the bush

and Margaret felt a trifle awkward. Did he blame her for the whipping he had received? "Your father is looking for you."

Jeremy did not reply.

"You were supposed to go fishing with him and your uncle Bernard."

Still no reply.

"I think your father is concerned about you, Jeremy."

"No, he's not. He doesn't care about me at all." Digging up a handful of dirt, Jeremy clutched it in his hands.

The bitter words shocked Margaret. She crouched down, trying to see his face. "How can you say that? He's your father and naturally he cares about you."

The boy sifted the dirt through his fingers, revealing a fat slug. "He's not my father."

"What? Of course he's—"

"No, he's not!" Jeremy threw the slug away and looked up. Bright, defiant eyes stared into hers. "I heard the maids talking at Grandpapa Barstow's. They said I was a bastard." A small sniff escaped him. "I asked my friend, Brandon, what that meant and he said it means my father isn't truly my father."

Margaret sank onto her knees beside him, unheeding of the soil staining her dress. She put her hand on his shoulder, but he shrugged it away. For a moment she felt helpless, then anger for the loose-tongued maids surged through her. How dare they name an innocent child so?

"Even if it's true, Jeremy, I'm sure your father loves you very much and considers you his son."

Jeremy scrambled to his feet. "No, he doesn't. He's always frowning and scolding. He never calls me 'son.' Brandon's father always calls *him* 'son.'"

Margaret felt out of her depth. Rising to her feet,

she brushed the dirt from her dress, wondering how she could reassure Jeremy, or if she should even try. She had no idea if the story was even true. Studying Jeremy, she could see many of Cecilia's features, and none of Geoffrey's, but that proved nothing. Really, Cecilia or Geoffrey needed to talk to him. "Why don't you go fishing with your father and ask him about it?"

"No, I don't want to." His mouth a stubborn line, he tilted his chin up in a strangely familiar way. "I don't even care, not really."

In spite of his proud words, she could see the misery in his dark eyes. Unable to comfort him, not knowing what to say, she decided to change the subject, hoping to distract him. "If you don't want to go fishing, would you like to go to Wynch Bridge with me?"

A spark of interest lit his eye. "Maybe." He wiped the palms of his hands on his breeches.

Before Margaret could say anything more, Bernard returned. "There you are, Jeremy!" he exclaimed. "Your father and I have been looking for you everywhere."

Jeremy hunched his shoulders. "I don't want to go fishing."

Bernard frowned and opened his mouth.

"I told Jeremy I would take him to Wynch Bridge," Margaret said hurriedly.

"You will have to ask Geoffrey," Bernard said. "Perhaps he can go with you."

"Mama said I mustn't ask Papa to take me there. He couldn't go on the bridge because of his leg."

Bernard's frown deepened. "Then I will have to escort you, if Geoffrey gives his permission."

Margaret's heart sank. She had hoped to try out the bridge. Bernard's presence would spoil everything. "I don't think that's necessary."

"Margaret, you cannot go gallivanting around the countryside with only a boy. People would think you eccentric to say the least."

"I don't care what people think," she muttered in a low, cross voice.

Unfortunately, Bernard heard her. Shock rendered him momentarily speechless.

"You . . . don't . . . care?" he sputtered. "But I thought . . ." His voice trailed off and he stared at her as if she were an anarchist. "You've changed since we came here," he finally said. "Next thing, you'll be talking to Phillip."

She tried to keep the blush from rising in her cheeks, but she knew she had not succeeded when Bernard's expression grew incredulous.

"Margaret—" he began, then stopped, looking down at Jeremy's wide-eyed face. "Jeremy, run and ask your father if you may come with us to Wynch Bridge."

Jeremy scampered off, and Bernard turned back to Margaret, standing before her like a judge. "Now, Margaret," he said. "What is this lunacy? Do you truly pretend to have heard Phillip's ghost?"

Irritation rose in Margaret. "I pretend nothing," she snapped. "I have seen him."

"You have actually seen him? Good Lord!" Bernard stared speechlessly at her.

"I know you must think I am insane. I think so myself, sometimes. But certainly something has been in my room every night."

"In your room? Margaret, do you mean to say that *he visits you in your room at night?*"

Bernard could not have sounded more shocked if she had confessed to having intimate relations with the devil himself.

"You are overreacting." Margaret spoke sharply. "He is a ghost. A phantasm. He never stays later than midnight, and he cannot touch me, even if he so desired, even if I would allow it."

"That is beside the point. The point is that a person of the male sex is in your room at night! Dear heaven, has he even seen you in your night rail?"

He has even seen me without it, Margaret was tempted to say. Fortunately, Jeremy came back, shouting, "I may go!" and prevented her from committing that particular indiscretion. Instead, she only said coldly, "This entire discussion is beside the point."

The trip to the bridge was silent. When they arrived, Jeremy immediately shot out of the carriage and ran off.

"Stay off the bridge, Jeremy!" Bernard shouted after him.

Margaret followed Jeremy, her pace quickening. When she caught up to him, he was looking longingly at the bridge. "Would you like to come out on the bridge with me?" she asked.

"Oh, Miss Westbourne! Yes!"

"You know I told you the bridge is not safe." Bernard huffed, coming up behind.

Margaret hesitated. She didn't want to endanger herself or Jeremy—

"I insist you stay here, Margaret."

"You may stay if you like," she said. Grabbing Jeremy's hand, she moved out onto the structure.

It did sway most alarmingly, she thought, grabbing the cold iron chain that suspended the bridge with one hand and holding firmly onto Jeremy with the other. Together, they inched forward on the wooden slats, out toward the middle of the bridge.

It was like being in some fantastical fairy world. Rainbow mist sparkled all around her, enveloping her in a cool layer of spun gossamer. Jeremy shouted something at her, but she could not hear him over the roar of the falls. The bridge began to sway again, and Margaret felt as if she were flying. Exhilaration swept through her and she laughed out loud.

A hand latched onto her elbow. Startled, she turned to see Bernard standing behind her, his face pale, but determined. Her grip on the iron chain tightened. She half expected him to drag her off the bridge, but to her surprise he merely stood there, waiting.

After a while, Margaret beckoned to Jeremy, and they all returned to the side.

"That was prime! Thank you, Miss Westbourne," Jeremy said before running ahead to the carriage.

Margaret followed with Bernard. She peeked at him sideways, wondering if he was going to lecture her. He still looked a bit pale.

"Is something the matter?" she asked.

"I don't care for heights," he replied.

"What!" She stopped, staring at him in astonishment. "Why, I remember when you climbed to the top of the tallest tree in the orchard to get the last cherry for me."

"You will also remember I fell and broke my leg. Even at that age, looking down a long way made me dizzy."

"Oh," Margaret said blankly. She had not known. She'd never even suspected. Looking over her shoulder at the swaying bridge, guilt pricked at her. Going out on the bridge must have been torture for him. "I'm sorry, Bernard. You should have stayed at the side."

"As I said before, the bridge is dangerous, and I wanted to be at hand if you needed help."

He had truly been worried for her, she realized in amazement. Her guilt increased. "I appreciate your concern."

He pulled her to a stop, and faced her, his expression serious, his chin for once thrust forward. "I am always at your service, Margaret, for anything. Even if I don't approve of your actions." His gray eyes darkened. "Such as your consorting with Phillip. I shudder to think what has been going on between you two."

Margaret shuddered to think what Bernard would say if he knew. Her guilt made her reply sharper than it might have been otherwise. "There is nothing going on between us. He is trapped here because of the curse, that is all, and I would appreciate it if you would keep your base imaginings to yourself."

A dull flush colored his face. "Forgive me. I did not mean to imply . . . of course you would not do anything improper. I don't know what I was thinking."

Margaret turned her face away so he wouldn't see her burning cheeks. "Please, let us not discuss it."

The journey home was silent. It wasn't until Margaret was dressing for dinner that it finally registered. Bernard, after his initial disbelief, had not doubted that she saw a ghost, and in fact, had tacitly admitted that Phillip did indeed exist.

14

Bernard knotted his cravat haphazardly, paying little heed to the process. Ignoring the protestations of his valet, he shrugged on his dark blue dinner coat and slipped his watch into his pocket. The result was perhaps less than perfect, sartorially, but Bernard was too worried to care that a crease marred his sleeve or that his cravat was a trifle askew.

Something was wrong with Margaret, and the more he thought about it, the more worried he became. She had changed, and he had a sinking feeling he knew why.

Phillip. Margaret could *see* Phillip.

Waving aside his fuming valet, Bernard went downstairs. He was too early for dinner, so he wandered into the picture gallery. Stopping before the portrait of Phillip, he stared up at the painted visage.

All through his early childhood, Aunt Letty had filled his ears with tales of Phillip. Brave, dashing, man-about-town Phillip. Witty, charming, wizard-with-the-women Phillip. As a child, Bernard had often played here in this room, saving England from foreign armadas, rescuing ladies from fiery dragons, dueling with the villainous Lord Mortimer. Pretending he was Phillip.

Those imaginary games had stayed with him even when he went to school. They had sustained him through the days when older boys had bullied him and laughed at his interest in his studies. While he learned to keep his chin down and be invisible, those games had been the only bright spot in his life.

Until the summer he met Margaret.

Margaret. Even now, he could remember his first sight of her, waltzing down the path, a dandelion chain hanging crazily on her glossy brown curls. When she had seen him, she had stopped, staring at him with enormous blue eyes for a moment, before she invited him to join her game.

After that, he had frequently escaped from the gloomy confines of Barnett Manor to seek her out. His time with her was a happy, sunny world that made up for the cold misery of school. By the time he turned sixteen, he had fallen hopelessly in love with Margaret.

He never mentioned it, knowing his father would sneer. So when Lord Barnett had suddenly proposed a marriage, Bernard had been ecstatic.

It hadn't lasted, of course. Margaret had denounced Lord Barnett in church, and seeing the disgust in her face, Bernard had been shamed to the soles of his boots. He had known then that she would never agree to marry him unless he could show her that he was nothing like his father.

He had worked hard at it, and he thought he had succeeded—she had accepted him, even in spite of the way his wretched tongue had mangled the proposal. Now he feared it was all for naught.

He sensed he was losing her.

Because of Phillip? Thinking of his boyhood idol, Bernard's mouth tightened. Phillip might be charming and witty, but he was also a selfish womanizer. A *dead* selfish womanizer.

Bernard stared up at the painting. Phillip's mocking gaze stared back.

"You can't have her," Bernard said through suddenly clenched teeth. "Dammit, Margaret is mine."

Later that evening, Margaret was about to go up to her room when Bernard stopped her.

"Margaret, may I speak to you for a minute?"

Margaret gripped the balustrade. Bernard had been in an odd mood ever since they'd returned from Wynch Bridge. He had frowned all through dinner, and barely spoken. Even Geoffrey had commented on his gloom.

Was he going to question her about Phillip again?

Bernard pulled out his watch. *Click, snap.* "I was wondering . . ." *Click, snap.* "That is, er . . ." He put the watch back in his pocket and took a deep breath. "I was going to play a game of billiards, and I wondered if you might join me," he said in a rush.

His invitation was so unexpected, Margaret gaped. "But I don't know how to play billiards," was all she could think to say.

"I would be more than happy to teach you."

Good heavens! What had come over Bernard? What he suggested was shocking. Not only was he asking her to indulge in the unladylike occupation of billiards, but he was asking her to do it late at night. Just the two of them. *Alone.*

But what if Phillip was waiting for her?

The memory of her behavior last night made her cheeks turn hot. How could she possibly face him? Suddenly, a game of billiards sounded like a good idea.

She looked at Bernard warily. Why was he proposing something so improper? Was he testing her moral fiber perhaps?

She didn't care if he was, she decided. For the first time in eight years she was enjoying herself, and she saw no reason to stop now. She smiled. "I would love to, Bernard."

Located in the east wing, the billiards room had hunting scenes hanging on dark walnut paneling, a deep red carpet, and a massive fireplace. In the middle of the room stood the billiards table.

Bernard took down two cues and handed one to Margaret.

She inspected the long narrow pole and laughed. "What would Lady Creevy think if she could see me now?"

"Why does everyone put such store in her opinion?" Bernard muttered as he placed two balls, one red, one white, on the green baize cloth of the table. "I can't abide her."

Margaret almost dropped the cue. "Bernard! That's . . . that's heresy!"

He hunched his shoulders and looked at the table. "I will take the first shot, to demonstrate," he said. Using the cue, he took careful aim, and drove it against the white ball, which rolled toward the red one, striking it. The red ball spun toward a pocket and went in. "That is called a winning hazard," said Bernard, straightening. "Three points for me."

Margaret, thoughts of Lady Creevy still occupying her, paid no attention. "I never liked her either. She always complained to Mama about my unladylike behavior, reporting every instance she caught me without shoes or a bonnet. I think she considered it her Christian duty to invite Mama and me to join that silly 'sewing society' of hers. Mama was in alt—she'd been trying to wangle an invitation for months—and how furious I was! Do you remember, Bernard? I couldn't play with you for the whole month of July because we had to go to Lady Creevy's every day."

Bernard shrugged and retrieved the red ball, placing it within a semicircle outlined in white on the green cloth.

"I was ever so glad when it broke up." A reminiscent smile curved her lips. "I told you, didn't I, how she opened her sewing basket one day, and a score of beetles flew out? All the ladies had hysterics. They were hideous—the beetles, I mean. Purplish black and huge—"

"*Carabus violaceus.*" Nodding absently, Bernard's gaze met hers.

Suddenly, he began to apply chalk to the end of his cue with great industry, his eyes avoiding hers. An insane suspicion formed in her brain. "Bernard—you didn't—"

"Margaret, I brought you here to play billiards, not to talk about Lady Creevy. The object is to try to hit the other balls."

Margaret stared at him, trying to remember what—if anything—she had said to him about the beetles in the sewing basket. She couldn't remember exactly, although she was almost certain—

"Margaret! It's your turn."

She jumped. "Oh, I'm sorry Bernard." She would have to think about the beetles another time.

Focusing her attention on the game before her, she decided it looked easy enough. She picked up the cue and bent over the table, holding the stick as Bernard had done. Her gaze fixed on the ball, she asked, "Like this?"

"Mm-hm."

He sounded distracted, but Margaret paid no attention. Taking careful aim, she shoved the stick at the ball. She missed completely, the cue swinging up in the air.

"Hold the cue steady and drive it straight ahead," Bernard instructed.

Feeling foolish, Margaret thought perhaps this wouldn't be so easy after all. She positioned herself again. When she was ready she glanced over her shoulder for approval from Bernard. He seemed to be staring at her backside.

Flushing, Margaret straightened. "Bernard!"

Startled, he looked up, then flushed also. "Oh, I beg your pardon." He moved to the other side of the table. "Please proceed."

Rattled by his incomprehensible behavior, she pushed the cue forward once more. She barely nicked the ball.

"No, no." He moved to her side, and his hand closed over hers on the cue. Bending over with her, he held the cue straight and steady. "You are swinging up, like this, Margaret. You must shoot straight, like this."

She barely heard him. It felt very strange to have Bernard so close. His body was compact, his hands strong over hers. She could feel his breath against her cheek, could smell a vetiver scent. The earthy, woodsy fragrance surprised her. Normally, she would not have associated such a smell with Bernard. She rather liked—

"Enjoying yourself, Margaret?" a sarcastic new voice intruded.

15

Margaret straightened up abruptly, her head hitting Bernard's chin. Phillip, arms folded across his chest, stood watching from the other side of the table.

"What are you doing here?" she exclaimed, blushing a little as she met his gaze, trying not to think of last night.

Grimacing, Bernard rubbed his chin. "Teaching you to play billiards, I thought."

"Is that what he was doing? They called it something different in my day."

Margaret's embarrassment faded rapidly. Her fingers tightened on the cue stick. "You are disgusting."

Affronted, Bernard drew himself up. "If you feel that way—"

"Oh, not you, Bernard."

"Not—do you mean to say he is here?"

Margaret bit her lip.

Bernard looked suspiciously around the room. Addressing a spot about five feet from where Phillip stood, Bernard said, "I will thank you, sir, to go away and leave my fiancée alone."

"I expect you would, bird's-nest."

"*Bernard,*" Margaret corrected him.

"What?" said Bernard.

"What astounding wit," sneered Phillip. "I wonder he doesn't set himself up as a pundit."

"Phillip . . ." Margaret said, an edge to her voice.

For a moment, Phillip was tempted to say something that would really shock her, but after a brief struggle, he restrained himself. "I must talk to you. It's urgent."

Alarm rose in her. "Has something happened? Are you ill? I mean, is something the matter with you?"

"I can't discuss it here, Margaret."

"Oh." She glanced hesitantly at Bernard. "He says he needs to talk to me."

Bernard tensed. "Can't he wait?"

Margaret looked at Phillip. He shook his head. "I don't think so, Bernard. He says it's urgent. Besides, it *is* very late. Why don't we meet here after breakfast tomorrow?"

Bernard nodded stiffly. His face set, he watched her leave. With a muttered curse, he threw the billiard cue down on the table and glared at nothing in particular, until the bellpull in the corner caught his eye. His frown lightened. Striding over, he gave it an urgent tug.

"What is it, Phillip?" Margaret asked worriedly when they were in her room.

He didn't answer immediately. Watching him pace about the room, Margaret grew more and more alarmed. "Phillip, you must tell me! What has happened?"

Mouth taut, he came to a halt in front of her. "I don't think it's a good idea for you to be alone with Bernard so late," he said.

"You don't think . . ." Margaret's voice trailed off then rose again in angry disbelief. "*That's* what you wanted to talk to me about?"

"You're very innocent, Margaret. You may not realize what it does to a man to—"

"How dare you?" Margaret was so angry, she wanted to stamp her foot. "Bernard is my fiancé! If anyone should be complaining, it is he!"

"And so he should be, the fool," Phillip muttered.

"What? What did you say?"

Phillip was tempted to tell her, but he restrained himself. It wasn't easy. Seeing Bernard bending over her had raised an angry demon in him. It wasn't jealousy—that would be foolish. He had merely wanted to order her out of the room and thrash Bernard to a pulp. Then he wanted to throw her on the floor and show her exactly what she did to men, what she did to him. He wanted to make passionate love to her the way he had ached to do last night. The way he ached to do now.

But to his frustration, making love to Margaret was as impossible as thrashing Bernard. He would have to deal with Bernard in some other way. In the meantime . . .

"I'm simply advising you to be careful with Bernard," he said coldly. "Or you may regret it."

Furious, she opened her mouth to reply, but a knock at the door interrupted her. Much to her annoyance, Phillip vanished as Yvette bustled in. "You're ready to change for bed, miss?"

With an effort, Margaret smiled at the maid. "Your timing is perfect, Yvette." She moved behind the screen just in case Phillip was still lurking somewhere. Although after last night, she supposed modesty was a bit useless.

"Oh, it was Lord Barnett that told me." Efficiently, Yvette dealt with the buttons and started on the corset strings.

Margaret inhaled deeply. "Lord Barnett?"

"Yes, he rang and told me how tired you were and could I please come up right away. That man is so thoughtful!" Yvette released the last corset string.

"Yes." Margaret's breath came out in a deep whoosh. "Yes, indeed."

The next afternoon, Bernard was still angry at how Phillip had spirited Margaret away. The thought of that . . . that rogue in her bedroom made him gnash his teeth. He wanted to demand that Phillip stay out of her room, to forbid Margaret to talk to the ghost. Unfortunately, even if Margaret obeyed, Bernard had no doubt Phillip would not.

He had to find another way to fight Phillip.

This morning's billiards session had failed miserably—at least as far as Bernard was concerned. At breakfast, Margaret had invited Geoffrey and Cecilia to join Bernard and her for the lesson. Before he could think of an excuse to prevent it, Cecilia had accepted. The resulting game had been hilarious and much enjoyed by everyone—except himself. He had wanted to be *alone* with Margaret.

He was determined to do better this afternoon. He had planned to spend the day observing the *Geotrupes sterocarius* in its natural habitat. If he invited Margaret to come with him, he could spend some time with her while he worked. Margaret would enjoy herself, he was certain.

Margaret, gripping the banister tightly, stared at Bernard in horror. "You want to do *what*?"

"A little field research." He stood two steps below her, looking up. "On the dor beetle."

"But I was just going to have my luncheon."

"I'll have Cook pack a picnic basket. Please, Margaret, you will enjoy it, I promise."

Margaret sighed in frustration, wishing he wasn't so persistent. Nothing could sound more unappealing than sitting around watching a bunch of creepy, crawling little creatures. "I hate insects."

"Yes, I discovered that many years ago," he said wryly.

She looked at him sharply, noticing the slight quirk to his lips. Indignation filled her. "You're referring to the 'present' you gave me for my ninth birthday, I suppose?"

"Mm-hm. My ears rang for days with your shrieks."

"Can you blame me? If I'd known what was in that box, I never would have opened it."

"A *Curculio betulae*." Bernard smiled reminiscently. "Green with magnificent orange spots. It was a mark of my high esteem for you."

"Hmph." But she couldn't help smiling a little, too. "Oh, very well. I will accompany you."

They drove the dogcart down to the river for the picnic, and to Margaret's relief, Bernard refrained from mentioning insects while they ate. And although the day was hot, the shade was cool on the mossy bank where they sat and a pleasant breeze fanned her chest and throat where the neckline of her plum satin walking dress dipped.

She took a final bite of tart green apple, then lay back on the blanket with a sigh of repletion. Bernard had been right—she was enjoying the outing. "That was delicious." A pleasant languor was stealing over her. "Perhaps I will take a nap while you look at your insects."

Bernard tossed a chicken bone in the picnic basket. "Wouldn't you rather look, too? You shouldn't be so prejudiced, Margaret. In form and composition, there is no other creature of such phenomenal artistry."

"Phenomenal artistry?" she said doubtfully. "I don't know, Bernard. I've always thought insects were hideous."

"Surely you can't be so blind to their beauty. Look at that butterfly. Look at the brilliant hues, the perfect symmetry of pattern, the delicacy of form. How can you say it is not beautiful?"

Margaret's gaze followed his pointing finger to where a butterfly rested on the trunk of a beech tree perhaps ten feet away. The dark blue wings had an elegant tracery of black lines and bright orange spots rimmed the edges.

"It is a *Polyommatus icarus,*" Bernard said. Rising, he silently approached the tree and, with unexpected speed and grace, captured the butterfly in his cupped hands. Returning to the blanket, he knelt beside her and extended his hands. "Smell it, Margaret."

She sniffed. A sweet, rich aroma filled her nostrils. "Why, it smells like chocolate!" She inhaled again, not quite able to believe an insect could smell so good.

"This particular butterfly uses scent to attract mates." He smiled down at her.

Margaret blinked a little, suddenly conscious of her position and the way he was bending over her, his hands hovering above her chest. She sat up, the abrupt movement startling Bernard. Leaning back, his hands dropped to his sides and the butterfly fluttered up between them. "Are you studying butterflies, also?" she asked, keeping her eyes on the bright blue wings fluttering away.

Suddenly awkward, he rose to his feet. "No, no. Only the *Geotrupes stercorarius.*" He scrambled up the slippery bank to the dogcart, and for a moment, she thought he was going to leave without her. But he merely retrieved a small sketchbook and pencil and returned to sit on the blanket, a discreet distance away. Keeping his gaze averted from her, he scanned the underbrush until he found what he was seeking and began to draw.

After several minutes had passed, curiosity got the better of her. She inched forward and peered over his shoulder. "Good heavens, what is that supposed to be?"

"A dor beetle." With his pencil, Bernard pointed at a large black beetle resting on a twig. He looked down at his less than satisfactory effort and sighed. "I am working on a monograph that has excited some interest from the Entomological Society. I thought a few accompanying illustrative sketches would not come amiss."

"You're presenting a paper to the Entomological Society?" Margaret was impressed. "On what subject?"

"The Relationship between British and Egyptian Coleoptera of the Scarabaeidae and Geotrupidae Families—Comprising an Account of Their Metamorphoses, Habitations, and Mating Rituals."

"Good heavens," she said faintly. She supposed she shouldn't be surprised. He had always been brilliant. Unfortunately, the same could not be said for his drawing. "Why don't you let me sketch the beetle?"

He looked at her in surprise. "You would do that?"

"Certainly. As long as I don't have to touch it and it doesn't have to touch me."

He surrendered the book and pencil gladly.

She studied the beetle a moment, then drew a very competent outline. "You can't possibly think this is beautiful," she muttered as she began detailing its small, monstrous head.

Bernard, making some notes in a small journal, looked up. His lips quirked. "Perhaps not, but it is very interesting, nonetheless. It is related to the scarab beetle, which was sacred to the ancient Egyptians. The scarab's activities were seen as a reflection in miniature of the world around them and was a symbol of rebirth."

Margaret looked at the ugly black beetle, then at Bernard. "Truly?"

"Yes, truly." He leaned over to look at her drawing. "That is very well done, Margaret."

"Thank you." She finished adding striations to its back, then craned her neck to see behind the twig. "I can't quite see the legs, Bernard."

"I will hold it if you like."

She hesitated. "It won't jump out of your hand on me, will it?"

"No, these beetles fly only in the evening." Carefully, he picked up the beetle and held it in the palm of his hand.

Margaret repressed a shudder. How could he bear to touch it? She watched the thing warily, until satisfied it wouldn't attack her, then she returned her attention to her drawing. As she added several hairy legs to the sketch, she asked, "Were dor beetles sacred here?"

"No, but in some parts of Europe, it is believed they have magic powers to curse or conjure up a fortune," Bernard said. He smiled with the amused superiority often felt for the superstitions of one's ancestors. "Some even believe they are familiars of the devil—"

Before he could finish his sentence, the beetle flew up in the air and fell straight down the low neckline of Margaret's dress.

"Eek!" she screeched. Jumping to her feet, she brushed frantically at her bodice. The insect dropped lower. She could feel it crawling between her breasts, its wings fluttering. "Bernard! Get it out! Get it out!"

He hesitated a split second before plunging his

hand in after the insect. His warm fingers probed the cleft of her breasts, grazing the soft curves before he grasped the beetle and pulled it out.

"I have it, Margaret."

His voice sounded a bit odd, and she looked at him. She was still shaking, whether from the insect, or embarrassment, she wasn't quite sure. Mortification flooded her. Had she truly ordered him to stick his hand down her dress? "You did that on purpose!" she said shrilly.

Bernard turned pale. "No! Margaret, I swear—!"

She didn't let him finish. Stalking to the dogcart, she climbed into the seat and sat there stiffly until he drove her home, protesting his innocence all the while.

She told Phillip that night, and he listened sympathetically, making small noises of outrage at the appropriate moments. He was glad she was angry at Bernard, but he still did not like the side effect of the little incident. Bernard had actually *touched* her.

"But maybe it was an accident," she said, calming down a bit. "Bernard is too much of a gentleman to do something so lewd. He respects me."

Respected her! Why he'd wager the idiot was wallowing in lewd thoughts this very moment. "Bernard ought to be shot," he growled with more sincerity than he had shown till that moment.

She looked at him in surprise, then with dawning suspicion. "Phillip—"

Hastily, he rose from the settee. "Dear Margaret, I must go now." He patted his vest as if searching for his watch.

"Why?" Her suspicion increasing by the moment, she folded her arms across her chest.

"Ghost business." Ignoring her outraged expression, he smiled sweetly and vanished.

The next night, after everyone had retired, Bernard walked to Margaret's room and raised his hand to knock. His determination faltered for a moment, and he lowered his hand to his side again.

Would she like the idea? Or would she think it foolish? He didn't know, but he knew he had to take the risk. He was beginning to feel desperate.

Margaret had been a little distant all day, although she had finally accepted his apology. He did not try to proclaim his innocence again—he suspected he knew who he had to thank for the incident with the beetle.

He hoped he could recover some lost ground tonight. *If* she liked the idea and didn't think it foolish. With a deep breath, Bernard raised his hand and knocked.

Margaret's maid answered the door, opening it barely a crack. "Yes?"

Bernard cleared his throat. "May I speak to Margaret?"

The woman frowned. "She's getting ready for bed."

"Who is it, Yvette?" Bernard heard Margaret call.

Reluctantly, the maid opened the door all the way. Bernard saw Margaret, standing behind a dressing screen, her dress draped over the edge, her bare shoulders just visible. His throat tightened.

"Bernard! What do you want?" Her bright blue eyes looked curiously at him. "Is something wrong?"

"No, no, not at all." He had to clear his throat again. "I wondered if you would like to go for a boat ride on the lake."

"Now?" she gasped.

"Why not?" he asked. "The moon is almost full and it's still warm."

Margaret stared at him for a moment, wondering at the odd invitation. First the billiards, then the picnic, now this. Bernard hadn't been so . . . *friendly* since they were children. What was behind it all?

The answer came to her, so clear and obvious, she didn't know why she hadn't thought of it before. He was trying to reestablish their childhood friendship. A warm glow filled her. Perhaps he wanted to let bygones be bygones. Perhaps he missed her companionship as much as she had missed his. She smiled brilliantly. "Why not, indeed? Yvette, come help me put my dress back on."

Grumbling, the maid did so, and in a few minutes, Margaret and Bernard were walking toward the lake through the sweetly scented night.

She hesitated a moment when she saw the weathered wood of the old rowboat. "It won't sink, will it?"

"Don't worry, it's seaworthy. I checked it today." He helped her climb aboard, then pushed off and jumped in. Picking up the oars, he began to row.

Still a bit tense, Margaret relaxed slightly when the boat glided forward.

"Worried your dress might get wet?"

Startled, she looked at him. Was he actually *teasing* her? Although the light was dim, she could see his half smile. Involuntarily, she smiled back. "It's not my dress that concerns me. I can't swim."

He stopped rowing to stare at her. "You never learned? Why didn't you tell me? I would have taught you."

When they were children, he had always been trying to coax her into the water, she remembered. She had turned up her nose in disdain to cover her fear. Ever since she had fallen in a lake as a child, she had tried to avoid large bodies of water.

"I'll still teach you," he said as he resumed rowing, "if you would like to learn."

"Perhaps someday," she murmured.

The lake was like a silver mirror, perfectly still, except for where the boat cut through it. The only noise was the slight splashing made by the oars, and the creak of wood. The last of her tension flowed out, leaving her with a pleasant lassitude. What a wonderful idea this was! It surprised her that Bernard had thought of it. But he had surprised her quite a bit the last few days.

"It is important to have some knowledge of swimming," Bernard continued. "You never know when it will save your life."

She thought she detected a grimness in his voice. Curious, she asked, "You sound as though you speak from experience."

"Yes, I almost drowned once in India."

"Drowned!" Margaret straightened. "What happened?"

"When I first arrived there, I heard about some bees that made their nests in the Marble Rocks at Jubbulpore. Since the Marble Rocks stand up out of a lake, I had to hire a boat in order to observe the bees. Due to an excess of enthusiasm, I rowed too close to a nest, and a swarm attacked me. I was forced to dive overboard. Every time I surfaced, the bees attacked. Fortunately, I was a skilled enough swimmer to escape finally."

"Dear heaven," she breathed. "That wasn't much of a welcome to India."

He shrugged. "India isn't always welcoming to foreigners. The British especially. Just the heat is nigh unbearable—the air is thick with humidity, and the sun so fierce one can't hold a gun, or anything else made of metal, without gloves."

He paused, gazing out across the lake, with a distant look in his eyes. "But on a night like this, you can go down to a water hole and see deer, jackal, leopard, and wild boar. In the garden of my villa, I often saw bulbul, hoopoe, and mynah birds. There was even a green parrot that stole plums from my tree. The villa itself smelled of sandalwood, and the windows and doors were always open for air and for visitors. The hospitality of the people is unlimited."

Margaret could not take her eyes away from him. "You sound as if you enjoyed it," she whispered.

He looked at her. He shook himself slightly, as if coming out of a trance. Picking up the oars, he began to row again. "As I told you before, it's not so romantic as it sounds. In the rainy season, snakes prefer a dry house to a wet garden. Many are poisonous. Sudden disease and death are common. It's not comfortable, Margaret."

No, it didn't sound comfortable at all. But did she want to be comfortable? "Don't you think one can become *too* comfortable?" she asked.

He gave her an odd look. "Perhaps."

He didn't say any more, and she considered what he had said. Although much of it was negative, there had been a tone in his voice and a look in his eye that made her think Bernard wasn't as stodgy as he sometimes appeared. In fact, she was sure of it—look how he'd invited her on this boat ride. Leaning over, she trailed her hand in the water, reveling in the pleasant coolness, and feeling more in charity with Bernard than she had in a long time.

They were some distance from shore when Bernard stopped rowing. "I wanted to talk to you where we wouldn't be interrupted," he said, pulling up the oars. "I've been wanting to elucidate a few matters." He sounded serious.

"Oh?" Margaret pulled her hand out of the water, shaking it to remove the moisture. "What matters?"

Bernard handed her a handkerchief. "Your father, for one."

"My father?" Margaret stopped drying her fingers to look at him. She couldn't read his expression. "What about my father?"

He hesitated, as if choosing his words. "What he said about 'upping the ante,'" Bernard finally burst out. "That wasn't true."

Upping the ante? Oh. She remembered how her father had implied he'd had to increase her dowry to persuade Bernard to marry her. "It wasn't?" she said coolly.

"I mean, he did, but I never . . . that is, he was the one . . . what I mean to say is, I certainly never asked for anything from your father. I've done very well for myself in India. I would have been glad to marry you even if you didn't have a penny."

"You would?" The handkerchief slipped from Margaret's fingers and she had to grope around the bottom of the boat to find it. She didn't know what to make of his words. Was he merely trying to be polite? If he truly wanted to marry her, then why did he always seem so distant?

Looking up at him, her lips parted in unconscious invitation.

He leaned forward. "Margaret—"

A sudden cold breeze swept across the lake, rocking the boat. Strangely, the breeze swept back again, from the other direction, rocking them even more violently. One of the oars tipped into the lake. Bernard, reaching out to grab it, leaned dangerously far over the edge of the boat. The cold wind swept by for the third time, and Bernard fell overboard, almost as if he had been pushed.

With an exclamation, Margaret reached out to help him, only to overbalance. Her arms windmilled in an effort to save herself, but it was useless. With a loud splash, she fell into the cold, dark water.

16

A black nightmare world closed around her. She was a four-year-old child again, weak, helpless. Terrified, she tried to claw her way to the surface, but her swirling hair and heavy skirts hindered her. She managed to pull the skirts away from her legs, but although she had instinctively taken a breath before falling in, she was quickly running out of oxygen. Panic-stricken, she thrashed in the water, heart pounding, lungs bursting.

She was certain she was going to die when a hand seized her arm and pulled her to the surface. "Margaret!" Bernard exclaimed. "Are you all right?"

"Bernard!" She locked her arms about his neck and wrapped her legs around his hips. Pressing her face against his chest, she clung like a starfish to a rock.

"Margaret." His hands came up to her waist, and she burrowed closer to him. "Margaret! The water's only five feet deep."

Tremors reverberated through her bones. She could barely make sense of what he was saying. Something about the water.

"You can stand up, Margaret. The water's only five feet deep."

Five feet? Margaret's breathing slowly returned to normal. Becoming aware of the intimate way she was clinging to him, she abruptly released her death grip. She splashed awkwardly in the water until she found her footing. "I'm sorry, Bernard." She blushed furiously. "Thank you."

"Are you all right?" Bernard asked again, keeping hold of her arm.

"I'm fine," she replied. "But we'd better get inside."

Abandoning the boat, they waded to shore and hurried to the house, Margaret dragging her heavy sodden skirts. Inside, she headed straight for the stairs, when Bernard caught her arm again.

His dark brown hair looked almost black against his pale skin. "Margaret—"

"Tomorrow, Bernard," she said, her teeth chattering. "I'll talk to you tomorrow." Pulling away, she hurried up to her room.

She threw the door open so violently, it crashed against the wall. Shivering and dripping, her hair plastered to her scalp, water trickling down her nose, she glared around the room.

Phillip was not there.

Furiously, she stomped over to the bellpull and yanked.

With much clucking, Yvette helped Margaret change. When the maid left at last, Margaret climbed into bed and waited, arms folded across her chest.

Half an hour passed. Muttering dire imprecations under her breath, she picked up her book and forced herself to read. By the time Phillip finally made an appearance, she had herself well under control.

From the corner of her eye, she saw him hesitate, then try that engaging grin of his. As if she were one of those foolish women who found him irresistible, she thought. As if he expected her to smile back.

Her lips tightened; she ignored the smile. That wind had not been natural and it had confirmed her suspicions about the beetle incident. She wanted an apology. A *protracted* apology.

Phillip watched her quietly for a few moments. Her eyes looked bluer than ever against her pale skin and the dark gold of her slightly damp hair. She was sitting up in bed, leaning against a mass of pillows, reading a book. He studied her tilted chin, raised brows, and pursed lips.

She looked amazingly adorable, even though she appeared a bit miffed. He supposed it hadn't been a good idea to rock that boat. He had never meant for her to get wet, only her stick of a betrothed. He hadn't realized she couldn't swim.

"I'm sorry I rocked your boat, Margaret."

Her face remained cold. Perhaps she was a bit more upset than he'd thought. He tried again. "If I'd known you can't swim, I wouldn't have done it. I didn't mean to frighten you."

Still her lips remained pursed and he discovered he did not like seeing that expression on her face after all. She should be happy, her eyes glowing with love. His stomach clenched in a peculiar manner. And quite suddenly, he was determined to make her smile.

"You look lovely tonight." He smiled his most charming smile, the one that caused women to sigh, to melt, to swoon.

She did none of those things. Nor did she look charmed. In fact, if it wasn't for the disdainful arch of her eyebrows, he would have thought she hadn't noticed. She turned a page in her book and stared at it intently.

He sighed noisily. Pulling out a handkerchief, he laid it on the floor. At least, he tried to. It floated slightly above the carpet. He pressed it down, but it immediately rose again as if it, or perhaps the floor, gave off some repelling force. Oh, well. He rested one knee on the handkerchief. "I humbly ask forgiveness for being the inadvertent cause of your midnight swim. My intentions were honorable—I had hoped to wash some of the starch out of the noble Barnyard."

"Bernard," she corrected, with a fierce frown.

"As you say. Tell me you forgive me or my life will be ever blighted." He paused, placing a finger to his temple. "Hold, that's not right. My *death* will be ever blighted? That doesn't sound quite right either."

"You are ridiculous." She snapped her book shut.

"Smile upon me please, fair maid. Say you forgive me."

Her lips twitched.

"One word from thine beauteous lips will spare me the agony of *undying* remorse. There, that is much better, isn't it?"

She laughed. The sound was like rippling bells. Her whole face softened, the contours somehow rounding with laughter. Even her blue eyes, shimmering with mirth, seemed to curve upward at the corners.

The sweet sound caused his stomach muscles to contract again. He stared at her, an unnamed longing rising in him. He wanted . . . He wished . . . For a moment, his smile slipped, and the darkness pulled at him. It was becoming more and more difficult to ignore.

"Very well, you impossible man. I forgive you." Her light voice tugged him back. "Though I really shouldn't."

Jeremy was sitting forlornly on the bottom step when Margaret came down the stairs the next morning.

"Papa and Mama are fighting," he said when Margaret asked him what was the matter.

"Oh, dear," Margaret said. She knew Geoffrey had received a letter from London yesterday. Cecilia had not looked very happy about it. "Would you like to go for a walk with me?"

Jeremy shrugged. "I don't know." He glanced at her sideways, a sly gleam in his eyes. "There is a fair over at Middleton. Yesterday, I asked Mama if we could go, and she said she didn't want to, and she didn't think Papa could maneuver on his crutch very well in a crowd." The gleam intensified. "Uncle Bernard is going today."

"He is?" She frowned a little. Why hadn't he mentioned it to her? Did he think she was upset about last night? If so, she must reassure him—she wanted to become friends again. And what better place for friends to go than the fair? "Perhaps I will ask if I may accompany him. Would you like to go, too?"

"Miss Westbourne, do you mean it? Oh, that would be prime!" His eyes shone and he almost smiled.

Margaret held up a hand. "I must convince your uncle, so don't get your hopes up," she warned.

"Oh, I'm sure you can convince him, Miss Westbourne." The glow in his eyes was undimmed. "He's always staring at you with a silly look in his eyes. He's batty over you."

Margaret smiled at Jeremy's innocent interpretation of what had probably been a glare of disapproval, but she did not correct the child. Jeremy's excitement was contagious and she felt exhilaration pumping through her veins. She grinned down at him and took hold of his arm.

"Let's go find Bernard then. And we will see if you are correct about my persuasive powers."

*　　*　　*

Bernard stared at Margaret in dismay. He didn't want to say no, but he had some business to attend to at the fair. He couldn't let her interfere.

"Don't you think you should rest today?" he tried to dissuade her. "You may take a chill after your soaking."

Margaret laughed. "Nonsense. I'm healthy as a horse." With a beguiling smile, she pleaded, "Please, Bernard, Jeremy and I truly would like to go to the fair."

He swallowed. How could he refuse her when she smiled at him like that? When she smiled like that, it made his pulse race, his heart pound. It reminded him of how enticing her rounded bottom had looked when she bent over the billiard table and how soft the skin between her breasts felt. It reminded him of how she had clung to him last night, her breasts pressing against him, her arms and legs wrapped around him like a lover's. . . .

"Please, Bernard?"

A fine sweat broke out on his forehead as he remembered how close he had come to kissing her before the boat tipped. Had she guessed he'd wanted to sweep her into his arms and kiss her until they were both breathless?

He shook himself, mentally. What was the matter with him? Where had all these carnal thoughts come from? He had to control them—and himself. Margaret was too fine and pure to be subjected to such base desires. He couldn't allow lust to sully his love for her.

"Bernard?"

Reluctantly, he agreed. He would have to make certain she was otherwise occupied while he conducted his business. He couldn't delay it. Last night's incident had been no accident. He had been pushed, and he knew who had done it. And although part of him was grateful that he had been prevented from kissing Margaret and ruining everything, today he was determined to do something to get rid of Phillip.

He hoped she wouldn't interfere.

As they drove to the fairgrounds, Bernard made several more attempts to change Margaret's mind. He would gladly drive her home if she decided she didn't want to attend the fair after all.

"I hope you won't regret this, Margaret," he said, deliberately giving his voice the direful tone of a clergyman predicting hell and damnation.

"I don't think I will." He saw her glance at Jeremy, who was bouncing on the seat. She smiled and whispered, "Even if I don't like the fair, it's worth going just to see Jeremy so animated, don't you think?"

"We'll be lucky if we're not robbed," Bernard warned as they drove along. "There are all sorts of unsavory characters at these affairs."

Leaning forward, Margaret grabbed Jeremy's arm to prevent him tumbling out the window. She didn't reply.

"The amusements are low, too."

Margaret nodded absently. Jeremy was attempting to swing from one of the carriage straps, not too successfully.

"Not at all the sort of thing to appeal to a lady. I can't understand why you want to go to this."

"Why do *you*, Bernard? If you disapprove so much, I'm surprised you planned to go at all."

Caught off guard, he flushed. "I have a fancy to have my palm read," he muttered.

"You wish to see a fortune-teller?" Margaret couldn't conceal her astonishment. "Surely you don't believe in such nonsense?"

"Certainly not. But it will be amusing."

She looked at him strangely, and he decided not to say any more.

The fairground was a mass of milling people. A few stalls had been set up, but hawkers mostly walked through the crowd. Women with yokes slung over their shoulders to hold trays sold everything from ribbons and lace to cricket balls and tops. Tempting smells wafted from the wheelbarrows and carts of men selling pickled whelks, fried fish, and hot green peas. Puppet shows and players drew small knots of people, making passage through the grounds even more difficult.

Bernard directed them toward a group of tents a short distance away. Margaret stepped forward, and a child bumped into her.

"Watch out for that little ragamuffin, Margaret. He is probably a cutpurse," said Bernard. The boy tugged at his cap, muttered, and darted away.

"Look, kidney puddings!" Jeremy exclaimed. "May I have one, Uncle Bernard, please?"

"I don't think it's a good idea. You don't know what's in them."

"I would like one, too," Margaret said. "Please, Bernard?"

He grumbled, but he bought the puddings. As they walked along, Jeremy wolfed his down. Margaret, after removing her gloves, ate hers more slowly. Bernard tried not to watch as she savored it. When she was done, she licked her fingers discreetly.

Looking up, Margaret saw Bernard staring at her. Thinking he was disgusted, she hastily pulled her gloves back on, half expecting him to lecture her on her manners. Instead, to her surprise, he stopped and tugged out his handkerchief. "You have a spot of pudding on your chin," he said gruffly, lifting the cloth to her face. Gently he wiped her mouth.

"Uncle Bernard, a talking pig!" Jeremy tugged at Bernard's jacket. "Isn't that amazing? We must go in and see it."

Bernard's hand dropped and he glared at Jeremy. "No, I don't want to see the talking pig; it is a hoax of some sort. I've never heard of anything so ridiculous."

"But Uncle Bernard, the sign says—"

Margaret noticed a sign on another tent. It said Madame Razinski—Amazing Seer into the Future.

A Gypsy . . . a Gypsy! It was so obvious, she didn't know why she hadn't thought of it before. Who better to ask about curses than a Gypsy? What incredible luck that she'd come to the fair with Bernard. . . .

Bernard.

A suspicion formed in her brain. Had it truly been a coincidence? She looked at him, a question in her eyes.

He flushed a little, but nodded. "It seems the logical way to get rid of—I mean, this curse business upsets Aunt Letty so, I thought we should try to break it."

"Of course!" She reached for the flap.

"Margaret, what are you doing? Surely you don't intend to go inside that filthy tent? You and Jeremy can wait outside. Margaret!"

Margaret ducked under the flap and paused to let her eyes adjust to the dim light. Bernard, entering right behind with Jeremy, bumped into her.

"I beg your pardon," he said stiffly. "Margaret, are you certain this is wise?"

She ignored him, her gaze fastening on a Gypsy sitting on a cushion in front of a low table. The woman had coarse black hair and a large dark mole on one cheek. Gold hoops dangled in her ears and numerous gold and silver chains were draped around her neck and arms. Her tattered red dress had a crazy assortment of patches, partially concealed by an enveloping moth-eaten shawl.

"Welcome, *gorgios*," she said, not lifting her eyes from the cards she was laying on the table. Her low, scratchy voice had the exotic accent of some faraway land.

Margaret knelt on the cushion opposite the Gypsy. Bernard and Jeremy did not move from their positions by the flap. Raising dark, beady eyes, the woman inspected Margaret thoroughly. Her gaze flickered briefly to Bernard and Jeremy before returning to Margaret. "What can Madame Razinski do for you, pretty lady?"

Margaret glanced at her companions. Jeremy's eyes were round, while Bernard stood with his arms folded. With a small toss of her head, she tugged off a glove. "I would like to have my fortune told."

The woman lifted Margaret's hand and stared hard at the palm. "Ze picture is unclear," she said.

Margaret followed the Gypsy's gaze. "How odd."

"I believe she wants some money," Bernard said.

"Oh, of course." Margaret fumbled for her reticule. With an exasperated sigh, Bernard tossed a few coins onto the table.

The Gypsy took her hand again. "Ah, it becomes more clear. I see a man. His face is hidden." The Gypsy nodded significantly. "I see a long journey, across ze water . . ."

Bernard snorted. "Perhaps this wasn't such a good idea. We are wasting our money on this fraud."

"Wait. We should at least ask about it." Margaret shifted her weight. Even though the cushion was soft, she was not used to kneeling, and her knees were beginning to ache. Bernard's disapproval and Jeremy's wide-eyed curiosity did not ease her discomfort. "Do you know anything about curses?"

"I do not deal in ze black arts," the Gypsy said, her gaze shifting from Margaret to Bernard and back again.

"I don't want to know how to lay a curse. I want to know how to break one."

"Ah," said the Gypsy. "Zis I can do. When a witch curses someone, she sends an object into ze body of ze victim. For a small fee, I can extract zis object."

"What kind of object?" Jeremy piped up.

"It could be one of many zings. A fish bone, a pig bristle, a straw. I myself once removed a maggot from ze stomach of a curse victim."

"Coo!" breathed Jeremy. "I'll bet Uncle Phillip has thousands of maggots in him."

A vivid and most unpleasant image made Margaret wish she hadn't eaten the pudding. "Unfortunately, the victim of this curse has been dead for over seventy-eight years. Is there another way?"

"A bottle of holy water sometimes works. Ze cost is a mere three shillings."

"Margaret . . ." Bernard's foot tapped on the packed earth.

"Or, I could retrieve ze curse token for you," the Gypsy said. "Zat is more expensive."

"What is a curse token?"

"Ze person laying ze curse usually has in her possession somezing zat belongs to ze victim—a personal item, such as a ring, or handkerchief. A hair, or fingernail clipping is even better. To break ze curse, you need only return ze token to ze victim."

Bernard had had enough. "If we want to retrieve a token, we will do it ourselves. Come along, Margaret." Reaching down, he pulled her to her feet.

Hastily, Margaret dropped another coin on the table. "Thank you," she said over her shoulder as Bernard yanked back the flap, and pulled her outside into the bright sunshine.

Jeremy began to babble. "Coo, this is prime. Are we going to help Aunt Letty break the curse?"

"We'll talk about it later, Jeremy," Bernard said with a stern glance.

Margaret staggered as someone bumped into her,

and Bernard reached for her arm to steady her. "Are you hurt?" he asked.

"No, I'm fine."

Her thoughts were busy while they walked around the fair. Although the Gypsy hadn't seemed very credible, it was possible that one of her methods would work. Of the three options Madame Razinski had offered, Margaret thought retrieving a "curse token" sounded the most feasible.

Excitement bubbled in Margaret. Although she knew the chances of finding a token were almost nonexistent, at least she had something definite to do. Perhaps they would get lucky. And surely Bernard would help. . . .

She glanced sideways at him. His brow was furrowed, and he was frowning. Silently, she sighed. What was the matter with him? She would have to ask for his help later when he was in a more propitious humor. For now she would enjoy the fair.

"It's late," Bernard said, a few hours later, glancing up at the sun. He pulled out his watch. Looking at it, he frowned and shook it, then wound it a few times. Putting it back in his pocket, he said, "It's time for us to go."

"What?" Jeremy said. "But I only got to ride the roundabout three times, and I haven't seen the talking pig, or—"

"Perhaps we can come another day, Jeremy," Margaret tried to console him. "We must get back. Lord Mortimer is coming to dinner tonight."

"That's hours and hours away. Besides, who cares about him? He's mean to Aunt Letty and his grandfather was the one that cursed her. I hate that old dilberry."

"Jeremy!" Margaret exclaimed.

"Watch your tongue, young man," Bernard frowned.

"Yessir." Jeremy's words were respectful, but he maintained a sullen silence once in the carriage.

In spite of his appalling rudeness, Margaret sympathized with Jeremy. She wasn't looking forward to Mortimer's visit either. But she also couldn't wait to tell Phillip what she had discovered about the curse.

17

Mortimer, wearing too much jewelry and too much cologne, arrived late, but he didn't bother to make any excuses to the assembled family. Sitting next to Margaret at dinner, he let his cold gaze wander over her blue satin dress in the same manner as he had last week. She felt as though a slug had just crawled over her skin.

"Very nice," he said. "Barnett, you must have gained some finesse over the years to be able to bag this little bird."

Margaret stiffened.

Malicious amusement entered Mortimer's eyes. "Please forgive my frankness," he said smoothly. "Bernard and I are such old friends, I sometimes forget to mind my tongue."

Doing her best to hide her revulsion, she said politely, "I didn't know you and Bernard were friends."

"Yes, indeed, although we've had our differences. By any chance has he told you about our duel?"

Margaret did not like the spiteful smile Mortimer directed at Bernard. Glancing at her fiancé, she saw that he was staring down at the roasted pigeon on his plate, but making no move to eat it.

"I don't think I want to hear—" she started to say.

"Please, I insist. The tale is most amusing. It happened about ten years ago. Bernard was a tad . . . clumsy, shall we say?—as a youth. He had a habit, you see, of tripping over his own feet. Naturally, he was the target of many good-natured gibes."

"Mortimer," Aunt Letty said hesitantly. "I don't know if—"

"Wait." Mortimer waved his hand, causing the light to reflect and sparkle off his rings. "I haven't told you the best part. When Bernard was perhaps sixteen, he and I got into an argument over some small thing. I was three and twenty, my manhood well established and would you believe he challenged me to a duel? The fellows and I had a good laugh, and naturally I accepted. I planned to teach him a thorough lesson—being an expert swordsman—so we met in a clearing in the oak spinney behind Durnock Castle, and you know what happened?"

Bernard did not look up from his plate, but his knuckles looked white where he gripped his fork.

Margaret saw Mortimer looking at Bernard's hands. His lips curved and his icy green eyes met hers for a brief moment.

He hates Bernard, Margaret realized with a jolt as she looked into his eyes. His gaze returned to her fiancé as he finished his story.

"He tripped and somehow managed to stab himself with his own sword!" Mortimer laughed.

For a moment, Margaret thought Cecilia would forget all dictates of etiquette and say something rude, but Geoffrey laid a hand on her arm and she remained quiet.

"Bernard's family and mine have been friends for generations," Mortimer continued. "Ever since my grandfather and Bernard's great-grandfather collaborated to get a murderer hanged."

Margaret stiffened. What did he mean?

Aunt Letty also stiffened. "Phillip was not a murderer."

"I don't understand," Margaret said. "Who was Bernard's great-grandfather?"

"Baron Robeson," Mortimer supplied. "The Lord High Steward on the case."

Robeson! How could she have forgotten Robeson was one of Bernard's lesser titles? No wonder the name had sounded familiar when Phillip mentioned it. But what could this mean? Margaret felt a slow dread rising in her. With an effort she pushed aside her disturbing thoughts and concentrated on the conversation.

Mortimer was apologizing to Aunt Letty.

"I beg your pardon. I had forgotten how fond you were of Phillip. Miss Westbourne, I take it Letty has told you the story of the infamous Phillip Eglinton. Did she also tell you she sometimes hears his ghost whispering to her?"

"Ah . . ."

"Don't be embarrassed, Miss Westbourne. I don't hold Letty's eccentricities against her. We are good friends. She comes every month to my card parties." He swallowed some more wine. "I pride myself on my little parties. I'm having one Saturday. You and Bernard must come. And you, too, Mr. and Mrs. Barstow. Letty, you'll be there, won't you?"

"I wouldn't miss it," Aunt Letty said.

"Excellent. Card games are one of the few breaths of civilization in this benighted part of the country. I have something of a reputation for cards," he boasted to Margaret. "In fact, why don't we play a few hands when we're all done here?"

"Unless you'd prefer to play billiards," Bernard said. "You have something of a reputation for that also, don't you?"

To Margaret's surprise, Geoffrey and Cecilia both laughed, although they tried to stifle it. Mortimer flushed.

"Don't tease our guest, Bernard," Aunt Letty admonished. "We will play cards."

Mortimer must be an exceptionally poor billiards player, Margaret decided.

They all went into the front parlor, except for Geoffrey, who excused himself, claiming his leg was paining him. Cecilia professed a lack of interest in cards, so she sat and sewed while the others played.

The game went on for quite a while. Margaret noticed that Aunt Letty seemed totally immersed in play. Her eyes had a feverish gleam. Bernard was competent, but nothing more. Margaret herself was not very good, and her luck was definitely out. Over the course of the evening, Mortimer cleaned out the small amount of funds she had allotted for the evening's entertainment.

"Barnett, have another drink," said Mortimer, pouring out some more wine.

"I've had enough," said Bernard.

"One can never have enough. When will you understand that, Bernie?"

Mortimer drank heavily throughout the evening. Every time it was his turn to deal, he shuffled the cards skillfully, his rings flashing. Especially the large ruby.

It looked familiar, but Margaret couldn't quite think why.

"That's a magnificent ring," she commented when the hour had grown late and the game was nearly done. "Is it an heirloom?"

"Of a sort. My grandfather won it in a game of hazard." Mortimer dealt out the last hand. The ring blinked and sparkled. Something nagged at Margaret's brain.

Mortimer won the last of their money and rose to his feet. "That was most enjoyable. Are you certain you don't wish to continue? I'd be glad to extend you credit."

"I prefer not to indebt myself," said Bernard.

"You must learn to enjoy yourself, Bernie." Mortimer slapped Bernard on the shoulder and the ring flashed again. It was very large, Margaret thought. And she could almost swear she had seen it somewhere before. But where?

"Lord Mortimer, would you mind if I looked at your ring?"

"Not at all, Miss Westbourne." He approached her and held out his hand.

She hesitated. She had thought he would remove it.

As if reading her thoughts, he said, "I never take it off. It's too valuable. But you may hold my hand."

Reluctantly, Margaret took hold of his smooth hand and lifted it up. His palm was cold as ice. Trying to ignore the shivers of revulsion she felt, she studied the ring. The base was wide and deep and ornately wrought. Excitement bubbled up in her. She recognized it now! It was exactly like—

Margaret felt a pressure on her fingers. It was repeated, and hastily she dropped Mortimer's hand.

The creature had squeezed her hand!

"Now I must bid you all good night," he said with a leer in her direction and a bow to the others.

Aunt Letty rang for the butler, but he did not come. "That's odd," she said. "Gibbons is usually so reliable."

Margaret wished Gibbons would hurry. As far as she was concerned, the sooner Mortimer left, the better. Besides, she was eager to see Phillip and tell him all she had discovered.

Fruitlessly, Aunt Letty rang the bell a few more times, then looked apologetically at Mortimer. "I will show you out myself." She opened the door to the dark hall.

Bernard picked up a lamp to light the way. Margaret followed him, eager to go upstairs. Cecilia drifted behind.

"I will see you next week, Letty," Mortimer was saying. "I look forward to—"

"Eeeeeekkkkkk!" Cecilia shrieked.

All heads swiveled. Cecilia pointed a shaking finger toward the front door. Everyone turned. There, a noose around its neck, a ghostly figure hung suspended in midair, dangling in the dark shadows.

18

"Dear heaven!" gasped Margaret.

"Phillip?" Aunt Letty asked vaguely.

Bernard stood frozen and Margaret was similarly afflicted.

"Eeeeeeekkkkkk!" Cecilia screamed again, hands on her cheeks.

Bernard snapped out of his stupor. He held the lamp up high and walked forward. As he approached the grisly figure, light illuminated it, and Cecilia abruptly stopped screaming.

"Why, it's only a dummy," she said, her hands falling to her sides.

And indeed it was. A makeshift figure, covered by a sheet with a crude face drawn on it. The rope was tied to the chandelier.

Margaret was dumbfounded. "Who would do such a thing?"

Cecilia apparently reached her own conclusion. "That boy! I saw him with a bundle of clothes and some rope, but I never dreamed . . . I'm going to blister his backside." She stormed up the stairs.

The remaining three looked at each other.

"Where's Lord Mortimer?" Margaret asked, realizing he had disappeared. Everyone looked about the hall.

"There he is." Aunt Letty pointed to a figure huddled under a table at the far side of the room. "Mortimer, come out. It was only a prank by that foolish boy."

Bernard walked over and tapped him on the shoulder.

"Is . . . is it gone?" His face was white with terror.

"It's nothing. Only Jeremy's idea of a hoax."

"Oh." Mortimer stood up. He was still shaking, but now his face turned red with anger. "I hope someone will give that brat the thrashing he so richly deserves."

Grabbing his hat and gloves, he stormed out of the house.

"Dear me," said Aunt Letty.

Bernard's expression was carefully blank.

"I think I will go to bed." After one quick survey, Margaret avoided looking at anyone's face. "Good night."

She walked sedately up the stairs. Once out of sight, she hurried down the hall, beginning to gasp. She rushed into her room, slammed the door behind her and burst into laughter. She laughed so hard the tears rolled down her cheeks.

"Your evening was amusing?" asked a cold voice.

"Phillip!" Margaret wiped her streaming eyes, her soul filling with a ridiculous joy. She smiled radiantly at him.

He looked rather strange, but in her excitement she didn't pay too much attention. "I think I have discovered how to break the curse!"

"Oh?"

"Yes. I visited a Gypsy today. She said we must retrieve a token—such as a strand of hair or watch or ring of yours—and the curse will be broken!"

"I see." He turned away from her and studied the panel of her dressing screen where Actaeon was being torn apart by his dogs after spying on Diana bathing.

Margaret's excitement began to dim. She had expected a more joyous reaction from him. She had expected him to be thrilled. Instead he sounded cold and distant. "Aren't you excited?" she asked uncertainly.

"About what? About looking for a strand of my hair? Frankly, it could be in any of a thousand places. But if you wish it, then by all means let us begin searching. I will look here and you can go search your beloved Bernard's room."

Margaret stiffened. "You need not be sarcastic," she said indignantly. "And I don't think we will need to search at all. Lord Mortimer has a ring—like the one in your portrait."

"Very possible. Mortimer's grandfather did win such a ring from me." He didn't turn around from his study of the screen.

"Phillip, stop looking at that silly screen! How can you be so calm? Don't you understand, it must be the token!"

He turned, his gray eyes cold and silvery. "Forgive me. You may be correct, but how will we get the ring from Mortimer? He is unlikely to give it up."

"Perhaps he would if I explained."

"I doubt it. The Mortimers were ever a greedy, spiteful bunch."

Margaret ignored his pessimistic remark. "We are going to a card party there Saturday. I shall ask him then."

"It won't do you any good."

"Do you have a better idea?" she asked in exasperation.

"Perhaps I can come along and take the ring if he's not wearing it."

Margaret's jaw dropped a little. "Can you do that? Go to another house?" Somehow she had thought he must stay at Durnock Castle.

Frowning, Phillip stared into the dark corner. "I'm not sure," he said slowly. "It would be very difficult. Perhaps it might be easier to hire some thugs to do the job for us. They could steal the ring."

"Thugs! But they might hurt Lord Mortimer!"

"Forgive me if the possibility does not make me weep."

Actually, she didn't much care either. But still . . . "I don't think I could condone illegal activity."

Phillip rolled his eyes. "It's only fair that you be recompensed for the money he stole from you tonight."

"Are you saying he cheated at cards?"

"Of course. All Mortimers cheat."

Margaret considered for a moment, then shook her head. "I still don't like it."

Phillip's temper flared at her stubbornness. "Why such concern? He doesn't deserve it. But then, it seems women have always been attracted by the Mortimer brand of oily charm. Have you fallen victim to it, too?"

Margaret gaped at him.

"Tell me," he continued, the glow around him taking on a reddish tinge. "Did you enjoy having that slimy bastard squeeze your hand?"

"How did you know about that?" The implications of his earlier remark about Mortimer cheating finally struck her. "Were you *spying* on me?"

Arrogantly, he looked down his nose at her. "I only wanted to see Mortimer's spawn. The sight was as unpleasant as I expected. Almost as unpleasant as watching him slobbering all over your hand. I actually felt nauseated. If I had known I'd have to watch you and him making calf's eyes at one another—"

"Calf's eyes! Why you—"

"Don't bother to deny it. I see now that you are not to be trusted. You consort with my enemies—"

"I was not 'consorting' with Lord Mortimer! The man is repulsive."

"And do you find Bernard equally repulsive?"

"Bernard? What do you mean?"

"I mean Bernard, your fiancé, is descended from Robeson. Do you dare deny it?"

"No. At least, I believe he must be—"

"Tell me, how does it feel, knowing you are marrying the descendent of the man who sentenced me to hang? Or have you changed your mind? Perhaps you intend to throw over the namby-pamby Bernard so you can pursue that slimy villain, Mortimer."

Margaret stared at him incredulously. "Are you insane?"

He glared at her, his aura shining brightly. A muscle in his cheek jumped. Then slowly, gradually, the light around him began to fade. His aggressive stance softened and he passed a hand across his eyes. "I . . . I apologize, Margaret. I don't know what's the matter with me." Weariness lined his face and his glow dimmed even further. "Knowing they can touch you . . . when I cannot—" He stopped abruptly and looked at her, his eyes dark, intent.

Then with a sigh he faded away.

19

The next night, when the clock chimed midnight, Margaret realized that Phillip wasn't going to appear. She took off her cherry satin robe and carefully folded it over a chair. Pulling back the covers, she crawled into bed and lay staring up at the underside of the pagoda canopy.

She thought of the picture there, concealed by shadows. She could visualize each fluffy white cloud—even the one with the coupling man and woman.

Impulsively, she reached over for the lamp and held it high above her head, illuminating the picture of the sleeping Chinese man and his dreams.

She examined the man's face. It was unlined and a blissful smile curved his lips. For the first time, it occurred to Margaret that perhaps the scene was meant to represent death, not sleep. A peaceful serene death, where one dreamed of beautiful places and adventures and love.

Her gaze moved to the lovers. This time she did not look away. She studied the position of their arms and legs, the look of ecstasy on the couple's faces. Would she feel pleasure like that? she wondered.

Knowing they can touch you—when I cannot . . .

Abruptly, she blew out the candle and lay back down, resting her head on one hand, holding the blankets beneath her breasts with the other.

Why hadn't he come tonight? She wanted to talk to him. To say something. To tell him . . . what?

She didn't know exactly. Words were so difficult sometimes. It would be much easier if she could take his hand in hers and hold it as tightly as possible. Or if she could wrap her arms around him and hold him against her breast. She wished she could give him everything, but she was afraid she couldn't give him what he wanted.

If she couldn't, though, she wanted to talk to him. She knew her heart would somehow find the right words. She would have to tell him tomorrow night.

But Phillip did not appear the next night, or the following night, either, and Margaret grew more and more worried. Was he gone forever? Had something terrible happened to him? She was not sure terrible things could happen to a ghost, but he supposed it was possible. Perhaps she would never see him again.

No. There must be some other explanation. He was probably resting. Or perhaps he was still angry at her for her "flirtation" with Mortimer. Phillip would come back.

He must.

He must. The curse wasn't broken yet. She still had not thought of a scheme to retrieve Phillip's ring. Once they had the ring and broke the curse, then . . . well, she would not think about what would happen then.

The day before Mortimer's card party arrived and Margaret was moping in her room when she heard a firm knock on her door.

It was Bernard, with a frown on his face.

"Margaret, I wondered if you would like to take a turn in the garden with me."

She hesitated. "I don't know, Bernard."

His frown deepened. "What is the matter with you? Are you ill? You didn't come down for breakfast."

"No, no. I am merely a little homesick, I suppose."

"Do you wish to go back to Motcomb House?"

"Oh, no! I think I'm just suffering from a case of the doldrums. A stroll will be exactly the thing to perk me up."

The unusually hot August had turned suddenly cool. Outside, there was a chill in the air and a cold breeze was blowing. Shivering, she huddled under her shawl. Although the bright blue wool was warm, she wished she had worn her mantle.

They passed Jeremy, bouncing an India rubber ball against the house, and Margaret could see his cheeks and nose were bright red. He looked rather lonely and forlorn, reminding Margaret of what he had said about being a bastard. She wondered again what she should do, if anything, about his problem.

"Shall we take the honeysuckle walk?" asked Bernard. "It is in bloom right now and will afford us some shelter from the wind."

The honeysuckle walk was actually a tunnel of thick vines supported by an arched trellis. Yellow flowers cascaded from above and fallen blooms carpeted the dirt pathway, surrounding them in a golden cocoon.

Bernard stopped in the middle of the path. Glancing up, Margaret saw he was staring at her intently. She looked back into his eyes. They were a peculiar colorless hue. Gray, actually. Almost the same shade as Phillip's.

"Margaret, please tell me what is wrong."

She looked away and plucked a flower from the honeysuckle vine, trying to decide what to say. She didn't want to tell him she was concerned about Phillip. Somehow it seemed inappropriate to tell her fiancé she was worried about another man—even if the other man was a ghost.

"Margaret—"

Searching for some subject to distract him, she suddenly remembered Jeremy. Why hadn't she thought of it before? Surely Bernard would know how to handle that situation.

"I'm worried about Jeremy," she said.

"Jeremy! What is the matter with Jeremy?"

"He told me something he overheard." She hesitated briefly. Drawing a deep breath, she plunged ahead, keeping her eyes on the flower. "He heard some servants say he is a bastard."

Total silence met her statement.

Glancing sideways, she saw that his face had reddened, but she could not quite read his expression. Was he embarrassed? she wondered. Embarrassed because she had spoken of such an indelicate subject? Or was he shocked? Perhaps he had not known his sister had been unfaithful to her husband.

"I see," he finally said in a quiet voice. "Thank you for telling me. I will take care of the matter."

She could tell nothing from his voice either. He was very calm about her revelation. She wished she knew what he was thinking, but Bernard had never been an easy person to read.

"Is that all, Margaret?"

"I beg your pardon?"

"Is that *all* that is bothering you?"

Heavens, he was more perceptive than she had realized. "Why, yes." He was watching her closely, and she couldn't prevent the blush that burned her cheeks.

"Very well," he said, his mouth tightening. "If you cannot trust me, your fiancé—"

"Oh, no, that's not it," she said hastily. "It's only that I am worried about Phillip."

Bernard tensed. "*Him* again!" he said, almost under his breath. "I might have known." In a louder voice he asked, "What is the problem?"

"I am trying to think of a way to get Lord Mortimer's ring."

"Mortimer's ring?" Bernard's jaw dropped a little. "Why do you want his ring?"

"It belonged to Phillip. I believe it may be the key to breaking the curse."

"Margaret, you don't believe anything that old charlatan said, do you?"

She tilted her chin. "Why not? It's not impossible. Besides, it's worth a try at least."

"It would be worth almost anything to get rid of him," Bernard muttered. "Very well," he said more loudly. "I will offer to buy the ring from Mortimer."

Startled by his abrupt turnabout, she stared at him. "Do you think he would sell it?"

"Mortimer is greedy. If I offer enough, I think he will."

Hope curled in her. "Would you do that?"

"Certainly. I will ride over there tomorrow morning, first thing."

Tomorrow she might have the ring. Surely Phillip would come back then. Happiness filled her. Impulsively, she hugged Bernard. "Thank you, Bernard."

His hands came up, his long slender fingers almost spanning her waist. She stepped back, but his hands continued to rest on her hips. She glanced at him in surprise.

Coming to his senses, he snatched his hands away, as if her dress had suddenly sprouted brambles. A flower fell on his sleeve, and he spent an inordinate amount of time brushing away each and every petal. Finally, still flushing, he offered his arm and they started back for the house.

They were almost at the front door when Bernard, gazing up at the gargoyles, asked, "Why are you so fascinated by Phillip?"

Startled, Margaret stumbled, almost falling. Only by clutching Bernard's arm did she prevent it. Regaining her balance and her breath, she said, "Why, because he's a ghost, I suppose."

He did not argue the matter, nor did he look particularly disbelieving, but for some reason she felt compelled to explain further.

"I find him interesting, that is all. He is so exciting. So charming." Bernard was still silent, so she added, "I admire his courage, too."

"I see." Bernard's face was shuttered. "Margaret, I think your maid should sleep in your room at night."

She stopped in the middle of the path, staring at him. "Whatever for? Because of Phillip? That's absurd. Besides, he hasn't visited me for the last three nights."

She thought she saw a flicker of relief in his eyes, and he said no more.

His silence made her nervous. What was the matter with Bernard? He had been acting very strange all week. Ever since she told him about Phillip, in fact. Did he perceive Phillip as some kind of threat?

Silently, she shook her head. That was ridiculous. She enjoyed Phillip's company, she enjoyed the excitement of his visits, but that didn't change anything. She still wanted to marry Bernard. She wasn't going to give up her goal—to be accepted by society— because of a ghost.

But somehow it was more—and less—than that now. Less because being accepted by society seemed less important than it had before. More because Bernard was more than she had expected.

After spending these last few days with him, memories had come flooding back. Memories of the friendship they had once shared—a friendship she would have sworn could never be broken. Now she longed to find that closeness again.

But could she find it with Bernard?

She wasn't sure. Something was missing. Was it because he had changed so much? Or had she? Her fingers tightened on Bernard's arm as they entered the house and walked up the stairs to her room. After a brief bow, he walked away. She watched him go, an odd ache in her throat.

She opened the door of her room. The scent of tobacco assailed her nostrils.

"Phillip!"

The dull ache vanished, and a flood of emotions rushed through her: gladness, relief, and another sentiment she couldn't quite define, but which made her smile radiantly.

Closing the door, she walked toward him, stopping barely a foot away. "Where have you been?"

He stood very still, drinking in the sight of her beautiful face, the sparkling blue of her eyes, the sweet curve of her lips. Had it only been three days since he had seen her? It had seemed a lifetime, an eternity.

"Phillip? I was worried."

He had meant to stay away longer, but a hunger had been growing in him. He couldn't stay away and it frightened him. Frightened him more than he had been frightened for a very long time.

"I missed you, Phillip. Where have you been?"

He didn't like the effect her voice had on him. It seemed to flow inside him and curl around his heart.

"Margaret—" With an effort he steadied his voice. "We must find a way to break this curse."

The light in her eyes dimmed. She turned and moved away, her shoulders a little stiff.

"Margaret—"

He stepped toward her, then stopped, clenching his fists. He wanted to gather her in his arms, hold her against his chest and stroke her hair. He wanted to murmur soft words in her ear. He wanted the impossible. Didn't she understand that if he acknowledged the emotion swirling around the room, his pain would be increased a hundredfold? He stepped back, resolve filling him. He was determined to hold on to his sanity—and hold her at a distance.

She faced him again, back straight. "You're right, Phillip. In fact, I'm glad you came, because I wanted to tell you that I spoke to Bernard and he is willing to help. Tomorrow he is going to Lord Mortimer to try to purchase the ring."

Phillip froze, all good intentions fleeing at the mention of her fiancé's name. Jealousy, raw and ugly, whipped through him. "I told you already Mortimer will not give up the ring willingly."

"It's worth a try at least."

"It's bad enough that you're actually going to marry that blockhead; must you involve him in this, too?"

"Bernard is not a blockhead! Considering how bizarre all this is, I think he has been very understanding."

"Only because he lacks the understanding to realize all this *is* bizarre."

"You are impossible! I refuse to listen to any more aspersions on Bernard's character." She placed her hands over her ears and turned away.

"You don't like to hear the truth, do you?" He followed her across the room, raising his voice as he went.

Margaret pressed her hands more tightly to her ears and closed her eyes.

He stood next to her, shouting in her ear. "You are marrying that buffoon for security, because you're too cowardly to go after what you really want!"

"Stop it, stop it, stop it!" she cried.

"Margaret, dear, are you all right?" a new voice intruded.

Margaret spun around, her hands dropping to her sides. Aunt Letty's face was peering uncertainly around the edge of the door.

"Aunt Letty! Er, yes, I am fine. Please come in." Margaret took Aunt Letty's arm, sitting down next to her on the settee. From the corner of her eye, she saw Phillip fade away.

"I'm sorry to bother you, dear," Aunt Letty said, settling herself comfortably. "But I wondered if I might ask a small favor of you."

"Certainly. What is it?" Discreetly, Margaret glanced around the room to make sure Phillip wasn't lurking in some corner. He was nowhere in sight. Good riddance, she thought angrily.

Aunt Letty hugged her jar. "I find myself a little short of funds. Would you consider lending me a few pounds? I will pay you back tomorrow night with my winnings from Mortimer's card party."

Margaret retrieved her reticule from her dressing table and absently opened it. "How much do you need?" How dare Phillip accuse her of being a coward? She wasn't a coward at all. It took a lot of courage to marry a man she didn't truly love—

"Do you have a hundred pounds, dear?"

"A hundred . . . ?" Margaret forgot her angry thoughts and focused her attention on Aunt Letty. Staring at the old woman's innocent face, snatches of conversation came back to her: Mortimer's voice saying, "I can't wait much longer," and Aunt Letty's reply, "I'm sure my luck will turn soon." She also remembered the elderly woman's feverish absorption the night Mortimer had played cards with them.

"Aunt Letty," Margaret said slowly. "Are you in debt to Lord Mortimer?"

"My dear, whatever gave you that idea?" Aunt Letty laughed nervously. "Well, perhaps a little. Nothing to signify. A pound here or there. But I am an excellent cardplayer. It is only that sometimes my luck runs out. But it always turns, and you must keep playing or you will miss that turn."

"Aunt Letty . . ." Margaret felt a deep foreboding. "Have you signed anything?"

The old woman's face crumpled. "Oh, Margaret, I never meant to, but I've signed a mortgage on the castle, and Mortimer is insisting upon payment. But if you will lend me only a few pounds—it doesn't have to be a hundred, fifty will do—I am sure I can win it all back. I'm feeling especially lucky."

Margaret sank onto her bed, her brain numb. "Doesn't the castle belong to Bernard?"

"Oh, no. It was part of my sister's dowry. Phillip felt it only fair to leave it to me when he was hanged."

"Admirable," said Margaret grimly. "Exactly how much do you owe?"

"I'm not sure precisely. Maybe ten thousand pounds or so."

"Ten thousand!" Margaret reeled from shock. She could hardly imagine such an enormous sum. "How could Lord Mortimer allow you to lose so much?"

"People lose to him all the time. In fact, I wish there was another place to play, because it does seem that people lose excessively there. It's simply not a lucky house. Why, two men blew their brains out after losing their families' fortunes. But there is nowhere else to play, and I do so enjoy a good game of cards."

"But why do people keep going?"

"I think almost everyone owes Mortimer money; they have to try to win some to pay him. Besides, no one wants to offend the man. He's terribly influential. I do wish Jeremy hadn't played that little prank. Mortimer does have a tendency to hold a grudge and he's terrified of anything to do with ghosts."

"How odd," Margaret murmured, still trying to comprehend the enormity of Aunt Letty's debt.

"Not so odd, actually. He tries to hide it, but once, when he was a bit tipsy, he told me he has nightmares about ghosts. He didn't say what exactly, but I could tell it frightened him terribly."

Margaret didn't care about Mortimer's aversion to the spirit world, and she wished Aunt Letty wouldn't ramble on so. Didn't she understand she was in danger of losing Durnock Castle? "Do Bernard and Geoffrey know about this?"

"About Mortimer's nightmares? I don't think—"

"No, no," Margaret interrupted. "About the money you owe Lord Mortimer."

"Oh, no. I have been very careful not to let them find out. They would be sure to scold dreadfully."

Speech failed Margaret. She gave Aunt Letty the fifty pounds.

The old woman clutched the bills, crumpling them in her gnarled hand. "Oh, thank you, dear! I'll pay you back tomorrow night—with interest! Good night!" She trotted out, smiling happily.

"Convinced?" a voice said in Margaret's ear.

She looked up, her brain numb. Phillip was there, a sardonic expression on his face. "Did you hear, Phillip?"

"Yes, I heard."

"Whatever are we going to do? Aunt Letty is going to lose her home. And, dear heaven, what will happen to you if Lord Mortimer has possession of this house?"

"Very likely I will be doomed to eternal ghostdom.

But it won't come to that. I have an idea."

Margaret looked dazedly at him. "An idea?"

"Yes. I'm coming with you to Mortimer's card party tomorrow night. And I'm going to help you win everything back—including the ruby ring."

20

Leland Carew, Earl Mortimer, walked around the ballroom, checking to make sure everything was ready for that night. On the sideboard, bottles of wine were waiting to be poured; on the walls, the mirrors were adjusted to exactly the right height; and on each table a special deck of cards rested. He glanced around once more, satisfaction filling him as his gaze lingered on the heavy gilt trimming the doors and windows. Everything in the house, from the expensive furniture to the crystal chandelier, reeked of wealth and prosperity. Mortimer reveled in it.

Long ago, at his grandfather's knee, Mortimer had learned about wealth and power. The first earl had had both—land and business interests to furnish the wealth, and titles and political interests to provide the power. With his connections to the powerful families of Durham and stakes in York's financial markets, the first earl had played the game and played it well.

But things were different now. Laws, regulations, and the new morality sweeping the land made it difficult to attain that kind of dominance. The thought gnawed at him sometimes, that he would never match his grandfather. Still, he had done well enough. He had influence and wealth. Few in the area would dare cross him and in addition to the several questionable enterprises he owned and operated, he had these gaming parties to provide a steady income.

Sitting down at one of the tables, he picked up a deck of cards, shuffling them with practiced ease. As he did so, the ruby glinting on his finger caught his attention. He studied the ring, and his lips curved in a cruel smile, remembering the stories his grandfather had told him.

The first earl had explained how Phillip had tarnished the family name and honor and how cleverly he had won his revenge. "I told them Alicia's ghost appeared to me," the old man had cackled more than once. "And they believed it!"

The ruby ring, won from Phillip in a card game, represented the triumph of the Mortimers over the hated Eglintons. The night the first earl died, he had given the ring to his grandson.

Remembering that night, Mortimer's smile faded and the motion of the cards slowed. He had been wakened by a terrifying scream. Running to the earl's room, he discovered his grandfather thrashing in the bed moaning, "No, stop laughing. Stop! You're dead, dead, I say!"

Wakening him, Mortimer had been startled when the earl pressed the ring into his hand. "Take it, take it," the old man whispered. "And remember, you can never have enough wealth, or power. Or revenge."

The first earl had died, and since his own father had passed away a few years before, Mortimer became the second earl. Fierce elation had filled him when he was finally able to assume the title.

He had not spared more than a thought for the old earl. Toward the end, the old man had grown bent and senile, undeserving of the Mortimer name. It was fitting that the title should pass to one younger, more worthy.

But it turned out the title was not the only thing the earl had passed to him. Exactly one year after his grandfather died, Mortimer experienced the nightmare.

That first time he dreamed of the hanging, he hadn't been afraid. He had been fascinated. In the dream, a body, suspended from the gallows, swung on the rope while Mortimer smiled. But his smile died when the corpse's eyes opened and it started laughing. The laughter was like no sound Mortimer had ever heard, like the creaking of a coffin's hinges, like the wind whistling through a deserted graveyard, like demons cackling from hell.

The nightmare had come every year after that. He always woke trembling, the sheets wet from his cold sweat, his heart pounding with indescribable terror. After the first few years, he had learned to stay awake the entire night. The few times he had passed out, or fallen into a doze, the dream had been there, waiting for him.

In two more days, it would be the anniversary of his grandfather's death. Mortimer's palms grew clammy, his fingers slipped, and a card fell face up on the table. The knave of hearts.

"Lord Barnett to see you, my lord," the butler interrupted his thoughts.

Barnett? Here? Mortimer frowned. What did that imbecile want? Was he coming to taunt him about last week's debacle?

"Show him in." Picking up the fallen card, Mortimer's fingers tightened on the deck, remembering what a fool he had made of himself. When he had seen the hanging figure, he had thought, for an instant, that his nightmare had come true. He had reacted with blind terror, not knowing it was only the brat's idea of a joke.

Damn that brat, and damn the old woman and Barnett, too. They would all pay—but most especially Barnett. Mortimer bent the card in his hand. He had always hated Barnett. Even as a puling lad, there had been something about his steady gaze that always infuriated Mortimer; a sort of moral air that made Mortimer want to grind him to dust.

The swordfight had taught the boy a much-needed lesson, and in the following years, Mortimer had taken great pleasure in regularly reminding him of it.

Until the billiards episode four years ago. That story had made the rounds for months, even years, afterward. Even now, whenever he visited London, some wag always asked about his billiard game. Every time he thought of the humiliation he had suffered, his hatred of Barnett increased.

Just watching him walk into the room made Mortimer's blood pressure rise.

"Good afternoon, Mortimer. I hope this isn't an inconvenient time for me to call."

Mortimer subdued his dislike. He rarely allowed his emotions to interfere with his dealings. Waving Bernard into the chair opposite, he said, "Not at all, Barnett. I'm merely making some last-minute preparations for tonight. What can I do for you?"

Stiffly, Bernard took a seat. "I'm interested in acquiring your ruby ring."

Mortimer felt a jolt of surprise. "My ring? Why do you want it?"

"My fiancée has admired it. I would like to purchase it for her."

"Come, come. There must be more to it than that." His curiosity aroused, Mortimer studied Bernard's face. He could read nothing from the other man's stiff expression.

"Miss Westbourne believes it once belonged to Phillip Eglinton, my aunt's brother-in-law. She—Miss

Westbourne—would like to give it to my aunt as a remembrance of him."

"Hm." Pretending to consider, Mortimer's thoughts were busy. Did the fool expect him to believe such nonsense? Obviously there was something else, something Bernard wasn't telling him. And somehow, Miss Westbourne was involved.

Mortimer's thoughts dwelled for a moment on Barnett's fiancée. How had such a clod managed to win such a prime piece of womanflesh? he wondered. Although her breasts were small, her lines were good, and the curve of her lips belied the coolness of her eyes. His fingers caressed the cards in his hands. He would not mind having a piece of her himself.

He remembered she'd exhibited little skill at cards. He would have to make sure he played a few hands with her. It might be useful having her in debt to him. Very useful indeed.

As for Barnett's clumsy attempt to buy the ring— he would refuse, of course. He only wished there was some way to pry out the full story.

Surreptitiously, he studied the stolid, patient face of the man opposite him. He sighed. There was little chance of prying anything out of Barnett. Old Bernie was as closed as an unwilling woman's legs. Oh, well. It didn't matter. He would never give up the ring and he would derive great enjoyment from refusing Barnett's request.

Shaking his head as if he had just come to a decision, Mortimer said, "Sorry, Barnett."

"I'd be willing to pay a great deal."

It was that important? Mortimer's spiteful pleasure increased. He shook his head again, but much to his disappointment, Bernard only frowned slightly, showing no other sign of frustration.

"I will take up no more of your time, then." Barnett rose to his feet.

Mortimer rose also. "I hope you and your delightful fiancée will be able to attend tonight?"

"Yes, we're looking forward to it. Good day, Mortimer."

"Good day, Barnett." Smiling, Mortimer sat down and began shuffling the cards again, mentally picturing what Miss Margaret Westbourne would look like without her clothes.

A summer squall blew up as Bernard rode home across the fields. Angry raindrops pelted against him, and he slouched forward, his spirits at low ebb. Ever since visiting Madame Razinski, a fear had been gnawing at him. He feared it was impossible to get rid of Phillip.

His failure to obtain the ring compounded his bleak mood. He didn't actually believe the ring would help, but as Margaret had said, it was worth a try. He was even tempted to go back to the fair and buy that hag's "holy water." At this point, he was willing to try almost anything.

If only he had managed to buy the ring. Although it might not break the curse, at least it would have made Margaret happy. She might even have hugged him again.

Remembering that moment in the honeysuckle walk, his heart increased its rhythm. Her waist was so tiny, his hands had spanned it. He had wanted to pull her hips against his and kiss her until she was breathless, until he drove all thought of Phillip from her mind, until she was as hungry with want and need as he was. . . .

His horse stumbled, bringing Bernard to his senses. Automatically, he steadied the bay gelding with a firm hand and mentally castigated himself for his lustful thoughts. He had other problems to worry about—such as Jeremy.

Bernard frowned, remembering what Margaret had said. He needed to have a talk with Geoffrey. Not only about Jeremy but about the London post, too. He would talk to the other man today, and perhaps to Margaret, also. He would tell her how much he cared about her. He would tell her to forget about Phillip. . . .

Margaret thought Phillip charming and exciting. When she had told him that, he had wanted to shake her. Couldn't she see how superficial those qualities were? How insubstantial? Respect and consideration counted for more, he had wanted to tell her. But before he could speak, she had added courage to Phillip's list of attributes.

Courage.

The insinuation was there, although perhaps unintentional—she thought he lacked courage. Was he a coward? He thought of the times in his life when he had been too frightened or ashamed or even too lazy to stand up for what he believed, and despair filled him. It was true. He was a coward. How could he ever hope to win her away from Phillip?

Deep in gloom, Bernard almost passed the path leading to the village, but the church steeple in the distance caught his eye. He pulled back on the reins, easing the gelding's pace, as an idea formed. The vicar was a good friend of Bernard's—they had gone to school together. Perhaps, just perhaps . . .

With sudden determination, Bernard turned the horse onto the path.

Margaret sat in the parlor, unenthusiastically sewing a small piece of lace to the garland she planned to wear in her hair tonight. Sighing, she rethreaded her needle and wondered what on earth was taking Bernard so long.

"Are you not feeling well, dear?" Aunt Letty asked.

"No, no, I'm fine," Margaret assured her hastily.

"That's good. I wouldn't want you to miss the party. Geoffrey, Cecilia, are both of you going to Mortimer's tonight?"

Geoffrey, who was playing draughts with Jeremy on one of the gilded baroque tables, didn't look up. "Only if he'll play billiards."

Cecilia chortled.

"What is this business about billiards?" Margaret asked.

"Bernard hasn't told you?" exclaimed Cecilia, pausing in her beadwork. "It's a most amusing story. Geoffrey, you tell her, you were there."

With obvious relish, Geoffrey complied. "It was about four years ago. Bernard had come back from India for a visit and dragged me along to his club, when who should walk in but Mortimer. As soon as he saw Bernard, he told everyone who would listen about their duel, then challenged Bernard to a game of billiards. Mortimer expected to win, naturally, so when he lost, he was furious. Instead of taking his loss like a gentleman, he accused Bernard of cheating. Bernard immediately tapped his claret."

Tapped his claret? Margaret gasped. Bernard had *hit* Mortimer?

"Your turn, Papa," Jeremy said.

Geoffrey moved one of his draught pieces before continuing. "His nose bleeding everywhere, Mortimer challenged Bernard to a duel. I'm sure Mortimer thought to humiliate Bernard again, but Bernard turned the tables neatly. He accepted the challenge and named his weapon—billiard balls."

"Billiard balls?" Margaret stared incredulously at Geoffrey.

"Clever, wasn't it?" He blocked Jeremy's last move, then grinned. "The gentlemen in the club howled, thinking it a fine joke. Naturally, they all insisted on attending the duel. Mortimer's ball went wide, fortunately, since it appeared he was aiming for Bernard's head. Then, cool as you please, Bernard popped Mortimer in the leg, dislocating the knee. Mortimer was out of commission for nearly three months."

"Good heavens," Margaret said blankly as Cecilia and Geoffrey laughed heartily.

"Papa, it's your turn," said Jeremy with the long-suffering air of one who has heard the same story many times.

Aunt Letty shook her head indulgently at Geoffrey and Cecilia. "You two are terrible. Are you coming tonight, or not?"

Geoffrey stopped laughing and glowered down at the draughts. "I wouldn't be caught dead there," he muttered.

"But Papa," Jeremy said solemnly, "just imagine Lord Mortimer's fright if you *were* caught dead there."

"Jeremy, don't forget our little discussion." Cecilia tapped a warning finger on her chair.

"Sorry, Mama." The glint in his eye vanished. Ducking his head, he jumped one of his father's pieces.

"Then Bernard and Margaret and I will go." Aunt Letty peered at the mantle clock. "In fact, it's almost time."

Almost time! Margaret gathered up her sewing things. "I think I will start preparing."

She hurried up to her room. Where was Bernard? She needed to know if he had been successful in his efforts to obtain the ring. She prayed he had been. Phillip's plan was entirely too risky.

As she reached her door, she noticed it was ajar. That was odd, she thought. Usually the maids cleaned in the morning. Unconsciously holding her breath, she pushed the door open.

To her utter amazement, she saw Bernard tiptoeing around her room, sprinkling what appeared to be water from a small glass vial. Her pent-up breath expelled in a single exclamation. "Bernard!"

Bernard jumped and turned, a guilty flush spreading over his face. Quickly, he slipped the glass vial into his pocket.

"What are you doing?" asked Margaret. "What is in that vial?"

"Er, nothing."

She looked at him suspiciously. He wasn't taking after Aunt Letty, was he?

"Er, that is, I was looking for you," he continued. "I wanted to tell you about Mortimer."

Excitement filled Margaret and she forgot about the glass vial. "What did he say? Do you have the ring?"

"He refused to sell."

"Oh." Disappointment welled up in her. She had not truly expected Mortimer would sell the ring, and yet she had hoped. Now everything was riding on Phillip's plan.

"Never mind, Bernard. We will think of another way." She made her voice playful, even though her next words were actually quite serious. "Perhaps I can win the ring from Lord Mortimer at cards tonight."

Bernard smiled. Small lines fanned out from his eyes and a crease appeared in his cheek.

Margaret smiled back. He had a beautiful smile. She had forgotten how nice it was. And how nice he could be. Although he had failed to purchase the ring, she appreciated the fact that he had made the attempt.

She would like to tell him about Phillip's plan, she

thought as Bernard left. Very likely he could help somehow—if Phillip would allow it. Margaret sighed. If only the two men weren't so hostile toward each other!

Some time later, Margaret stood before the mirror in her room studying her appearance. She felt like a soldier going into battle, although certainly no soldier ever wore a pale pink organdy dress to face the enemy. But the gown might help her cause—she hoped the lecherous Lord Mortimer would be distracted by the way it was cut low off her shoulders, with only a bit of lace draped around her upper arms and pinned between her breasts by an artificial rose. The corsage formed a point at her hips, and the skirt flared out over an underskirt with row upon row of lace. Two gold bracelets adorning her arms were her only jewelry. In her hair was the small garland of roses, with a piece of lace attached; on her feet she wore white silk evening boots.

A knock at the door signaled that the carriage was ready. She grabbed up a fan and hurried downstairs to join Aunt Letty and Bernard. Bernard stared at her for a long moment, his eyes dark and inscrutable, before moving forward to offer his arm.

Outside, thunder rumbled and a cool breeze blew. With a glance at the gathering storm clouds, Margaret climbed into the carriage.

As the horses trotted down the road, Margaret's fingers tightened on the lace-covered sticks of her fan. If she failed tonight, Aunt Letty would lose her home. The old woman would be devastated, and Margaret felt certain Mortimer would not show any mercy.

She must win.

Her grip on the fan tightened even more when they arrived at Mortimer's, only to find a crush of carriages in the drive, forcing them to wait in a long queue. Their carriage crept forward at a snail's pace. Margaret held the fan in both hands, bending the sticks into an arc.

Would she be able to do it? She was no cardplayer and she was not accustomed to high stakes. To try to win ten thousand pounds—*and* Phillip's ring—in one night from an expert cardsharp seemed not only impossible, but insane. Could she possibly succeed?

Click, snap.

The sudden noise almost caused Margaret to snap the fan in two.

Click, snap. Click, snap.

She glared through the dark at Bernard, but of course he couldn't see her. Her irritation faded though, as the rhythmic sound continued, strong and steady. Strong and steady. That was how she must be. Determination filled her. She must succeed—Aunt Letty's and Phillip's futures depended on it!

The carriage arrived at the front door and they were able to alight. She grimaced a little at the ornate gold trim that decorated the ceiling, door frames, and furnishings in the hall. Mortimer was nowhere to be seen, so they milled forward with the crowd into the ballroom, which had been converted into a gaming hall. Long tables were set up around the room. To the left, Margaret could see games of macao, vingt-et-un, and baccarat in progress. Along the opposite wall, people appeared to be playing Napoleon, whist, and faro. In the center of the room, a roulette table was set up, and beyond it, a table where Mortimer sat.

There was a hush to the air, people moving and talking quietly, that was quite unlike the parties Margaret had previously attended. There was no music, only the clacking roulette ball and tumbling dice. In spite of the gaily colored frocks, sparkling jewels, and brilliant lights, the people seemed somber, intent on the various games.

How many others were gambling away their homes and futures? Margaret wondered.

She glanced around, looking for Phillip. She did not see him, but before she could explore further, Mortimer spotted them through the crowd.

He waved them over. "Good evening, Letty, Barnett, Miss Westbourne. Please, sit down."

Bernard and Aunt Letty did so, but Margaret remained standing. "I think I will look around a little first." Seeing Mortimer's frown, she added sweetly, "It all looks so fascinating."

Mortimer nodded, his smile smug. "It is indeed. But you must promise to join us later, Miss Westbourne."

Margaret inclined her head politely before turning and moving away, her gaze searching the crowd. She must find Phillip. Walking around the room, she stopped by each table, hoping to find him lurking somewhere, but he was nowhere in sight. She squeezed past a fat gentleman, dodged a lady who appeared to be tipsy, and passed through an archway into a smaller chamber, pausing by a pillar. The crowd was thinner here, only a few tables set against the far wall. Seeing no sign of Phillip, she was about to leave when she heard two women on the other side of the pillar whispering.

"I'm completely broke." The first woman sounded near to tears. "What will I do? Charles will murder me."

"Don't look at me. I lost everything at the faro table." The second woman's voice was peevish and disgruntled.

"Elizabeth—" the first woman lowered her voice. "Do you think it is possible that Mortimer cheats his guests?"

"I don't know, but I have my suspicions. I wish I'd never started coming. Now I'm so far in debt, I daren't stop, lest he call in my debts."

"Surely he wouldn't do that! Good heavens, if he calls in mine, Charles will find out." The woman shuddered. "Come along, Elizabeth. Let's play one more hand of whist. Perhaps our luck will change."

"Very well." Elizabeth sighed, then added, "I just wish that he would lose—really lose for once." They headed off toward the whist table.

"Shall we oblige them?"

"Phillip!" She had never been so glad to hear his voice. She peeked around, but didn't see him, even though she could smell his tobacco.

"Softly, now. I'm right beside you."

She looked, but still could not see him. Then she thought she saw a faint glow, hovering to her left.

"Phillip? Are you all right?" she whispered, stepping back farther into the shadow of the pillar.

"I'm fine," he replied. "Although this is a bit more difficult than I thought it would be. You won't be able to see me, but I can talk to you, and that's all that we need to defeat Mortimer." She could sense the smile in his voice. "Are you ready?"

21

"*Are you?*" Margaret asked.

"Not quite. I want to watch the game for a while. It's an interesting one. I've not played it before. I also need to see what methods Mortimer uses. He's a clever rascal."

His voice was moving toward the other room and Margaret followed. "You truly believe he is cheating?"

"Certainly. Ah, watch him closely now, and you'll see it. He has a stacked deck in his hand. There, did you see him switch the decks when he pretended to sneeze?"

Stopping in her tracks, Margaret exclaimed, "The scoundrel!" Several men at the roulette table stared at her. Flushing, she started walking forward again, head held high. She heard Phillip chuckle.

Ignoring his inappropriate humor, she raised her fan to cool her heated cheeks, then used it to conceal her mouth while she whispered. "Phillip, how can I possibly win if he's cheating?"

"Don't worry, Margaret. Now, listen carefully. I want you to play by yourself for a while, so I can discover all his tricks. When I'm ready, I will whisper my instructions to you. Understand?"

Margaret nodded.

Mortimer looked up as she approached. "Miss Westbourne! Are you ready to play now? Wonderful, wonderful. I insist you sit here, next to me. Ogglethorpe, get up and give Miss Westbourne your seat, you're done up anyway." With unctuous charm, Mortimer seated her. After Ogglethorpe departed, Bernard and Aunt Letty were the only others at the table. Bernard nodded at Margaret. Aunt Letty, jar at her elbow, didn't look away from the cards in Mortimer's hands. "Hurry and deal," she said.

"Miss Westbourne, are you familiar with the game brag?" Mortimer asked as he shuffled the cards.

"I've played a few times," Margaret responded. It was a simple game as she recalled. The object was to get either a pair or a triplet. The ace of diamonds, knave of clubs, and nine of diamonds were all wild cards.

As Mortimer dealt out the cards, the ruby ring on his finger flashed. He must have noticed Margaret staring at it, because he said, "Sorry I couldn't accommodate you about this ring, Miss Westbourne. It has a special significance for my family—a talisman of sorts."

Because it sealed the curse on their enemy, Phillip Eglinton? Margaret's determination grew stronger. She must win tonight and she must get that ring.

Looking at her cards, she saw she had received three sevens. Taking a deep breath, she bet a pound.

To her surprise, she won.

"Nice hand, Miss Westbourne," Mortimer said as she raked in her winnings. "It appears you will be lucky tonight."

And indeed, for the next hour, her luck was phenomenal. She couldn't lose. Excitement began to mount in her as she won hand after hand and the pile of counters in front of her steadily grew. Perhaps she would be able to do this by herself, without Phillip's help, she thought.

At one point he whispered in her ear, "I'm going to check out some of the other tables. I'll be back shortly." She nodded without even glancing at him.

He must have been wrong about Mortimer's cheating, she thought as she laid down another winning hand. And perhaps she had been mistaken when she thought she saw Mortimer switching decks—it had happened so quickly, she couldn't be certain. One thing was clear, though. She was doing extremely well.

The room and people around her faded as she concentrated totally on the game.

The first time she lost, she wasn't too concerned. The pot had been small. And she won the next three hands. But on the fourth, she lost badly. Struggling to recoup her loss, she bet heavily on the next hand, and lost again.

She lost the next three hands in succession.

"How unfortunate." Mortimer frowned with simulated concern. "But don't worry. Your luck will turn."

But as the game continued, Margaret lost more. Although she won an occasional hand, the pile of counters in front of her diminished steadily. In what seemed like minutes, the pile dwindled down to nothing.

She was staring disbelievingly at her last hand when Phillip returned.

"What the devil!" his voice growled.

"If you would like to write a note, Miss Westbourne, I would be glad to advance you some cash," Mortimer said smoothly.

"What happened?" Phillip demanded. "How did you lose everything so quickly?"

"I don't know," she said dazedly.

"It's done all the time," Mortimer said.

"Dammit, we'll have to start from scratch. Sign the note, Margaret."

"Do it?" she murmured, horrified.

"You'll do it? Excellent," said Mortimer. A servant brought pen and paper.

"Make it for a thousand pounds," ordered Phillip.

A thousand pounds! Holding the pen over the paper, Margaret hesitated. What if Phillip's plan failed? What if they lost and she ended up owing Mortimer a thousand pounds? But she must do it for Aunt Letty's sake. And Phillip's. Biting her lip, she scratched her name onto the paper.

Glancing at the IOU, Mortimer's eyes widened. Then with a smile he leaned toward her and lightly rested his hand on her knee under the table. "You are a woman after my own heart, I see. You and I must try another game later."

Gripping her fan tightly, Margaret dug one end of it into Mortimer's wrist. With a curse, he drew back.

"Planning another game is a bit premature, Lord Mortimer." She pinned a smile on her face, trying to ignore the barely restrained rage in his eyes. "This one is not over yet."

Phillip barked with laughter. "You're a cool one, Margaret Westbourne. Are you ready to begin?"

She nodded almost imperceptibly.

"Good. Now watch Mortimer's hands closely," Phillip instructed. "It will make it more difficult for him to switch cards."

Obediently, Margaret stared intently while Mortimer shuffled the cards. He took a long time about it, hesitating once or twice. Finally he dealt.

"Very good," Phillip praised her. "You've got him beat. Raise the bet."

Margaret did so, but Mortimer promptly threw in his cards. Frowning, Margaret gathered in the small pot.

"Curse it all, I forgot about the mirror," Phillip said. "Mortimer can see your hand. You'll have to switch seats."

Margaret glanced over her shoulder. Sure enough, a mirror behind her was reflecting every card in her hand. She jumped to her feet. "Aunt Letty. Would you please exchange seats with me?"

"Whatever for, dear?" Aunt Letty asked.

"Perhaps changing seats will change my luck."

"Oh, that is a good idea. It often works for me."

Bernard watched them switch, a frown on his face. "Margaret, perhaps it would be wise—"

"Now, Barnett, don't be a spoilsport," Mortimer interrupted. "Deal the cards."

The game continued.

Following Phillip's directions, Margaret managed to win two out of the next four hands.

"Dammit," Phillip said when the deal came back to Mortimer. "He slipped you a second, Margaret. Throw in your cards."

"Oh, dear." Margaret placed her cards facedown on the table. "I don't think it would be wise of me to meet your wager, Lord Mortimer."

She looked up to find Mortimer staring at her with narrowed eyes. Margaret smiled sweetly.

"Perhaps we need a fresh deck," Mortimer said, signaling a servant.

A new deck appeared forthwith, and Mortimer dealt.

"He has the ace of diamonds up his sleeve," hissed Phillip. "Keep your eyes on his sleeve so he can't change the card."

Mortimer waved his hand in the air, but Margaret did not move her eyes from his left arm. He shifted in his seat, but Margaret kept her gaze fastened to his sleeve. He shifted again and his elbow caught his glass, sending wine spilling across the table. Margaret's eyes flickered to the spreading stain, then quickly came back to his sleeve, but it was too late.

"Dammit Margaret, I told you to keep your eyes on his sleeve!"

"I'm sorry," Margaret muttered.

"It wasn't your fault, Miss Westbourne." Mortimer spoke jovially. He lifted a finger, summoning a servant to clean up the mess. "Now, let's see what we have here." He laid down two kings and the ace of diamonds.

"This isn't going to work," Phillip said through clenched teeth.

"What can I do?" Margaret murmured.

"Keep trying, Miss Westbourne." Mortimer gathered up the cards. "Your luck is bound to change, it always does. You have to keep trying."

"Cheat, Margaret," said Phillip.

She swallowed. "I don't think I can."

"Nonsense, Miss Westbourne. You're a very good player. Surprisingly good. You simply need a bit of luck."

"You're probably right." Phillip's voice was full of frustration and the glow was a little brighter. "It takes a great deal of skill to cheat a cheater and I have a suspicion he's using 'splitters'—cards that are trimmed on the ends and sides. Dammit! We must do something or all is lost."

Despair washed over her. She had known from the beginning that this idea was insane. How could she possibly beat Mortimer at his own game?

"I wonder." Phillip's voice had a new note in it—a note that made her very nervous. She had a foreboding he was about to do something outrageous.

From the corner of her eye, Margaret saw the glow moving across the table toward Bernard. She watched with frozen horror as the flicker of light entered Bernard's body.

Bernard jumped.

Margaret's eyes widened as his chin came up, and his mouth tightened. His shoulders straightened and grew square. A bright gleam entered his gray eyes.

Phillip inhaled deeply, feeling the air expand his lungs and the blood rush through his veins. He was alive again! An array of sights and smells and sounds assaulted him. How extraordinarily acute all his senses were. As a ghost, he had not realized how muted everything was. Picking up the deck of cards, he flexed them between his fingers. The cards felt smooth, slippery. He could feel the softness of Bernard's clothes, the slight discomfort of the high collar where it poked his chin, the tightness of his boots pressing against a corn on his toe. He could smell Aunt Letty's soft lavender scent, Mortimer's acrid, stale odor, and, most of all, Margaret's sweet rose perfume.

He looked at Margaret for a moment, drinking in the sight of her. She was staring at him with those wide blue eyes of hers. How lovely, how incredibly lovely she was. The pink of her dress lent a glow to her cheeks, and the huge bell of the skirt made her waist look impossibly small. The low neckline revealed smooth white skin and the tops of her breasts curved invitingly above her bodice. She was so close, he could reach over and—

"Deal, Barnett. The night's young."

Mortimer was staring at him, too, Phillip saw. Did he suspect something? Casually, Phillip pulled out his watch, and clicked it open. "You're correct, Mortimer. But I must confess, playing for these chicken stakes is becoming tedious. What do you say we excuse the ladies and play a real game?"

Mortimer gaped a little, then a cunning gleam lit his eyes. "Certainly, certainly, if that is your wish."

"But, Bernard!" wailed Aunt Letty. "I'm not ready to quit."

"Aunt Letty," Margaret intervened smoothly, "let's watch for a few hands. Please?"

The old woman grumbled, but said no more.

Snapping the watch closed, Phillip laid it on the table and shuffled the deck, fumbling slightly. A card dropped to the floor. He picked it up, raising it high to show Mortimer the crease now running across its length.

"How clumsy of me," Phillip apologized. "I've bent the card. I'm afraid we'll need a new deck."

Mortimer frowned, but since he had no choice, he called for a fresh deck.

Phillip took the new deck and fanned the cards out on the table. With a flick of his finger, he turned them over before gathering them back up. He felt the sides and ends, then held up a card, tilting it at an angle to the light. On the plain white back he saw a small spot.

"Dear me," he drawled. "How unfortunate. This deck appears to have some sort of defect. The glaze on the cards is not evenly applied. Perhaps we should have another deck, Mortimer."

Their eyes met. Mortimer's expression of astonishment gave way to wariness, and then to dark anger. His fingers clenched the stem of his wineglass. The line of his mouth tightened, and he nodded curtly to the servant. "A new deck. Make sure it has no . . . blemishes."

Phillip repeated his examination of the new deck. Satisfied, he nodded, and the game began.

In the hours that followed, Phillip won hand after hand. He steadily increased the bets until enormous amounts of money were riding on each deal. A crowd began to gather around, watching the silent duel, until almost all the other tables were empty.

To the watchers, it seemed the Viscount Barnett had an uncanny knack for knowing when his hand couldn't beat Mortimer's. Time after time he threw his cards in, allowing Mortimer to win only a small pool. At other times, Phillip drove the pool so high, the onlookers gasped. Occasionally Mortimer would stare at Phillip, his expression a mixture of rage and bewilderment.

"Ready to quit, Morty, old fellow?" Phillip asked after Mortimer suffered one particularly devastating loss. "Seems your luck is definitely out tonight."

The crowd murmured as Mortimer threw down his cards and stood up. His face reddened with fury, veins throbbing at his temples. "Perhaps that would be wise," he said through gritted teeth.

"It is always wise to quit when your courage fails you," said Phillip, shuffling the cards negligently through his strong fingers.

In the sudden silence, the only sound was Mortimer's rasping breath. The two men's gazes locked and battled. Then Phillip tilted his head back slightly and smiled.

Mortimer's face grew pale. "No one can question my courage," he snarled. He looked around at the watching faces. No one moved. His face paper white, he sat down again.

The game went on.

They stopped a few times, to send for paper and ink so Mortimer could write out an IOU, but other than that, they did not pause. It was almost dawn when Mortimer finally said in a queer voice, "That's it. You've won everything I own, Barnett." His breathing was shallow and erratic. Sweat rolled down his face.

Phillip tapped his fingers against the watch lying before him. "I'm willing to play one final game, Mortimer."

"Don't toy with me," Mortimer bit out. "I have nothing left."

"Actually, you do have something. Something I want. The ruby ring on your finger. I'm willing to wager everything I've won tonight against that little bauble."

Hope glimmered in Mortimer's eyes. "Done," he said.

Phillip dealt the cards slowly. Mortimer picked them up with shaking hands. His eyes flickered from his cards to Phillip's face, then back to his cards. A savage smile lit his face. With a triumphant laugh he laid down his cards. Three aces. "You should have stopped when you were ahead, Barnett." He reached out for the slips of paper littering Phillip's side of the table.

"Wait."

One by one, Phillip laid down his cards. The ace of diamonds. The knave of clubs. The nine of diamonds.

Disbelievingly, Mortimer stared at the cards. With a roar of rage, he leapt to his feet. Pulling off the ruby ring, he threw it down on the table, and turned on his heel.

"You may call on me tomorrow, Mortimer, to settle the rest of your debts."

Without replying, Mortimer stormed out of the room.

Phillip picked up the ring and tossed it high in the air. Catching it deftly, he turned and flashed a grin at the stunned crowd.

A laugh rang out, then a few more.

Soon the room was filled with the sound of howling, roaring laughter.

Margaret, laughing along with the rest, grabbed his arm. "Phillip! You did it! Aunt Letty has her home back!"

He had done it! He laughed out loud and swept her into his arms, swinging her around in a wide arc. Her helpless laughter was sweeter than any music, the feel of her in his arms more heavenly than any paradise. Setting her back on her feet, he pressed the ring into her hand, and did what he'd been longing to do for an eternity.

Margaret barely had time to see the glint in his eyes and think, *No, he wouldn't, he couldn't—not in front of all these people,* before his lips were on hers and he was kissing her hard.

The room whirled, and Margaret didn't even hear the ragged cheer that went up. She was too wrapped up in Phillip's—Bernard's?—warm mouth, his strong arms, his lean body. Who would have thought that a mere kiss could make her blood sing, her heart dance, her body flame?

Abruptly, the kiss stopped.

Margaret looked up, dazed, into Bernard's confused eyes.

22

Margaret felt numb. Huddling in the corner of the carriage, her eyes tired and gritty from lack of sleep, she knew she should be feeling happy, triumphant. Mortimer had been defeated, Aunt Letty's home was safe, and the curse . . . was broken?

It must be. Why else would Phillip have disappeared? But everything had happened so quickly, she was having difficulty believing it. She hadn't known it would happen so fast.

She stared down at her hands, the clenched knuckles of her fists barely visible in the predawn light. For the first time, her mind registered that she did not have her fan. She must have lost it somehow, in the confusion at Mortimer's. After Phillip disappeared, people had crowded around, jostling and pushing her aside in their eagerness to congratulate Bernard on his victory. She must have dropped the fan then.

She did not care particularly about losing the fan. It had been an ugly thing and she was sure the sticks were permanently bowed from the abuse it had taken last night. She could easily purchase a new one at the haberdasher's, a much prettier one. She could bear losing a fan.

But she wasn't ready to lose Phillip. The moments she had spent with him were the happiest she could remember. Those hours had added brightness and excitement to her otherwise dull and ordinary life. How strange that someone who was dead made her feel so alive.

Was he gone? She hadn't even said good-bye. How could he be gone?

"Margaret, please say you forgive me!" Bernard's pleading voice penetrated her misery. "I don't know what came over me, but I swear it will never happen again!"

What on earth was Bernard babbling about? Oh. The kiss.

She averted her face, not wanting him to read her thoughts. Through the window, she could see sheets of rain pounding down. In the early morning twilight, everything appeared dark gray. Her life suddenly seemed to be the same lackluster color.

"It . . . it was the strangest thing. I just don't understand. All those people staring at us . . . frowning at us. What a scandal!"

"Oh, pooh," said Aunt Letty. "Everyone loved it. They were as caught up in the moment as you were."

Bernard shook his head. "I don't know what I could have been thinking to embarrass you like that, Margaret."

She hadn't been the least bit embarrassed, but Margaret remained silent, filled with the desperate desire to get home and reach the sanctuary of her room.

Bernard began playing convulsively with the catch on his watch. "I must have been insane. Perhaps I am ill. How else to explain it? Or to explain how I won all those IOU's. There was one for twenty thousand pounds. And one for . . . that reminds me. Aunt Letty, how did you ever come to sign the mortgage over to Mortimer?"

"Ah, let's see—"

Fortunately, Bernard was so bewildered he didn't wait for an answer. "And there was another for the deed to Mortimer's estate! I just don't understand," he mumbled.

Much to Margaret's relief, he fell into a brooding silence that lasted for the duration of the trip home.

At the castle, Margaret tried to make a quick escape to her room, but Bernard detained her.

"Margaret, I must know. Can you forgive me?"

She didn't want to talk right now. Her limbs felt leaden and her head ached. "Of course, Bernard. But please excuse me. I am very tired."

More tired than she had ever been in her life, she thought when she reached her room. But instead of ringing for her maid, or lying down, she seated herself at the dressing table and opened her fist.

The ruby ring rested snugly in the palm of her hand. She stared at it for a long minute, her brain reluctantly accepting the truth. She had been right; the ring had been the key to releasing Phillip from the curse. And now he was gone.

Margaret dropped the ring on the table and put her head down on her arms.

"Why so glum, Margaret?"

"Phillip!"

He stood before her in the early morning light, his glow a bit fainter, but his eyes glinting as usual. She jumped to her feet, taking an impetuous step forward, before she remembered and stopped.

He grinned wryly. "I wish I could kiss you, too, sweeting."

"That's not—oh, never mind." She was too happy

to try to conceal it. "What are you doing here? I thought the curse was broken."

"Apparently I must take the ruby with me."

"Oh." So it was only a temporary reprieve. Her joy dimmed. "I have it right here."

She picked up the ring. The weight of it in her hand felt like lead. It was extremely hideous, she thought, with ornate gold swirls and the ruby gleaming evilly like blood trapped in ice.

"Well?" His voice was abrupt. Startled, she dropped the ring. With a small bounce, it landed out of sight under the dressing table.

"Dammit!" she exclaimed.

"Really, Margaret, I'm shocked."

She blushed. "Oh, you are a terrible influence on me, you wicked man."

"You will be glad when I am gone, then."

Margaret reached under the table for the ring, not looking at him. She must let him go. Her brain urged her to do it quickly, before she made a complete fool of herself. "Yes, I will," she lied.

"That's not what your lips said to mine. You kissed me so sweetly, Margaret. And the feel of you in my arms . . . your hair is as soft as it looks, as soft as I had imagined. Dear God, Margaret, how I wanted to hold you forever, to kiss you forever, to—"

She couldn't look at him. She couldn't let him see how her heart was breaking. If he didn't stop, she would forget her sanity and plead with him to stay, she would take the ring and throw it in the deepest part of the river where it could never be found. "I . . . I . . . oh, look, here it is."

She held out the ring, barely able to see because of the tears filling her eyes.

She could feel him hesitating. Why didn't he take it and go? Through her tears, she saw his bright hand reaching out. Her fingers tightened on the gold for a moment. Forcing herself to let go, she dropped the ring into his waiting palm.

The ring fell through his hand and onto the floor.

"Hell and the devil!" Phillip glared first at his hand, then at the floor.

Margaret stared blankly at the ring. "Dear heaven, what can this mean?"

"It means the curse is not broken, obviously."

Happiness and relief flooded her, making her smile radiantly. But he had turned away and didn't see her expression.

"It means we are right back where we started and we have no idea how to break this damned curse."

Something in his voice stopped her burgeoning joy. She looked at him more closely. The bright glow outlining his tense shoulders ebbed and shimmered for a moment before brightening again, making her blink hard to clear her vision. Was it her imagination or was he glowing less brightly than before? Alarm coursed through her. "Phillip, are you fading?"

He turned back to look at her, brows drawn. "Yes, Margaret." She gasped and his mouth twisted into a grim smile. "Every time I appear, it uses up a portion of my 'strength,' I suppose you would call it. Stepping into Bernard's body was especially draining. If we don't break the curse soon, I will no longer be able to appear." He looked away from her and stared into the dark corner of her room. "Very likely seventy-eight years will pass before I have enough strength to try again."

The blood drained from Margaret's face. "I don't understand. What went wrong? The curse should be broken. Everything that belonged to Lord Mortimer is now in your—I mean, in Bernard's possession."

Suddenly, shockingly, pure venom wiped the resigned expression from Phillip's face. "Barnett!" he spat, each syllable filled with loathing. "Of course." His glow brightened and he began to pace around the room. "I'll wager your betrothed is somehow responsible for my presence. All along the coincidence of finding Robeson's spawn here has bothered me. Now the reason is clear. I'm here not because of some foolish curse, but to revenge myself on Mortimer's and Robeson's descendents!"

Margaret stepped back, a hand rising to her throat. "I can't believe that," she whispered. "Bernard has never harmed anyone."

"Perhaps not, but as the Bible says, 'The iniquities of the fathers shall be visited upon the children.' As you and I both know, justice is not always fair."

Not always fair? Margaret's hand dropped to her side and she stared at Phillip. That was his excuse for seeking revenge? For committing such wickedness against innocent Bernard?

Her initial dismay began to fade as anger took its place. "What nonsense!" she snapped, fists clenching at her sides. "Because you've been wronged, do you now envision yourself as some sort of avenging angel? Harming Bernard will serve no purpose and if you so much as say 'boo' to him I'll . . . I'll curse you myself!"

"So." Phillip strode around the room, his voice cold as the air surrounding him. "Even now you defend him. Now, when it's clear that it is he and only he that prevents me from leaving."

"You're wrong. I don't believe you've been trapped between life and death for over seventy-eight years just so you can wreak some horrible revenge on a man as good and kind as Bernard. There must be something else. Something the Gypsy didn't tell me."

Phillip stopped by the fireplace, his face averted, but

Margaret could see that he was listening. She spoke more calmly, her words coaxing and conciliating.

"I will go to the Gypsy and ask her. She will know what to do, I am sure of it. We are probably overlooking some silly thing, or maybe there is some sort of ceremony we must observe formally to break the curse. Phillip—" She stepped to his side, bending forward to see his face. "I will go to the fair this afternoon and talk to the Gypsy."

Phillip didn't reply. Margaret waited tensely, afraid that he intended to refuse her and continue his quest for revenge. Slow minutes ticked by.

The silence had grown almost intolerable when he gave a curt nod. "I will agree with one condition. You must summon the Gypsy here. I want to hear what she has to say."

Margaret went limp with relief. "Very well. I will send a servant to request that Madame Razinski come today. If I offer to pay her, I am certain she will come. We will find out exactly what we must do. We will break this curse, Phillip, I promise."

23

The Gypsy entered the west parlor regally, as if she were a queen. She looked very much as she had at the fair, only instead of the tattered shawl, she wore a flowing purple robe and her coarse hair was covered by a matching turban with a large paste diamond in the center. The mole on her face looked bigger than Margaret remembered. Margaret stared at it. Hadn't it been on the other cheek?

"This is your Gypsy? She looks like an actress from Drury Lane." Phillip was leaning against the wall—although not quite touching it—his legs crossed at the ankle, arms folded across his chest. Although his image was faint, Margaret could clearly see his expression of combined amusement and disgust. "This should be as entertaining as a play. Are there to be acrobats and a ballet, too?"

Margaret glared at him. His future—and possibly Bernard's—was at stake. The seriousness of the situation made his sarcasm inappropriate. Even if the Gypsy did look a trifle . . . well, theatrical.

"I am Madame Razinski," said the Gypsy. "How may I be of service, lady?"

Conscious of Phillip's derision, Margaret sat on the sofa, turning her shoulder so she wouldn't have to see his mocking face. She smiled at the Gypsy. "Madame Razinski, please sit down. I have a friend who believes one of his ancestors was cursed."

"Yes, I remember you asked about ze curse before." The woman sank down on the floor, her knees cracking loudly. She arranged the patched skirt around her.

"We tried to break it by retrieving a token of . . . of the ancestor's from his enemy. It did not work," Margaret said. "We don't know if we had the wrong token, or even if there is a token."

"Ah. Tell me of zis curse, lady. I need to know ze precise wording."

"Let's see." Margaret tried to remember. "I believe it went like this: 'Thee and thine, thy wishes will go wanting; thee and thine will falter and fail; thee and thine will diminish and die.' "

"And ze curse, it has come true?"

Margaret hesitated. "I think so. Although nothing truly terrible happened *after* the curse."

"I see." Madame Razinski placed her hands together and looked thoughtful. "I will have to commune wiz ze spirit world to discover ze answer."

Phillip snorted. "If this woman knows the first thing about curses or spirits, by God, I'll give you and Bernard my blessing."

Margaret ignored him. "Then pray do so, Madame Razinski."

"It will be of ze most difficult—and expensive."

Without a word, Margaret placed several bank notes in front of the woman.

The money quickly disappeared into the folds of Madame Razinski's gown. Raising her arms above her head, bracelets jangling, she began to sway and moan and sigh. She reached higher and higher into the air as if trying to catch hold of something, the moans increasing in volume to a high-pitched wail.

"She sounds like a paid mourner at a funeral," Phillip grumbled.

Suddenly, the noise stopped and the Gypsy slumped down. Her turban almost fell off, but she swiftly raised a hand to hold it in place.

Startled by the Gypsy's near collapse, Margaret jumped up and knelt beside her, patting her hand. "Madame Razinski? Are you all right?"

Moving her hand to her brow, Madame Razinski lifted her head and tilted it back. Her eyes were half shut and only the whites showed beneath her lids. "I have ze answer," she said in a faraway voice.

Margaret, her fingers tightening on the Gypsy's hand, grew still. "Yes?"

"Zere is a token."

Margaret leaned forward, excitement filling her. "Yes?"

"But ze curse, it is weak."

"Weak?"

"Yes, weak." Madame Razinski nodded her head in a wise fashion. "Because ze person zat cursed your friend's ancestor did not have possession of ze token."

"But would the curse work, then?"

"Yes, because ze item, it was of great significance to ze victim."

"I don't understand. What does this mean? Can the curse be broken or not?"

The Gypsy shrugged. "Zis is hard to say, lady. Perhaps. Perhaps not. For another small fee, I can seek ze answer to zis question also."

Dropping the woman's hand, Margaret sat back on her heels. She stole a look at Phillip. He had moved right behind her and was scowling at Madame Razinski.

Margaret averted her gaze and dug into her reticule once more.

Before she could give the woman any more money,
though, the door opened, and Bernard looked in.
"Margaret, may I speak to you?" He saw the Gypsy
and stopped, drawing himself up. "What is this old
fraud doing here? And why are you sitting on the
floor, Margaret?"

Margaret rose hastily to her feet.

"For once I agree with Bernard," Phillip said into
her ear. "This woman is obviously a charlatan."

"Oh, hush!"

"I beg your pardon?" Bernard drew himself up,
looking mortally offended.

"Not you, Bernard," Margaret said impatiently.

"Not . . . oh, you mean *he* is here?" Bernard glared
around the room.

Margaret shrugged.

The Gypsy looked bewildered. "Who? What are
you talking about?"

"A ghost," Bernard snapped. "Here in this room."

"A ghost? In 'ere?" The Gypsy stood up, her face
paling under her heavy makeup. "Where is 'e? Oi
don't 'old with no ghosts, oi don't!"

Margaret stared at the Gypsy whose accent suddenly sounded more cockney than foreign.

Madame Razinski headed for the door, eyes darting frantically. "Oi be leavin'. Oi don't like this talk of
curses and ghosts—Oi don't believe in 'em and nei-
ther should you. You would think a fancy pair like
yourselves would know the difference between wot's
real and wot's make-believe. Don't you know these
things is all in your 'ead?" With one more frightened
look around the room, the Gypsy left, slamming the
door behind her.

Margaret and Bernard gaped after her. A small
black spot on the floor caught Margaret's eye and she

leaned over to pick it up. It was the mole from the Gypsy's cheek.

"I'd say her mole was as authentic as the rest of her," Phillip remarked sardonically.

"Good heavens, who was that?" Aunt Letty asked wandering in. "She looked rather peculiar."

"Madame Razinski, a Gypsy," Margaret replied, still staring at the mole.

"A Gypsy?" Aunt Letty's brow furrowed for a moment, then cleared. "A Gypsy! How clever of you, Margaret. Did she say how to break the curse?"

"Er, she said we must retrieve a token—a personal item that belonged to Phillip and was used to seal—"

"Pardon me, Margaret," Bernard interrupted. "I would very much like to speak to you in private. Aunt Letty, would you mind?"

"Not at all. You young lovebirds want to be alone." She left the room muttering, "A token . . ."

Margaret looked at Bernard. His arms were folded across his chest, and her heart sank. Now what?

"Margaret, I've been thinking about last night."

She groaned silently.

"I must know," he continued. "Was Phillip *possessing* me?"

Margaret hesitated. She didn't want to lie, but lately Bernard had been quite unpredictable. How would he react, knowing Phillip had taken over his body? Before she could decide though, Bernard came to his own conclusion.

"Never mind. I can see by your expression he was." He fell silent, a deep frown creasing his forehead. "So," he muttered softly, almost as if to himself, "it was Phillip you kissed."

Margaret blushed. Bernard looked at her and she knew guilt was written all over her face.

"Margaret, do you love him?"

The blood drained from her face. What kind of

question was that, to ask if she was in love with a
ghost? She glanced over at Phillip, silently watching
the scene being enacted before him. Her gaze met his
for a long moment before she looked away, back to
Bernard, who was watching her closely.

"I told you, I—"

"Yes, yes. You admire his courage." He stepped
toward her. "Is he here now?"

She nodded.

Bernard closed his eyes. His brow furrowed, and
he appeared deep in thought. After a while, he sighed
and opened his eyes again. He glanced around the
room, his gaze stopping when it came to Phillip.

Margaret gasped. "Bernard! Can you—?"

His mouth tight, he inclined his head a fraction of
an inch. He didn't appear too pleased by his ability.

"But how?"

He sighed again. "I think I always had the capabili-
ty. I simply didn't care to exercise it." His level gaze
met Phillip's sardonic one. "Margaret, will you excuse
us for a few minutes?"

He wanted her to leave? Surely he must be joking.

"Go on, sweeting. I think Barn Owl has something
to say not fit for a lady's ears."

Bernard flushed, whether at the derogatory name
or the endearment, Margaret wasn't sure.

She glared at the two men, but they didn't notice.
They were too busy trying to stare each other down.
With a muttered exclamation and her skirts twitching, she swished out of the room, slamming the door
behind her.

So the idiot could see him. Interesting, Phillip
thought, a smile curling his lip. The situation
promised to be most entertaining. "You had something to say to me, Barnett?"

The mockery in his voice was plain. Bernard straightened, his lips tightening. "Why don't you go away and leave Margaret alone? We don't want you here."

Phillip's smile grew wider. "Are you certain of that, Barnett? Have you asked Margaret what she wants? I think you might be surprised."

Bernard's hands clenched into fists.

Phillip grinned.

"She's not for you, Holwell."

Phillip's grin faded. "What makes you so certain?" he asked coldly.

"You're a ghost! What kind of life will she have if she's in love with a ghost?"

Phillip turned away to study a painting of St. Adelheid over the fireplace. "Perhaps I will take her with me."

Bernard stared in horror. "You couldn't."

"Couldn't I?" Phillip laughed.

"Damn you, you're not good enough for her."

"And you think you are? You didn't even stand up for her when the village ostracized her."

Bernard grew even paler. "What do you mean? That's not true—"

"She wants a man, and even as a ghost, I'm more of a man than you are."

"What kind of man would take a woman's life? Do you even know what will happen to you when you leave here? I wouldn't be surprised if you ended up in hell. Is that what you want for Margaret?"

Phillip froze, fury rushing through him. "What I want is to make you suffer, Barnett. Just as your great-grandfather made me suffer. That's why I'm here, to have revenge against my enemies." Phillip smiled silkily. "That means you, Bernard."

24

Margaret paced the hallway anxiously. It seemed as if they had been in there forever. What was happening? She crouched down and pressed an ear to the keyhole, but all she could hear was the low murmur of voices.

She couldn't wait any longer. She had to know what was passing between them. Putting her hand on the knob, she started to turn it, when there was a commotion at the front door.

Mortimer stormed into the hall, his riding gloves still on, a crop clenched in one fist. Gibbons, right behind him, grabbed him by the arm, but at that moment, Mortimer saw Margaret.

Shaking off the butler, he strode across the hall. "Is Barnett in there?" he snarled.

Margaret stepped back, too startled to reply. With an impatient growl, he flung open the door, causing it to bang against the wall. Margaret heard Bernard say, "What do you mean—?" before Mortimer snarled again.

"Barnett, I want to speak to you."

Margaret scooted into the room behind Gibbons. The butler looked flustered. "I'm sorry, my lord; he refused to wait."

"Never mind, Gibbons. You may go."

After an almost imperceptible hesitation, the butler quietly closed the door.

Bernard surveyed the visitor in a cool manner. "What do you want, Mortimer? Are you here to settle your debts?"

Mortimer flushed. "Not yet, Barnett. First I want to know how you did it."

"Did what?"

"Don't give me that blockhead stare. All morning I've been trying to figure it out. I can't believe you've been fooling everyone all these years. It's simply not possible anyone could pretend such denseness. So tell me, how did you manage to cheat me out of my entire fortune?"

Bernard stiffened and looked his most pompous. "I never cheat."

"Hah!" Mortimer's frustration and fury were evident in the way he slapped the crop against his thigh. "Oh, I grant you, you were very clever. As closely as I watched, I could not catch you at it, but it's obvious you cheated royally."

"Do you impugn my honor?"

Mortimer gave him an incredulous stare. "Of course I'm impugning your honor, you half-wit."

Margaret tugged at Bernard's sleeve. "Bernard, come away. He's not rational."

"Stay out of this, you slut." The whip snapped against Mortimer's leg more quickly. Margaret had the uncomfortable feeling he was wishing he could use it on her.

Under Bernard's sleeve, Margaret felt his muscles tense. "Mortimer, your manners leave much to be desired. Apologize at once, or—"

"Or what?" Mortimer sneered. "You will challenge me to a duel?"

"If necessary."

Mortimer almost dropped the whip, his astonishment was so great.

Then he smiled.

"I refuse to apologize either to you or the slut," he said deliberately.

"Then name your seconds."

"Bernard—" Margaret gripped his arm. She couldn't believe this was happening. "This is madness."

Bernard shook off her hand. "Be quiet, Margaret."

"We'll have to forgo seconds," Mortimer said. "What with dueling in such disfavor these days, we might end up in prison."

"If that is what you wish." Bernard's expression did not change.

"And naturally, as I was the one challenged, I must select the weapon." Smiling, Mortimer fingered the crop. "I choose swords."

Bernard nodded tersely.

"Then what do you say to tomorrow? Night would be best. It will afford us some privacy, and the moon is still full. At the clearing behind the castle?"

"Very well."

"Tomorrow at midnight, then, Barnett. I look forward to it." With an evil laugh, Mortimer left the room.

"Are you insane?" Margaret half shouted at Bernard.

"A man must defend the honor of his fiancée and himself." He was wearing a particularly pigheaded look on his face.

"Honor! Who cares about honor? You could be killed!"

Bernard looked at her. "I thought this was what you wanted."

"What are you talking about?"

"You think I am a coward, Margaret." His gaze was unwavering. "Don't bother to deny it. Perhaps this will prove to you I am not."

"That will certainly comfort me when you are dead."

Bernard watched her steadily, ignoring her sarcasm. Something in his gaze made her flush and turn her head away.

"If you will excuse me," he said quietly. "There are some things I must attend to." He bowed and left the room.

Disbelievingly, she stared after him. What had gotten into him? She thought she knew him, but the Bernard she knew would never be so foolish.

"He's right, you know," Phillip said softly.

Margaret whirled to face him. "How can you say that? We must stop them!"

Phillip inspected his sleeve, not answering for a moment. Was that a speck of dust marring the fabric or had a tiny spot faded away? he wondered.

Smoothing a finger over the spot, he didn't look at her. "Why?"

"Why?" Margaret sounded close to tears. "Bernard barely knows one end of a sword from another. He will be killed."

Phillip looked up from the hole in his sleeve, anger kindling in him. Damn her, why must she always be so concerned for Bernard? Here he was, fading away, and all she cared about was her precious fiancé. Did she love Bernard? How could she love such a wooden block? He opened his mouth, intending to refuse to help, but the sight of the distress on her face stopped him.

Instead, he said coldly, "What can I do? There's not enough time to give him fencing lessons—even if I could hold a sword."

He knew the exact moment the idea occurred to her. The crease between her brows smoothed out, and her bright, pleading eyes turned to him. His anger increased. Could she truly be so naïve as to ask such a thing?

"Phillip, couldn't you step into his body again? You can fight with a sword. Aunt Letty said you were a master."

Incredible. He looked back at his sleeve, smoothing his fingers over the fabric, even though he couldn't feel it. "Letty was ever a flatterer."

"Oh, it's not true, then?"

"No, it is true. But do you realize what you ask, Margaret?" His gaze rose to meet hers. "If I do step into Bernard's body, I will very likely use up the last of my strength. I doubt I will be able to appear again."

Her hand rose to her throat and she stared at him. Then her eyes shut as if to deny his words.

For some reason, this made him even angrier. He started to pace around the room. In his anger, he strode right through the furniture, not bothering to go around.

"Why should I help Bernard?" he demanded, passing through the sofa. "If Mortimer kills him, then I will be avenged on both my enemies. The curse may be broken."

"You can't believe that, Phillip." Her voice was a whisper of sound, but it ripped at his conscience. "I can't believe your purpose here could be so wicked."

"Even if my purpose is not revenge, why should I risk waiting years for another chance to break this curse? What if I can't find another person who can see me? What if I wait forever?"

What if he stepped into Bernard's body and let Mortimer kill the idiot? Which was exactly what he wanted to do.

He stopped in front of her, glaring down at her white face. Didn't she understand what she was asking?

"I don't know, Phillip. You're right of course. I can't ask you to make such a sacrifice."

Her eyes were dark with confusion, pain, and worry. Looking at her, he felt his heart constrict and his throat tighten with some nameless emotion. He would miss her when he was gone. Strange, how she could make him feel so alive when he had been dead for over seventy-eight years. This time with her had been so sweet—perhaps a small recompense for the pain he had endured? Or perhaps a second chance to . . . to what? He stared deep into her eyes, seeking, searching for an answer to a question he couldn't even define.

The answer was there, although he still wasn't certain what the question was. But it no longer mattered.

He knew what he must do.

"I will be there, my dear," he said.

In the shadowy entry hall, Margaret stood quietly behind the suit of armor. Moonlight streamed through one of the narrow windows, lighting the stairs for Margaret's watching eyes. She had been waiting for Bernard since eleven o'clock to ensure that she wouldn't miss him.

She heard the muted chimes of a clock as it struck the quarter hour, the sound carrying clearly in the dark stillness. Only fifteen minutes until midnight. Where was Bernard?

Perhaps more to the point, where was Phillip? He had not come to her room after dinner, and it occurred to her that he had not actually promised to help Bernard. *I will be there,* he had said. Would he stand by and watch Bernard be killed to satisfy his thirst for revenge? She should have made him promise to help.

But what if Phillip was right? If he did help, would he fade away to exist in a kind of limbo, possibly forever?

Her stomach knotted. To help one, she must cause the other to suffer a terrible fate. What cruel providence had created such an impossible situation with such an impossible choice?

A light tread sounded on the stairway. Margaret ducked back into the darkest shadow. Bernard came into view, the moonlight gleaming on the blade of the sword he carried. He opened the door and went out into the night. Brushing away a cobweb, she pulled up the hood of her gray mantle and followed him.

The night was crisp and cold. Margaret shivered, wishing she had put on more than one flannel petticoat. She should have let Yvette help her get dressed, she thought.

Not wanting her maid to know she was going out, she had dressed herself. It hadn't been easy. She had had to leave off her corset, and she couldn't reach all the buttons of her dress. Fortunately, the mantle concealed most of her toilette's shortcomings.

And at least the thick cloth of her mantle and her woolen mittens were warm, she thought as she picked her way along the muddy path toward the clearing. She stayed several yards behind Bernard, scurrying from tree to tree in her efforts to stay out of sight. He paused once, head cocked, listening, and she froze, barely daring to breath. When he moved on, she released a sigh of relief and started picking her way more carefully along the winding path, watching for branches or leaves that might crunch underfoot and alert him to her presence.

She was peering down at the ground, stepping

over a small puddle, when a dark shape loomed up in front of her.

Margaret let out a stifled scream before she realized it was Bernard.

"Bernard!" she gasped, heart still pounding. "You frightened me half to death!"

Bernard was not overly concerned by her fright. He had suspected she might try something foolish. "What do you think you are doing, Margaret?" he asked quietly.

She tilted her chin. "I am going with you, Bernard. Don't try to talk me out of it."

"A duel is no place for a woman."

"It is no place for anyone. I cannot believe you are being so stubborn."

"We have already discussed this, Margaret. My honor is at stake."

"Hmmph. And what will fighting prove? That Mortimer is more skilled with a sword?"

"I'm not a complete idiot, Margaret. I have improved my swordsmanship since Mortimer and I last fought."

"But why take the risk?"

"You *told* him I abandoned you after the scandal."

Margaret was so taken aback by the change in subject she could only stare at him for a moment. Regathering her wits, she said in a cool voice, "Well, didn't you?"

"Is that what you think?" Bernard's face was pale and furious.

"What else can I think? You never came to the house—"

"That's not true! Your mother refused to let me in. I waited in the woods for you, but you never came."

"I was locked in my room," Margaret whispered faintly. "For a week."

He gave her a sharp stare. "I had left by then. I had some business that couldn't wait. When I returned to

Barnett Manor, my father and I argued, and he sent me to India."

"But you never looked at me that day in church."

For the first time, Bernard glanced away from her. "I couldn't, Margaret. My father was so callous and indifferent—and that girl was bearing his *child*. Don't you know how ashamed I was?"

"Do you know how hurt *I* was? No one spoke to me for over a year. After that I was constantly on trial. Any slip, and the silence returned. It wore me down, Bernard. I tried not to care, but I did."

Bernard was pale. "I didn't know. When I came home from India the first time, you were being courted by Lord Hugh. The next time I returned, I proposed, but I thought you hated me because of what my father did. I tried to show you I wasn't like him, but it didn't seem to work." He took hold of her hands, holding them tightly between his own. "I'm sorry, Margaret. God, I'm sorry. If I'd known, I would have come back sooner."

Even though he whispered, his voice rang in the still, dark night. The words flowed inside her, warming a small cold corner of her heart, easing an old ache that had been there so long she barely noticed it.

They had shared a childhood together, been friends for a long time. She had not realized how strong those bonds were, how much they meant to her. Looking into the dark gray of his eyes, she felt a glow of happiness, but also a curious dissatisfaction. She valued his friendship, yes. But she wanted more.

A crazy impulse seized her and she spoke without thinking. "Bernard, kiss me."

He froze for a second. His grip on her hands tightened, then abruptly he dropped them. "I would never cheapen our relationship by subjecting you to such behavior before we are married," he said in a cold voice.

Embarrassment burned her cheeks at his reproving

words. He must think her a forward hussy. But even worse than the humiliation was the disappointment. She should have known better than to hope . . . what? That she could ignite a spark that would make their relationship something more than friendship?

"Margaret, I have to go."

His impatient voice drew back her attention, reminding her of her original purpose. "Don't fight this duel."

"I must."

"Why?"

"To prove I am not a coward."

Her throat ached. "No one thinks you are a coward, Bernard."

He laughed shortly before turning and walking away. Over his shoulder he said, "Come if you wish, for I cannot stop you. But stay out of the way, for I don't want you to get hurt."

His lean figure quickly disappeared down the dark path. Biting her lip, Margaret picked up her skirts and hurried after him.

Mortimer was waiting.

Oak trees ringed the clearing like dark sentinels, silently waiting for the display of skill and strength, for the game of life and death to begin. Moonlight bathed the area in an unearthly glow and illuminated Mortimer's figure as he practiced a vicious sword thrust. The scene reminded Margaret of a picture she had seen in a book once—a picture of ancient Celts preparing a pagan ritual.

And Bernard would be the blood sacrifice.

Inside her mittens, her cold hands clenched into fists. Where was Phillip?

Hearing them arrive, Mortimer turned. "Ah, I see you brought a second after all. A most charming choice, Barnett. Perhaps after I kill you, I will show her what it's like to be with a real man."

Appalled, Margaret drew back against a tree. Mortimer laughed and pulled his cravat off, tossing it on a rock at the edge of the clearing where his coat already lay. Dressed all in black, he stood waiting like Death itself.

Bernard quickly followed suit. In his gray breeches and white shirt, he gleamed in silver contrast to Mortimer's dark shadow. "Are you ready to fight, Mortimer?" he asked, his voice as cold as the night air.

"Certainly. Are you ready to die?"

Margaret shuddered.

The two men saluted each other briefly. Then swiftly, before Margaret could even blink, Mortimer attacked.

Margaret's heart leapt to her throat as the wicked blade slashed through the air. Bernard swung up his sword, barely parrying the thrust in time. Without pause, Mortimer attacked again and the sound of clashing steel rang through the night.

Mortimer drove Bernard back across the clearing, his sword never ceasing its motion. He moved so quickly, it was difficult for Margaret to follow what was happening, but at least Bernard seemed to be holding his own.

Hope sprang forth in her breast, only to die as Mortimer backed Bernard up against a gnarled tree. His sword flashing like a hungry serpent, Mortimer made a lethal thrust.

Margaret buried her face in her hands, not wanting to look, not wanting to see the steel entering Bernard's body. She wanted to run away, back to the safety of her room, and hide her head under her pillow, away from the smell of hate and violence that permeated the very air. But she remained frozen in the shadow of the tree, even as she spread her fingers to see whether Bernard lived or died.

At the last possible moment, Bernard jumped aside

and the point of Mortimer's sword drove into the tree, the impact sounding like a pistol shot. Cursing, Mortimer yanked on the blade and whirled to face Bernard. But now it was Bernard who pressed the attack.

Mortimer backed in a circle around the edge of the clearing, his breath making white puffs in the air. Each parry seemed slower as he continued to back away from Bernard's onslaught.

Margaret watched in amazement. She never would have guessed it, but Bernard seemed quite proficient with a sword. As the duelists neared the spot where she stood, hope unfurled in her breast again. Perhaps he could defeat Mortimer after all. . . .

Before she could even complete the thought, Bernard's foot caught on an exposed root and he tripped. He went down heavily, his sword flying from his hand. As he stared up at Mortimer, a cold fear overwhelmed Margaret.

Bernard would be killed.

Phillip, where are you? she screamed silently.

Mortimer, his face dark with hate, snarled, "No one crosses me, Barnett, and no one makes a fool of me." His teeth flashed, while shadows hollowed out his cheeks and his eyes were black holes in his face. He looked like a grinning death's-head. "Or they die."

He thrust with all the force of his arm, the point of his sword heading straight for Bernard's heart.

25

He saw the point of a sword bearing down on him. Muscles bunching, he rolled with lightning speed toward his blade. Mortimer grunted when his thrust missed its prey.

He heard Mortimer's footsteps coming after him. Reaching for the fallen sword, he encountered only cold mud. The blade was barely beyond his grasp. In less than a second, he knew he would feel cold steel slicing into his flesh. Stretching his arm farther, all but dislocating it, he groped for the sword. As his fingers closed over the hilt, he heard the whistling sound of a blade slashing through the air toward him.

Death singing in his ears, he swung his sword in a wide arc. He deflected the thrust barely in time, trapping Mortimer's blade under his own and forcing him to his knees. Chest to chest, eye to eye, he looked into Mortimer's hate-filled gaze.

He tilted his head back slightly and smiled.

"Phillip," he heard Margaret breathe.

"Damn you, Barnett." Shoving Phillip back, Mortimer gained his feet. He took a hasty step forward, then stopped, his eyes widening.

Phillip leapt to his feet, hefting the weapon in his hand before closing his fingers tightly around the hilt. Lord, it felt good to hold a sword again! Fragmented memories of fencing with the masters of Europe flashed through his mind. In Spain, they had taught *la verdadera destreza*, "the true art"; old-fashioned, perhaps, but useful still. In Italy, they had preached the fundamental principles of the *stesso tempo*, or "single time," the parry and the counterattack combined. And in France—ah, France—there he had learned grace and elegance and pure mastery of the blade. The memories were perhaps a bit hazy, but it was small matter. He did not need to rely on memory to defeat Mortimer; he could rely on instinct. The sword felt like an extension of his right arm, as natural as if he had been born thus. Or as if he had been commissioned by the angel Gabriel to mete out punishment to Mortimer.

Adrenaline pumped through his veins. He felt powerful, when for too long he had been powerless. He felt in control, when for too long he had had no control. Raising the sword high, he laughed, then used the tip to beckon Mortimer forward.

Mortimer, shaking off his trance, attacked, looking angry as a jackal deprived of its prey. Their blades crossed, the steel scrabbled noisily as his sword slid down the length of Phillip's blade. Mortimer jumped back, then immediately attacked again, almost breaking through Phillip's guard. Barely in time, Phillip twisted to one side. They began to circle each other.

From the corner of his eye, Phillip caught a glimpse of Margaret standing in the shadows. Her hands were clasped together as if in prayer. Praying for him? Or Bernard?

Mortimer made a jab. Phillip parried, and feinted,

drawing Mortimer's sword to the left, before making a return to the left cheek, over the elbow.

Mortimer jumped back. Breathing heavily, he pressed his hand against his face. He stared down at the blood on his fingers for a long moment. When he looked up, his eyes were narrowed into vicious slits of hatred. He lunged.

Phillip ducked and turned. Mortimer's sword whistled through the empty air.

"Damn you, Barnett, damn you to hell." He made another thrust at Phillip.

"I prefer to save that particular fate for you, Mortimer." Phillip countered, nicking him on the shoulder. "Your grandfather awaits you, I'm sure."

"My grandfather?" Mortimer wiped the sweat from his eyes, his hand shaking almost imperceptibly.

"The first earl. The one who perjured himself to convict an innocent man." Phillip's sword teased Mortimer's.

"Phillip Eglinton, you mean? He got what he deserved. A Mortimer will always avenge any insult to his name and family."

"Then you will understand my desire to avenge Phillip since I am . . . related to him."

"You are related to Phillip?" Mortimer retreated a few steps, surprise flickering in his eyes, before he grinned evilly. "No wonder, then, that I've always hated you. It's in my blood. And how appropriate that I should be the one to dispatch you. 'Thee and thine will diminish and die.' "

Phillip lowered his sword, his gaze never leaving Mortimer's hate-contorted features. "What do you know of that curse?"

"Everything," Mortimer gloated. "Grandfather told me how he paid the Gypsy to curse Phillip and his descendants and how he contrived to get Phillip hanged. How we laughed over the court's gullibility!

Imagine believing a ghost would appear to name its killer!" Mortimer laughed loudly, but his humor did not erase his expression of cruelty and vindictiveness. "I suppose Letty told you the tale. You should have learned from it—my family is always very thorough in dealing with our enemies." He lunged forward suddenly, nicking Phillip in the shoulder.

Phillip parried too late. The cut was small, barely a pinprick, but to Phillip, the sudden pain was as intense as a fatal wound. For a moment, all sensation concentrated into that one small area. It felt as though his entire arm had been ripped open. As shock raced through him and black spots danced before his eyes, he hazily realized that the long years of sensory deprivation must have made him extremely sensitive to pain.

Cold blackness swept over him, bringing with it memories—memories of the long months of incarceration, of standing before the court listening to its verdict, of the ride in the cart to where the rope swayed in the breeze. Memories of the waiting, fear eating at his gut like vitriol.

Cold sweat poured down his face. The tip of his sword wavered. Through a blackish haze he saw Mortimer advancing. He tried to lift his blade, but his muscles seemed unresponsive. The haze thickened and darkened, sucking at him. Despair overwhelmed him. He had fought for so long, but he couldn't fight any longer. In another second it would be over. He had failed.

Suddenly, his sword snapped up, as if pulled by a string. Phillip stared at it in astonishment, the haze fading slightly. For an instant, he had the confused thought that the puppet had taken over the puppeteer. Without volition, his arms and legs began to move, blocking thrusts, retreating from Mortimer's attack. The motions felt awkward, sluggish, but familiar, as if they had been practiced frequently. *Circle of quarte . . . circle of tierce . . .*

Now Mortimer was on the defensive, unable to do anything but parry thrust after thrust. *Twice the counter of octave . . . twice the counter of octave and quarte . . .*

Blood dripped down Mortimer's cheek while more blood stained his shirt at the shoulder where Phillip's sword had pierced. His breathing was labored. *Bring the buckle of the left foot to the right heel . . . retire to the left foot. . . .*

Sweat gleaming on his brow, Mortimer made one more desperate lunge. The sound of ringing steel reverberated as Phillip struck a blow against the other man's blade, causing it to fly out of his foe's hand and fall to the ground with a soft thud. *Let your sword slide along your left thigh and come upon guard . . . throw your foil up and catch it under the guard and bring the buckle of the left foot to the right heel. . . .*

Feeling dazed, Phillip stared at Mortimer's fallen blade.

"Phillip!"

The blackness receded. Margaret's white face swam into view.

Margaret. Strength flowed back into him, dispelling the last vestiges of the frightening haze. That other consciousness faded, the awkwardness of his limbs disappeared. Phillip looked again at Mortimer's twisted features, and a fathomless rage filled him.

Dear God, how he hated this knave! He had spent over seventy-eight years of nothingness because of the spite and evil of a man like the one who now stood before him. At last, at long last, he had his chance for revenge.

"The world will be a better place once the stench of the Mortimers is gone from it."

The blood pounding in his veins, Phillip put the point of his sword to Mortimer's throat, and inhaled deeply. He had won. He only needed to apply the slightest pressure to cut the jugular and destroy his enemy. Sweat dripped down his brow, he could feel mud encrusting various parts of his body, his muscles were beginning to ache, and scrapes and bruises were announcing their presence, but the taste of victory was sweet in his mouth.

Preparing to drive the point of his sword home, Phillip unconsciously sought out Margaret, wanting to see her admiration, approval, awe.

Her face was filled with horror.

In the half-light, he did not look like Bernard. Margaret knew it was Bernard's body standing before her—but somehow it was hard to remember. By some trick of the light, he looked like Phillip. Or perhaps it was his expression—Bernard's eyes had never held the light of bloodlust.

His eyebrows drew together, his jaw clenched. Silently, she willed him not to kill.

"Don't kill me," Mortimer gasped. His throat moved convulsively under the sharp steel.

"Why shouldn't I?" The ruthless timbre of Phillip's voice sent a shiver down Margaret's spine. "Your family has been a blight to England for centuries."

"I'll do anything. I'll leave England. Go abroad. Never come back." Mortimer's breath came in quick choppy bursts.

"So you can prey upon other innocent people?"

"No, no. I swear I will never pick up a deck of cards again."

Phillip appeared to consider it for a moment. Even in the moonlight, Margaret could see the ugly gray hue of Mortimer's skin. The defeated man no longer looked evil or spiteful. He looked afraid. Surely Phillip would not kill him.

"How will you pay for your passage? You are penniless, as I recall."

"I . . . I . . ."

"Phillip, don't kill him." Margaret moved out of the shadows.

He raised a brow at her, the picture of cool control—except for the wildness in his eyes.

"How would we ever explain a dead body? Bernard would probably get arrested." Margaret forced her voice to sound calm and reasonable.

Phillip gave a harsh laugh. "How sensible you are, my sweet. But we can't simply let him go his merry way to practice his evil on others."

Mortimer watched them with an expression of slowly dawning terror. "I don't understand. Why does she call you—?"

Phillip stared appraisingly at him. "Haven't you guessed, Mortimer? Can't you guess who I am and why killing you would give me the utmost pleasure?"

Mortimer's face grew paler. "I don't believe it. You're lying."

Phillip laughed. Lifting his sword away from Mortimer's throat, he flexed the shining steel. "Don't you remember me from your nightmares? I certainly remember you. You thought I was dead, but surely you know the Eglintons always have the last laugh." And he started to chuckle, a low mocking sound that chilled Margaret's very blood.

It must have had the same effect on Mortimer, because terror carved deep lines into his face.

Phillip stopped laughing abruptly. "You're free to go, you scum, but remember this—if you ever so much as pick up a deck of cards, I will haunt your dreams, not just once a year, but every night for the rest of your miserable life. You will not be able to sleep, my laughter will keep you awake. You will slowly go insane. Do you understand?"

"Yes, yes. I swear I'll never cheat anyone."

"Good. Then there's only one more thing I want you to do." Phillip lowered his voice and whispered something Margaret couldn't hear.

Mortimer nodded. "Anything, anything."

"Remember, if you do not do exactly as I say, I will haunt you. Now go!"

Mortimer slithered away through the trees. When he was gone, Phillip turned toward Margaret.

Her heart almost stopped at the cold anger in his gaze.

"What was that all about?" he asked almost casually as he picked up his coat. He thrust his arms into it and draped the cravat around his neck.

"What?" she half whispered.

"That nauseating display of mercy."

Margaret stiffened. "There was nothing nauseating about it. Perhaps in the eighteenth century it was acceptable to go around killing people, but in the nineteenth, we are much more civilized."

"Like Mortimer?" he sneered.

"No, like Bernard," she retorted.

"Bernard!" Phillip practically spat the name. "Oh yes, he's civilized. So civilized he nearly got himself killed."

His sarcasm made her angry. "Very well," she snapped. "I thank you for saving Bernard." Turning on her heel, she stalked away.

She was halfway back to the house before he recovered his wits enough to follow.

"Where the hell are you going?" he snarled as he caught up to her.

Margaret didn't reply. She was shaking inside, the stress of the duel causing a roiling in her stomach. She kept walking until she reached the house. Inside, moonlight streamed through the windows and lit up the hall. She headed for the stairs.

He was right behind her. "Is this a game, Margaret? If so, I do not find it amusing."

Her hand on the balustrade, Margaret paused. "No game," she said finally, her voice shaking.

"Then what? What's the matter with you?"

"With me? What's the matter with you? You're behaving like a blood-crazed animal. You are angry because I deprived you of the pleasure of killing Mortimer."

"Forgive me if reality makes you nauseous. Wake up, Margaret. You got what you wanted. Your precious Bernard is safe."

"Barely. You certainly waited long enough before stepping in. I thought he would be killed."

"Ah, I see. You were worried about poor old Bernard."

"Of course I was, you buffoon!"

"You shouldn't have been. I waited until it was necessary for me to step in so that the risk of draining myself completely was small. It seemed reasonable to expect that Bernard would at least wear Mortimer out a bit. I suppose I should have guessed I would have to do the whole job myself," he finished sardonically.

Margaret ignored his sarcasm. "You should indeed. What if you had miscalculated? Bernard was almost skewered." She turned to go up the stairs.

Phillip put out the sword, blocking her way. "Would you have cared?"

Margaret drew back. She stared into his dark eyes. "Certainly I would have cared. What sort of a question is that? I am going to marry him."

"Ah, yes. How could I have forgotten?" Casually he leaned forward, sliding the sword past her as his arms came around to rest on the banister, trapping her. "But do you love him?"

Margaret shrank bank against the balustrade. She did not like the intense darkness of Phillip's face, the barely leashed emotion in his eyes. She managed to whisper, "Yes, of course I do."

With sudden violence, he threw the sword away. It crashed against the wall, then dropped to the floor, clattering against the flagstones. His hands seized her shoulders. "Don't lie to me, Margaret."

"I'm not! I do love him. I love him with all my h—"

His mouth stopped the rest of her words. His arms slid around her and held her tightly. Margaret struggled against him, hating him, hating herself.

She managed to pull her mouth away. "Stop that this instant, Phillip."

His lips traveled down her neck, causing the most delicious shivers to run down her spine; a glow ignited in the pit of her stomach and raced up to her breasts. His seeking mouth encountered the cloth of her dress and moved lower; her breasts swelled. He kissed the curves through the rough wool, and moved lower still to where her nipples had grown hard and aching. He bit them gently, causing her to cry out.

With her last ounce of willpower, Margaret tore herself away. She had to get away from him before she did something she would regret. Something that would change the whole course of her life. Bunching her skirt in her hands, her breath rasping in her throat, she ran up the stairs. They seemed endless, and somehow she could not catch her breath. Was he following? She could not hear him. She must hurry. But surely he would have caught her if he was pursuing her. Her steps slowed. Her legs felt leaden. She was barely halfway up the stairs. Something was compelling her to look around. Chest heaving, she paused and turned.

He was standing at the bottom of the stairs, his

face in the shadow. He was very still. When he spoke, his voice sounded distant, strange.

"Why do you run away, Margaret?"

Her heart began to pound with heavy painful beats. "I . . . this is wrong. . . ."

"Is it wrong for a man to make love to the woman he loves?"

Margaret's breath caught on a sob. "No! Don't say that!"

"Why, Margaret? It's true. And you love me."

"No!"

"Yes! Don't deny it. Don't, Margaret." She was not quite sure how it happened, but suddenly he was next to her, his hand tracing her cheek, his mouth dropping light kisses on her face. "Margaret, you love me. Say it. Say you love me. You know it's true."

Was it true? What was it about him that made her heart beat faster and made her glow inside? Why, ever since he'd come, did she feel as though she'd shrugged off a gray shroud hanging over her life and remembered what it was like truly to live?

His mouth closed once more on hers and he must have felt her surrender, for with a sound somewhere between a groan and a laugh, he lifted her in his arms and started up the stairs.

26

Laying her gently on the bed, he lit a single candle, then shrugged off his coat. Sitting on the edge of the bed, he pulled off his boots, slipped off her shoes, and tugged at her mittens. He lifted her hands, pressing a kiss into the palm of each one, before laying down beside her. His mouth covered hers, hot, seeking.

Margaret closed her eyes, inhaling the smell of sweet, rich tobacco. Sighing, her lips parted slightly. Immediately his tongue was in her mouth. Shocked, her eyes snapped open. He raised himself, his face dark and serious. Then it grew all blurry and his lips were against her ear, tracing the curves, and his warm breath tickled as he whispered to her.

"Margaret, please open your mouth. Don't be frightened. I won't hurt you. Please . . ."

Tender, persuasive, his voice lulled her momentary fear. His mouth pressed gently until her lips parted on a helpless sigh and his tongue slipped inside. It stroked her mouth in a strange rhythm, unfamiliar, and yet . . . her body seemed to recognize it and respond. Timidly, her tongue reached for his.

He groaned. With a single swift movement, he rolled off the bed, carrying her with him.

She stood before him, swaying a little, her body on fire, her thoughts confused. His hands were a trifle unsteady as he put them on her shoulders and turned her around, so that her back was to him. Then his hands were at her dress, undoing the long line of buttons. She could feel the warmth of his breath on her neck and hear the muttered curse as his fingers fumbled. When he was a quarter of the way through, his patience ran out. He pulled the gown off her shoulders, and halfway down her arms, effectively trapping them against her sides. She had not put her corset on, and his hands came around and reached inside her chemise. He covered her breasts with his hands and she heard him sigh deeply as he pulled her back against him.

She stiffened for a moment with shock and embarrassment. But she had repressed her emotions for so long, stifled her desires so rigidly, that now, once loosed, they surged through her in an unstoppable flood. She wanted to explore as many of these new sensations as she possibly could before she bottled everything up inside her again.

The hardness of his stomach and thighs pressed against her through the material of her dress. How strange and alien he felt, yet somehow, so right. His lips traveled across her neck, seeking out every sensitive spot, and his fingers on her breasts began a slow caress, circling closer, ever closer. . . .

Her knees buckled when he touched the taut nipples. His hands tightened for a moment, then he moved to a chair and sat down, pulling her onto his lap. He undid the ribbon on her chemise, tugged the material aside, and lowered his lips to her already aching breasts.

"Margaret, Margaret," he whispered. "Do you know how the memory of your breasts has tormented me? How I've longed to do this . . . and this . . . and this?"

His lips closed over a nipple, suckling gently at first, then more fiercely, driving her beyond caution, beyond sanity. She arched her back, wanting him to get closer, wanting to entwine her fingers in his hair and hold him there so the slow pulsing spreading throughout her body would never stop. . . .

"Phillip. Phillip!" She shifted in his lap, desperate to get his attention.

"Yes, my sweet love?" His voice was indistinct, almost unintelligible. "God, you are so beautiful. Don't be embarrassed, sweeting, don't."

"I . . . I'm not. I just . . . that is, I can't move my arms."

He lifted his head from her breast and stared at her. His eyes lit with laughter and he lifted her up from his lap. "How inconsiderate of me. Impatience seems to have addled my brain. Forgive me, my sweet, and allow me to assist you." He stood her by the bed and stripped off the dress. The chemise followed. He looked down at her lace-edged drawers and his eyes widened. "Margaret, that is the most indecent garment I've ever seen."

"Indecent?" She looked down at her demure pantalets. "What do you mean? There's nothing the least bit indecent about them."

Phillip could not seem to tear his eyes away. "You mean all women wear these?"

"Of course!"

"Ah. In my day, the ladies wore nothing."

"Nothing? That's much more indecent!"

"No." His eyes inspected the way the fine lawn revealed even as it concealed the flare of her hips, the hint of a dark shadow that could barely be seen

through the material at the juncture of her thighs.
"No," he murmured huskily. "More convenient, but
definitely not more indecent." He knelt before her.
"You weren't wearing these before."

Remembering the time she had taken off her nightgown, she blushed. "I don't usually wear them to bed,"
she murmured as he slowly pulled the pantalets down,
and stared at what he uncovered. His breathing grew
labored. Her blush deepened. Quickly he stripped off
his shirt, then fumbled with the flap of his breeches.

"How the devil? . . . Ah, I see." Unbuttoning the
breeches, he shucked them off.

Her heart beat in slow, heavy thumps as she stared
at the hard, angular planes of his body, ridged with
muscles, so different from her own soft curves. The
pounding of her heart became almost painful when
his hands undid the four small buttons of his drawers
to reveal . . .

Her eyes widened, and she covered her mouth with
her hand. She stared at that part of him that stood
out proudly, lusty, potent, threatening.

"Margaret—"

Her eyes flew to his face. His eyes were so dark,
they appeared black. There was a tight, almost pained
look to the line of his mouth.

Dear heaven, what was she doing? Had she disgusted him with her brazen stare? Hastily, she averted
her eyes. "I'm sorry," she whispered.

He laughed huskily. "Don't be, sweeting. It's only . . .
oh, the devil, I'll explain to you later. Later, you can
look all you like when I'm not so ready."

She was frowning, trying to make sense of this
strange statement, when he pushed her gently against
the edge of the bed and she fell back, her knees splaying wide. Blushing furiously, she sat up, straightening
her spine, pulled her knees tightly together and folded
her hands in her lap.

Phillip paused. "Who taught you to sit like that?" His voice was choked with laughter.

"Er, my mother." She suddenly realized how ridiculous her pose must look considering that she was completely naked except for a pair of silk stockings. She blushed again, feeling foolish and inexperienced.

"Phillip . . . I don't think . . ." Inhibition struggled to gain control over the passion he had unleashed. She groped for the sheet, but he gently caught her hand, raising it to his lips.

"Margaret, Margaret. I'm sorry, I didn't mean to laugh. It's just that I'm nervous, too."

"You?" She relaxed a little, barely noticing his fingers stroking the tops of her thighs soothingly as she considered this novel idea.

"Don't look so surprised. Naturally, I'm nervous." He rolled down one of her stockings. "It's been over seventy-eight years since I've done this. What if I've forgotten how?" He started on the other stocking, kissing every inch of flesh he exposed.

Suspiciously, she looked down at his bent head. "Phillip . . ."

He looked up and grinned wickedly, before returning his attention to her calf.

"Phillip . . ."

"Ssh." His lips on her ankle made her tremble. Electric fire ran up her legs and every muscle in her body began to melt. He looked up again, but now all humor was gone from his face. Staring into her dazed eyes, his voice husky, he said, "Margaret, please don't tell me to stop. Forget everything your mother told you. Don't think. Don't think at all. Just feel."

Just feel? If she felt any more, she would surely explode.

His hands were insinuating themselves between her knees. She resisted, even though her will to do so was barely an absurd flicker. He gently pushed her back down against the bed again, his lips going to her breasts once more, his fingers teasing the sensitive skin of her hips and upper thighs until she finally relaxed and let him have his way.

His fingers found her. He began to stroke her soft flesh. Margaret felt swollen, pulsing, as if something was about to happen. She gasped a little, surprised by this new sensation, but it felt so good, so right, she knew she didn't want it to stop.

"I love you, Margaret." He moved over her, his knee working to nudge her legs apart. His lips caressed her neck. "I've loved you since you were sixteen and told my father he could use the services of a good gelder."

Margaret stiffened. She had told *Bernard*'s father that. "Who . . . who are you?" she whispered, looking into dark gray eyes—Phillip's eyes . . . no, Bernard's eyes. . . .

His gaze flickered, then he kissed her, and went on kissing her until she forgot her question, forgot everything except the way he made her feel.

27

Her knees parted and he slid into her, smooth, hot, huge.

"Dear God, Margaret." His voice sounded strained. "You feel so good, so perfect." He prodded against her maidenhead and she felt a small bit of pain and then he was so deep inside her she gasped. He began moving in long strokes and all the wild sensations in her concentrated down to that point where his body reached inside to touch her. Then everything really did explode and she could feel him erupting inside her as she cried out against his mouth.

He should have answered her, he thought as the mad thumping of his heart slowed to a more regular pace. He should have stopped. But he hadn't. After waiting so long, he hadn't wanted to wait any more. He had wanted her so badly, he was willing to accept her confusion and even the knowledge that perhaps she wasn't completely certain who he was. Hell, *he* wasn't certain who he was.

He only knew he loved her. He had always loved

her, but tonight it was different. His love for her had taken on an intensity he had never felt before, never imagined. He loved her not only with his heart and mind, but with his body and all his senses as well.

Raising his weight onto his arms, he gazed down at her face. Her eyelashes were fanned against her cheeks, but a smile still lingered on her sweet lips.

"Margaret," he sighed, lowering his mouth to hers.

Margaret sighed, too. Her name sounded like a benediction, she thought hazily, aware that their bodies still joined. His body had a musky smell, sharp, but surprisingly sweet. Earthy, but with the barest hint of tobacco.

His lips moved to her ear, and dreamy eyed, she gazed up at the underside of the pagoda canopy. The cloud with the lovers was hidden in the shadows, but she could see the sleeping Chinese man. Now she knew why he was smiling.

"Did I hurt you?" he whispered, his breath tickling her ear.

"No, not really." She felt languid, replete, in spite of the slight ache between her thighs. She ought to be embarrassed, but she wasn't. She ought to be asking some questions, only right now she didn't want to spoil the delicious languor that was stealing over her. Besides, she already knew the answer. Even though her brain couldn't quite understand it, in her heart, everything was perfectly clear.

"You are very accomplished at this," she murmured.

His mouth paused in its exploration of the sensitive skin behind her ear. When he spoke, she heard a thread of humor in his voice. "I'm glad you think so. It seems I've been dreaming of this forever. Dreaming of making love to you in a hundred different ways."

"A hundred different ways?" she mumbled, half-asleep. "That's not possible, is it?" Sleepily, she lifted her lashes to find him staring down at her, a dark gleam in his eyes.

Her drowsiness faded. Why was he looking at her like that? Like a hawk espying some poor unsuspecting little field mouse? When he moved, she tensed a little, but he only pulled himself out of her and, rising from the bed, walked over to the washbasin. He came back with a wet cloth.

"Margaret," he said, smoothing away the perspiration from her neck and brow, "you have brought me such joy."

The cool cloth felt amazingly good on her hot skin. "I have?" she asked uncertainly.

"Yes, ever since I met you." He brought the cloth to her breasts, paying particular attention to the nipples. Her heart began to beat faster as he rubbed the cloth back and forth.

The gentle abrasion caused her breasts to tingle. "Since . . . since you met me?"

"You must know how I feel about you." His lips replaced the cloth and Margaret moaned.

She wished he would stop talking. She couldn't concentrate.

Abruptly, he tore his mouth away, leaving her aching. He moved the cloth to her thighs, wiping away the traces of their lovemaking. She stiffened, embarrassed to have him performing such an intimate task, but he was so gentle, after a moment, she relaxed again.

Finished, he rinsed out the cloth and handed it to her, his eyes black. "Your turn, Margaret," he whispered.

He sat on the edge of the bed, his back to her. Rising to her knees behind him, she hesitantly rubbed his back. His skin felt smooth, his muscles taut. She began to enjoy her task, seeking out each rib, his shoulder blades, his neck. She leaned forward, reaching over his shoulder to lave his chest, her breasts pressing against his back. He seemed to stop breathing.

She leaned forward farther, then back down, forward and back. She forgot she was supposed to be washing him, all her concentration focused on the pleasurable friction at her breast.

He bore it for as long as he could before he turned and pinned her back against the bed. "You know you are driving me insane." It wasn't a question and Margaret didn't answer. She pulled his head down to her breast, wanting to feel again the ecstasy of him.

His mouth barely brushed her breast. She tried not to feel disappointed when his lips did not linger there before moving lower. They moved down her side, then across her stomach and hip and lower still. . . .

Margaret stiffened when she realized his intention. "No! Oh, no, please, you can't—"

His mouth had almost reached its goal. He paused, his lips on the inside of her thigh. Waves of shock coursed through her. His hand reached up to caress her breast, quieting her, building her passion to an overwhelming need, leaving her without protection against the unthinkable thing that he surely would not do. . . .

His mouth closed over her and her body bucked. She heard him laugh softly and he brought both hands to her legs, holding them apart as he delved into her, until she was a mindless, writhing creature.

Soft cries broke from her throat as she climaxed. Satisfaction glinting in his eyes, he moved over her, and into her, quickly finding his own release, before collapsing on top of her.

During the course of the night, he took her again and again. She no longer thought of anything but him. He was the focus of her entire universe. She forgot all shame, all inhibition as the night wore on, letting him do what he would to her, doing things to him that she had never imagined. It seemed as though she, like he, was cocooned in a place between time, where nothing mattered, nothing existed, except the two of them.

28

A hand caressed her breast, filling her with languid warmth. It slipped down between her thighs, seeking out the wetness that immediately appeared there.

Margaret moaned.

The hand stilled. She wriggled a little and the hand withdrew with appalling suddenness.

"Dear heaven above!"

The unnaturally high voice barely penetrated the heavy fog in her brain. She opened one eye barely enough for the sunlight to pierce her throbbing head. Groaning, she shut her eye and tried to go back to sleep.

"Margaret. Good God, what has happened?"

Bernard? Her eyes snapping open, she sat straight up. Her gaze flew to Bernard.

He was staring at her bare breasts. Dear Lord, she had forgotten she was totally naked. With shaking hands, she pulled the sheet up, lowering her gaze from his face. But as she did so, her attention was caught by his muscular chest and all she could think was that she never would have believed Bernard could look like *that*.

"Miss Westbourne!" Now he pulled the sheet up to cover himself, blushing fiercely.

Margaret blushed, too. She blushed so hard her face felt hot and she was sure there wasn't any blood left in any other part of her body. She began to babble.

"I didn't mean to . . . I'm so sorry . . . what? . . . "

He was equally incoherent. "Please don't . . . I can't imagine . . . forgive me!" He yanked at the sheet, tearing it from her grasp, and wrapped it around himself, trying not to reveal any more of his anatomy. He kept his eyes averted from her, so perhaps he didn't realize he had divested her of her only cover, she thought a trifle hysterically. Frantically, she searched for something to replace the sheet, but the blankets had been kicked off the bed. In desperation, she grabbed the pillow and held it in front of herself.

Bernard, paying no attention to her plight, grabbed up his clothes, mumbled something, made an awkward bow, and fled, the sheet flapping.

A deathly silence settled over the room as Margaret sat frozen, staring after Bernard, her brain struggling to comprehend. She had thought . . .

What *had* she thought?

She didn't know. She only knew she'd never felt such disappointment in her entire life. Last night everything had seemed so wonderful, so right. Now everything was so confused, so wrong, and only one thing was clear.

She was the most depraved, fickle, *wanton* woman that ever lived.

Rolling over on her stomach, she covered her head with the pillow. She had given up her virtue outside of wedlock. And even worse, dear heaven, she hadn't even known who was making love to her!

She squeezed the pillow more tightly over her head. It was all Phillip's fault. She had been content before he came, filling her head with impossible dreams, making her aware of needs and wants she hadn't even known existed. Needs and wants that had translated into the most incredible pleasure she'd ever known. . . .

"No, no, no!" she groaned. It couldn't be, it couldn't have happened. It must have been a dream. In the morning light, last night's wild passion seemed too incredible, too intense to be possibly real. Real people didn't do things like that. Did they?

Hazy memories filled her brain. Images of writhing bodies; the sounds of moaning and panting; rough and smooth textures of skin and hair; the smell of . . .

Margaret stuck her nose out from under the pillow, sniffing. She groaned. It was there. The redolent smell of sin.

She cringed. Sin was hardly a strong enough word. Most young ladies committed sins like allowing a beau to steal a kiss. Most young ladies would never allow a man to do such . . . such *things*.

She trembled all over. She was ruined.

She would never be accepted in society. If they knew about her wild behavior . . . the things she had let Bernard—Phillip?—do to her . . . the things she had done to him . . . if they knew . . .

They must not know. No one must know. She had to make sure no one ever found out. Margaret threw the pillow away and jumped out of bed, frantically looking around.

The room screamed of wantonness. It reeked of lust. It revealed her guilt all too plainly. She must do something quickly, before the servants appeared.

She yanked her chemise and dress over her head, covering her nakedness, hiding her sinfulness. Fingers fumbling with the catch, she threw open the window, making fanning motions with her hands in a futile attempt to air out the room. She tore the bottom sheet off the bed, crumpled it up and stuffed it in the wardrobe. She stood on a chair to recover a stocking from the pagoda canopy, and got down on her hands and knees to retrieve her pantalets from under the escritoire.

As she clutched the pantalets, a glint of gold caught her eye. She reached for the object, her fingers closing over the cool, hard metal. Bernard's watch. She clutched it, panic rising in her. Dear God, she must get it back to him; otherwise someone might think that she and him . . . him and her . . . he and she . . .

Margaret tensed. She couldn't move or breathe or focus. Her ears rang. Only her sense of smell seemed to be functioning properly and very clearly she could smell a faint odor of tobacco.

"Margaret," a low voice whispered.

The paralysis vanished. Leaping to her feet, she screeched, "You! Look what you have done to me!"

Obediently, Phillip inspected her rumpled form, noting her disheveled hair, unbuttoned dress, and bare feet. His lips twitched as he saw she was clutching those shocking pantaletts in one hand and a watch in the other. She looked as though she had spent the night being passionately loved, he thought with satisfaction tempered by frustration—frustration because once again his faulty memory was playing tricks on him. Try as he might, he could not quite recall what had happened last night.

His memories were mostly of something he had never experienced before—a love that transcended the physical, that was so deep and true it made him ache with longing.

He did remember those pantalets, though. "No need to thank me," he drawled.

"Thank you! Why you . . . you . . ." Sinking down on the edge of the bed, she buried her face in the pantalets and burst into noisy tears.

"Margaret!" What was the matter with her? Surely she did not regret what had happened last night? Kneeling down in front of her, he tried to see her face. "Here, now, I'm sorry. I didn't mean to distress you. Please, Margaret, more than anything I wish I could make you happy. I love you, Margaret—"

She sobbed louder. "Love! How can you say you love me when you have ruined my chance for marriage?"

Phillip stiffened. Rising slowly to his feet, he stared down at her. An unnamed emotion, raw and ugly, ripped through him. "Is that what this is about? Are you afraid old Bernie will break your betrothal?"

She looked up at that, a militant sparkle replacing the tears. "Yes, I'm afraid! Ladies don't sleep with other men when they're engaged to someone else."

"You woke up with Bernard. If the simpleton has any sense, he will make sure you do so a thousand times more."

"He won't see it like that. Ladies aren't supposed to sleep with their fiancés either. He will probably break off the engagement."

"If he does, he is the worst kind of hypocrite," Phillip bit out. "It was as much him as me."

"How dare you!" She jumped up, arms folded across her chest. "Bernard would never do anything so . . . dishonorable!"

"You think not?" He turned away slightly. "Your Bernard has more to him than I ever guessed," he muttered.

"Why, you—"

Impatiently, he interrupted her. "Where is the dishonor? In loving you? In giving you pleasure?"

He heard her breath catch. Abruptly she turned away, the unbuttoned dress gaping to reveal a long vee of creamy white skin. Incredibly soft, smooth skin. He had a fleeting memory of how it had felt, like a butterfly's wing, and how it had tasted, like sweet honey. He stepped forward, his gaze traveling the beckoning expanse. On her back, near her neck, a small red mark was visible. Where he had kissed her, he was almost certain.

"I . . . That wasn't pleasure," Margaret lied through her teeth.

He had lost the thread of their argument. Tearing his gaze away from her back, it took a moment for her words to make sense, and when they did, anger surged through him. "What? Do you try to deny what you felt, Margaret?" He took another step forward. "The way you have spent your whole life denying what you are? You are a creature of passion, a sensual woman longing for escape from your drab existence."

"That's not true!" She whirled around, only to look startled to find him so close. She took a step back.

He followed.

He walked forward until her back was against a wall, but the mulish expression on her face didn't change. She turned her head aside, her mouth a stubborn line.

"You know it is true." He wanted to bury his hands in her soft, thick hair and force her to look at him, but he couldn't. Leaning forward until his mouth was by her ear, he whispered, "Ah, Margaret. We proved it is true."

Obstinately, she shook her head. He wanted to grab her into his arms, and kiss her sweet lips until she admitted it. But he couldn't.

Only Bernard could.

Jealousy and anger roiled through him. "You are

going to marry dull old Bernard and be bored out of your skull for the rest of your life. And for what? For security. Safety. So that you'll never have to risk anything, never have to discover what you really are. Do you know what your problem is, Margaret? You're afraid to live."

Her chin snapped up, her eyes a blaze of defiance, and words spilled out of her. "What of you? Isn't it about time you acknowledged what *your* problem is? I think Madame Razinski was right—this curse is working only because you believe it. Because you *want* to believe it." Her breathing made little choppy noises. "Because you're afraid to die."

The words echoed through the room. He tried to push them away, but they bore into him, drilling down to the very core of his brain. Brother Clement's voice rang in his head, *You'll roast in hell, You'll roast in hell.*

The black void, hovering in the corner, pulsed, expanded. It swept over him, almost overwhelming him, and he felt himself fading. He fought against it, the cold sapping his will, sapping his strength. He struggled to focus on Margaret's face.

"Phillip—" Her voice was distant, fuzzy. "Phillip!"

The blackness receded, leaving him weak as an infant, shaking like an old man. His vision cleared and Margaret's frightened face swam before his eyes.

"Phillip?"

Her soft voice broke the control he had maintained for over seventy-eight years. Feelings he had denied for most of his life exploded in a maelstrom of words.

"Dammit, yes. Yes, I'm afraid," he raged. For years he had held the fear at bay, years of nothingness, emptiness, loneliness. Now she had loosed it, and it spilled out in an uncontrollable flood of fury. "Is that what you want to hear? Is it?" he shouted. He leaned closer to her, and she pressed her head back against the wall, her face white and shocked.

He leaned closer, his face barely an inch from hers, staring into her wide, fearful eyes. Her chest rose and fell and he should have been able to feel her breath, but he couldn't.

Because he was dead.

Thrusting himself away from her, he paced around the room. "You don't know what it's like, having total darkness hovering, sucking at you. If I let go, I may never know anything again. It may be hell. It probably is hell, but that doesn't mean I can't fight. For seventy-eight years I've been fighting it and damned if I will let it win." He stopped in front of her again and glared down into her face.

Her eyes were huge pools of tears. "Phillip, you shouldn't . . . shouldn't be frightened. I wish I could make you believe that. I wish you could see that if you believe, you have nothing to fear."

She had a beautiful voice. It could almost make him forget his fear, make him believe anything. The rage in him waned, leaving him tired and drained. Black spots began to dance before his eyes. "Perhaps," he said wearily. "But dammit, I wasn't ready to die. There were still things for me to do. I should have done them when I had the opportunity, but I always thought there was time—time for the truly important things, time to have children, time to fall in love. . . ."

"Oh, Phillip—"

The black spots were growing bigger. Realizing what they meant, for an instant he felt a wave of panic. But the panic quickly faded, leaving a deep grief, a sorrow for all the things that might have been. He shook his head, trying to clear his vision before he turned and looked at her. "Listen to me, Margaret, I haven't much time."

"What . . . what do you mean?"

"I think you know, sweeting. Don't look so tragic. We knew my time here was limited. I can only thank God for allowing me this precious few weeks."

"Please don't—"

"Perhaps that was the real reason I came back. To fall in love with you." Her image was growing dim, her beautiful face blurring with her hair and dress.

"Phillip—"

"The time has been short, but incredibly sweet. I'm glad I came back. Otherwise I would never have known you. Never have touched you, loved you."

He could barely hear her voice, raw with aching sorrow, whispering, saying . . . what?

"Phillip, I . . . I—"

Then there was a knock at the door.

29

Margaret barely heard the knock. Her whole attention was centered on Phillip. She wished she could take back the dreadful thing she had said to him. He was fading quickly—she knew that in a few more minutes he would be gone forever.

Dear heaven, he did not have much time, and she was afraid she was going to cry.

"Margaret, may I speak to you?"

She turned to see Aunt Letty peering uncertainly around the door, a piece of paper in one hand, her jar in the other.

"I'm sorry to interrupt, dear, but—oh my, are you getting dressed?" Aunt Letty eyed the pantalets Margaret was clutching. "I *am* sorry."

"Oh," Margaret stared blankly at the pantalets before thrusting them behind her back. "No, I was just sewing on a bit of loose lace." She looked back at Phillip and her heart wrenched. He was barely visible.

"I see. Well, Bernard asked me to give you this." She held out the folded piece of paper. Margaret stared at it. She knew what it was, of course. Clutching the pantalets, she reluctantly held out her other hand, forgetting she also still held the watch.

It slipped from her loosened grasp, falling with a thud to the floor.

"Why, that's Bernard's watch," Aunt Letty said, clasping the jar to her breast.

Sunlight reflected off the watch, highlighting the ornate letter *P* scrolled on the case.

A *P*? Why would Bernard's watch have? . . .

Margaret froze, a horrible fear rising in her.

Her gaze flew to Phillip. He was also staring at the watch, but as if he felt her gaze, he looked up. His face was expressionless.

Dear heaven. Was the watch the token?

"Oh, dear, does Phillip want it back?"

Margaret's gaze swung to Aunt Letty. "Phillip?"

"Why, yes. He is here, isn't he? I can always sense when he is. He understands, doesn't he, why Bernard has his watch?"

"Yes, I believe I do." His voice was distant. "It has taken me a while to figure it all out—I should have realized when I had the watch at Mortimer's card game—but yes, I do understand."

She had forgotten. Phillip had had the watch. It could not be the token, or he would already be gone.

"Margaret?" Aunt Letty said.

"Phillip says he understands." But she didn't. What was the significance of the watch? Did it represent the wrong that Lord Robeson's family had done Phillip's?

"Oh, good. Here's your note, then. And one more thing—"

Margaret clutched the note in her fingers. Had Phillip been right?

"Would you give this to Phillip?" The old woman held out her jar.

Margaret draped her pantalets over one arm so she

could grasp the smooth glass with both hands. "Give Phillip your jar?" If he had taken his revenge when he had the chance, would he now not be fading away into nothingness?

"Tell him I've kept his hand all nice and safe, but he must take it back now."

"His hand? What do you mean, Aunt Letty?" What did it all mean? Or did it all mean nothing?

"His hand." Aunt Letty nodded at the glass container. "The witch paid the hangman to cut it off. But when the crowd dragged her away, I took it."

Margaret almost dropped the jar. She stared at the old woman in disbelief. "You have Phillip's *hand* in here?"

Aunt Letty nodded, smiling as if it were the most ordinary thing in the world to be carrying around a severed hand. Margaret stared at the innocent-looking object in the jar before quickly averting her gaze. Nausea rose in her throat. She knew Aunt Letty was eccentric, but this—this was positively gruesome. She swallowed a little convulsively, and looked over at Phillip. He was very faint, but she could still see his hands—both of them.

"But why . . . I mean, Aunt Letty, are you sure it's Phillip's?"

"Oh, yes, I'm sure," the old woman replied. "I had to take it or someone else might have gotten it."

"What an interesting enigma," Phillip observed, sounding for a moment like his old self. "Do you suppose ghosts are reunited with their missing body parts? Or do you think my ghost is reflective of how I looked at the moment of death, before my hand was cut off?"

Margaret shuddered. How could he sound so casual about it? Personally, she would not be thrilled to discover that parts of her body had been hacked off and stuck in a jar.

Aunt Letty reached over to pat the glass lightly, smiling reminiscently. "I preserved it myself so I would have something to remember him by. It's not at all difficult, you know. You just take the hand and wrap it in a piece of shroud drawn tight to squeeze out all the blood. Then you put it in an earthenware jar with saltpeter and finely ground dried long peppers. After two weeks, you dry it in the sun until it's nicely parched. That's all! I must tell you, it's been a source of great comfort to me."

Somewhere in the middle of Aunt Letty's speech on hand preservation, Margaret realized the truth. "Aunt Letty, the hand, it's—"

"It's the token. I'm certain of it." The old woman beamed proudly. "I figured it out all by myself. If I give it back, the curse will be broken."

Margaret gripped the jar. She looked at Phillip. He was so faint, he was almost invisible, but she could see him watching her. He said nothing, only looked at her.

She stared back. This was it. They both knew it.

Margaret tore her gaze away and looked at Aunt Letty. "Aunt Letty, will you leave—please?"

"Of course, dear." Margaret watched the old woman walk out of the room. The door closed gently behind her.

With a deep breath, Margaret faced Phillip again.

"So," he said. "It must be the curse after all, keeping me here."

"Yes, it must be." It was hard to get the words out. Her fingers tightened on the jar. She ought to give it to him immediately, but her limbs refused to obey as memories of the last few weeks tumbled through her brain.

She remembered that first night, when he had stood over her, demanding, "Who the hell are you?" She remembered his wicked grin as he told her that clothes were meaningless to a ghost, and the sympathy in his eyes when she told him about being shunned. She remembered the dark intensity of his voice as he asked her, "Is it wrong for a man to make love to the woman he loves?"

She would miss him—dear heaven, how she would miss him. She would miss the glint in his eyes, the smell of tobacco, his husky voice; she would even miss the swearing and teasing. She would miss his dark sensuality. . . .

Her throat aching, she took a step forward, gripping the jar more tightly.

Phillip stepped forward, too, so that only a few scant inches parted them. Only a few inches that might as well be a thousand miles, he thought bitterly. It wasn't fair. How could God play such a trick on him?

He loved her. He loved her more than he had thought it possible to love anyone. He loved everything about her, the sweet tartness of her, the subtle beauty, the sensual innocence. He loved her and he had to leave her.

Margaret knew he only had a minute or two left and she couldn't bear it. She felt as though her heart were being torn in half. How could he leave her? She wanted to be with him forever and ever and . . .

"Take me with you."

For a moment, the light around him blazed, bringing him into sharp focus. Then it dimmed, and he was fainter than before. His voice was gentle. "No, Margaret. You know I cannot."

"Why?" The lump in her throat was so big, the words hurt to speak. "There's nothing for me here."

He didn't answer for a moment. "What of Bernard?"

"Bernard? He will never forgive me for last night."

He shook his head, looking at her with sad, dark eyes. "That's not true. You know it as well as I. Look at him with your heart, Margaret."

"I don't know what you mean." Her eyes stung. "I just know I can't let you go. I don't want you to go."

"Dearest heart, I must." He faded to a soft glow.

Tears began to roll down her cheeks. She couldn't see him anymore and a great sob rose in her throat. But she could still hear his voice, low and intense, filled with anguish and despair.

"Please don't cry. Don't torture me anymore, I can't bear it. I must go. Please smile for me Margaret, so I will remember you smiling, not crying. Please, Margaret."

She couldn't. How could he ask her? It was impossible.

But, of course, she did. She smiled, even though tears were running down her face and she could hardly breathe for the pain in her chest. She smiled for him. Because she would do anything for him.

"Thank you, Margaret. I will remember you forever. Now give me the jar. Quickly."

Her fingers wrapped tightly around the glass jar. With every last bit of her strength, she lifted the jar toward him. A sliver of light reached out and enveloped the glass.

"I love you," she whispered.

The light brightened.

"And I love you." His voice rang in her ears. "Dear God, how I love you. Beyond life and death I love you. Thank you, Margaret," she heard him whisper. "I can face death now."

Immediately, a black coldness rushed into the room, washing over the furniture and Margaret, absorbing every bit of light, flowing toward the jar. It kept flowing into the glass container until it concentrated into one small black sphere, which pulsed like a disemboweled heart.

Her own heart beat in time to the black sphere. When it quickened, so did hers. It pulsed faster and faster and she felt the sorrow and the fear and the coldness.

The coldness. How could he bear it? It was like nothing she had ever felt; it went beyond mere coldness of her skin. This coldness was inside of her, part of her, as if the sun and the moon and the stars had been extinguished, as if the whole world were weeping with a grief so deep and so painful, it was like a silent scream that went on and on and on, as if nothing would ever be right again.

Just when she thought she could bear it no longer, the black sphere exploded in a brilliant flash of light. The glow expanded until it filled the room with gold and yellow and amber hues, the colors so beautiful Margaret's breath caught in her throat. Warmth and happiness and love washed over her, driving away the consuming fear. The glow brightened once more before contracting into a small, blindingly intense ball of light. Then in another flash, it streaked out through the window, and up into the sky, leaving behind a trail of brilliant, fiery sparks.

30

Margaret watched the sparks drift down until they vanished and the last trace of Phillip was gone. Numbly, she turned from the window, her chest aching. She wanted to cry, but she didn't. She couldn't. Phillip was finally at peace. Remembering the light, she was certain wherever he had gone, it was a good place. She was glad for that, at least.

She realized she was still holding her pantalets—the ones he had called indecent even while he was patently admiring them. She smiled a little, even though her chest was growing tighter.

Aunt Letty came in and peered around. Noticing the jar, the old woman leaned over to pick it up. It was empty.

"Oh, my," she said. A tear slid down her wrinkled cheek. "How I will miss him." Cradling the jar, she wandered out again.

The ache in Margaret's chest expanded up to her throat.

Yvette brought in a tray of food, her eyebrows arching as she glanced around the disheveled room.

Heaven only knew what she was thinking, but Margaret was beyond caring. In fact, she didn't care what anyone thought. She tried to remember why it had been important to her, but she couldn't. The years she had spent trying to conform suddenly seemed wasted. She had not accomplished anything by her efforts, only an arranged marriage with a man who didn't love her.

Bernard.

Remembering his shock and embarrassment this morning, her eyes began to sting again. How he must despise her. And in spite of her newfound disregard for society's opinion, she discovered she did care what he thought. She always had. It hadn't been the loss of society's regard that hurt so much—it had been the loss of Bernard's.

Last night, in his arms, she thought she had found everything she ever wanted, everything she ever dreamed. Only it hadn't been Bernard, it had been Phillip. Now Phillip was gone, and Bernard would probably never speak to her again. . . .

She straightened, remembering the note Aunt Letty had given her. Frantically, she looked around until she espied the small slip of paper on the floor. She didn't remember dropping it, but she must have done so when Aunt Letty gave her the jar. She opened the note.

Dear Margaret—
   After what occurred last night, I realize this situation can no longer continue as it is. You must make a decision.
                   —Bernard.

Margaret sank onto the bed, the note fluttering to the floor.

She hadn't thought it was possible for her to be any more miserable, but it was. Bernard was such a gentleman. Of course, he would never break the engagement.

Margaret began to cry. She cried with deep aching sobs that tore at her chest. Burying her face in the pantalets, she cried until they were soaked.

How had everything gone so wrong? She didn't understand. She didn't understand at all.

She cried until her eyes and nose were red. She cried until her head and chest ached from her sobs. She cried until her tears were all spent and then she cried some more. She cried until only numb acceptance was left.

She knew what she must do.

She must release Bernard. Even if last night had never happened, she knew she had been wrong to accept his proposal in the first place. He had offered from a sense of duty; she had agreed, hoping for social acceptance. If she had learned anything, she had learned that those were not good reasons for marriage.

Exhausted, she forced herself to rise from the bed. Slowly, she straightened her hair and clothes and washed her hands and face, taking her time until she was sure she had herself well under control.

Bernard's watch was on her dressing table. She picked it up and stared at it for a moment, then traced the *P* on the case. She would release him, and then she would . . . do what? Return home? The idea was not appealing, but she knew she must. Once there, she could start rebuilding her life.

But first, she must break her engagement.

With a heavy heart, she gripped the watch and started down the stairs. She would tell Bernard she couldn't marry him, and give him his watch. Or perhaps, she would give him the watch first, then tell him she couldn't marry him. Yes, that was what she would do.

In the entry hall, Cecilia was speaking to Gibbons.

" . . . on Saturday, so we will need the carriage then, and train tickets for London, and—oh, good morning, Margaret." Dismissing Gibbons with a nod, Cecilia smiled at her, but it was a wobbly effort.

Alarmed, Margaret placed a hand on her arm. "Cecilia, what is it? Has something happened?"

Cecilia nodded. "Geoffrey has accepted the post in London."

"Why, that's wonderful!" Margaret said. Then seeing Cecilia's strained face, she added uncertainly, "Isn't it?"

"I hope so." Cecilia's smile faltered. "I had a long talk with Bernard. He made me realize I've been a bit overprotective of Geoffrey. But you can't imagine what it's like to have someone you love almost die." With a visible effort, she pinned the smile to her lips again. "Geoffrey is over the moon. I don't remember seeing him so happy, not since the accident." Looking past Margaret, she said, "See what I mean?"

Margaret turned and saw Geoffrey entering the house, Jeremy at his side. To her shock, both of them were smiling.

"Mama! Mama! Papa said he will take me to Wynch Bridge, if you say I may go."

"Yes, you may, dear, but you'd better get a warmer coat. It will be cool at the falls."

"Hurrah!" With a shout, Jeremy ran away, jumping and leaping up the stairs. Margaret stared after him.

"My goodness," she said faintly. "He's . . . changed."

Geoffrey grinned. Actually grinned. "He does seem more like his old self." His face grew more serious. "Bernard told me what Jeremy said to you."

"Oh." Margaret blushed a little to be discussing such a personal subject.

"Please don't be embarrassed," said Cecilia. "Geoffrey and I were at our wits' ends, trying to figure out what was wrong."

Geoffrey adjusted his crutch. "I had a long talk with him, and explained the situation." He frowned with an echo of his old glower. "And you can be sure those gossiping maids will be discharged."

He continued to look angry for a moment or two, and Margaret was glad not to be in the maids' shoes. Then with a sigh, he added, "We should have told him long ago—not about the girl and Barnett, but about the adoption."

Shock reverberated through Margaret. What did he mean? Surely Bernard wasn't the father of? . . .

"Bernard?" she asked, trying not to let her voice tremble.

"What? Oh, no, of course not."

Margaret began to breathe again.

Now Geoffrey looked embarrassed. "Forgive me, I thought you knew. The old Lord Barnett got a servant girl with child. Jeremy is the product of that union."

This second shock, coming so soon after the first, made Margaret feel faint. "Good heavens. But how? . . ."

She could not finish the sentence, but Cecilia guessed what she was asking. "Bernard arranged it. He was very concerned about the girl. He brought her here to Aunt Letty, where she stayed for four months. By the time she had the baby, she had a sweetheart and Bernard used his entire year's allowance to give her a dowry. But then there was a little bit of trouble when the man balked over taking the baby."

Margaret remembered that Bernard had left Barnett Manor not too long after the church scene. She had always thought he had gone to London. She'd no idea . . .

"Cecilia and I, we were never blessed with children of our own," Geoffrey continued. "After my discharge, I was in a deep melancholy. And it was a very difficult adjustment for Cecilia, too. When Bernard suggested we adopt Jeremy, we agreed."

"*Bernard* suggested it?"

Geoffrey nodded. "Jeremy was a lifesaver for us both. He gave us purpose, someone we have come to love as much as if he were our own child—"

Jeremy came running back down the stairs, wrapped in a thick serviceable coat, preventing Geoffrey from saying any more. "Come on, Papa, let's go!" he cried excitedly. With an apologetic smile, Geoffrey allowed himself to be pulled away.

Margaret was dumbfounded. Given Bernard's high regard for appearances and propriety, she would have expected him to have nothing to do with the girl or her child. Obviously, the old Lord Barnett had cared nothing about their fate.

Bernard was an unusual person, she thought. She had known him for a long time, and yet sometimes she felt as if she did not know him at all.

"I must go, too, Margaret," Cecilia said. "I have a hundred things to do."

"Have you seen Bernard?"

Cecilia nodded. "I believe he is in the west parlor." With one last smile, she hurried up the stairs.

Still feeling a bit stunned, Margaret peeked into the parlor.

Aunt Letty and a little old man looked up. Aunt Letty was holding the empty jar with one arm while her free hand rested in the man's gnarled fingers. He looked even older than Aunt Letty. He was completely bald, with brown spots on his pate, and he hunched over the cane he still held even though he was sitting on the sofa next to Aunt Letty.

"Oh!" Margaret said, startled. Bernard was

nowhere in sight. "I do beg your pardon. I didn't mean to interrupt."

"Not at all, dear. I'm so glad you came down. Please come in. I want you to meet someone."

The old man leaned forward and he was standing. Or maybe bowing. "You must be Miss Westbourne, Barnett's fiancée. It's a pleasure to meet you," he wheezed.

Aunt Letty beamed. "Margaret, this is Mr. Gillingham."

"How do you do, Mr. Gillingham." Gillingham. The name was vaguely familiar. Suddenly it clicked. "Aunt Letty, surely this isn't? . . ."

"My old beau? Yes! The one I argued with when I was nineteen."

"Isn't it amazing?" Mr. Gillingham said. "Barnett invited me to come, and I knew I had to see Miss Chetwynd once more before I died." He looked fondly at his former sweetheart, who smiled back blissfully.

Margaret watched them with growing amazement. "Bernard invited you?"

"Wasn't that sly of him?" Aunt Letty said. "But I'm glad he did. As soon as I saw dear Mr. Gillingham, I popped the question!"

"Aunt Letty!" gasped Margaret. "Surely you don't mean? . . ."

"That I asked him to marry me? I do indeed. I knew the curse was broken, so why not? I'm a little old to be missish about it, don't you think?"

"You are forever young in my eyes," Mr. Gillingham interjected gallantly.

"Oh, Mr. Gillingham!" Aunt Letty giggled.

"We both knew immediately we were still in love," Mr. Gillingham said to Margaret.

"Fortunately, his wife is dead, so there is no obstacle," added Aunt Letty.

"That's wonderful. I mean, congratulations, Mr.

Gillingham. Aunt Letty, I wish you every happiness."
She hugged Aunt Letty and bent over to kiss Mr.
Gillingham on the cheek. He tottered.

"Please forgive me," he said, regaining his balance.
"It's past time for my nap. Miss Chetwynd, would you
be so kind as to summon a servant to show me to my
room?"

Gibbons appeared forthwith. Mr. Gillingham took
three steps forward, then paused to rest.

When he finally reached the door, Aunt Letty
called after him, "I will see you at dinner, dear sir. My
cook has a wonderful way with potatoes."

Mr. Gillingham paused. "Potatoes are my favorite
dish," he said, before continuing his snail-like pace
out into the hall.

"Did you want to ask me something, Margaret?"

Margaret tore her gaze away from Mr. Gillingham's retreating figure. "Er, yes. Have you seen
Bernard?"

"He is in the study, I believe. I see you still have his
watch. Be sure to give it back to him. It is the only
thing he has of his great-grandfather's."

Margaret paused. "Lord Robeson? I thought this
watch was Phillip's."

"Yes, that is who I mean. Didn't Bernard tell you?
Well, maybe he wouldn't. He's a dear boy, but he can
be a trifle stuffy at times. He doesn't like to tell anyone that his great-grandmother was unfaithful."

"His great-grandmother was . . ." Margaret's eyes
widened. "Are you saying Lord Robeson's wife had
an affair?"

"Yes, dear. With Phillip. He behaved very repre-
hensibly. Of course, Caroline was equally at fault.
Very foolish of her to get with child by a man other
than her husband."

"Phillip and Caroline had a child?"

Aunt Letty nodded. "Phillip didn't know, though.

No one knew. Lord Robeson swore Caroline to secrecy. He was furious, but he kept his mouth shut because he had five daughters and no sons and the estate was entailed. He ought to have been thankful, if you ask me, and perhaps he would have been, if the child hadn't been the spitting image of Phillip. But nothing could change the fact that he'd been cuckolded. Robeson was very glad to see Phillip hang."

"So that's why the sentence was so harsh."

"Yes." Aunt Letty frowned. "I told Caroline her husband deserved to be boiled in oil. But she said it was a worse punishment for him knowing that Phillip's son would carry the Robeson name."

Margaret could not quite take it all in. "But how do you know all this?"

"Caroline was my cousin. After Phillip died, she visited me often with little Charles. She told me the whole story."

The ramifications finally hit Margaret. "So Bernard is actually—"

"Phillip's great-grandson. Yes," Aunt Letty beamed. "I'm surprised you didn't guess. Didn't you ever notice the resemblance—especially around the eyes and nose?"

"I . . ."

"Never mind, dear. I really must go see if Mr. Gillingham has everything he needs." With a last burst of joy, Aunt Letty exclaimed, "Oh, Margaret, I'm so happy! Everything has changed now the curse is broken." She fluttered away.

Margaret barely noticed. A voice was echoing in her head.

Look at him with your heart.

Pictures flashed through her brain. Pictures of Bernard holding her arm in the middle of a swaying bridge; Bernard kneeling beside her, a butterfly in his cupped hands; Bernard challenging Mortimer to a duel to prove he wasn't a coward; Bernard saying, "I've loved you since you were sixteen and told my father he could use the services of a good gelder."

Margaret sank onto the rosewood sofa. Dear heaven, how had she been such a fool?

She loved Bernard.

She loved him because he was good and brave and kind. He was the companion of her childhood, the friend that could never be replaced. After the "incident," his absence had left a void in her life that had never been filled, that she had never even realized existed, until . . .

Until Phillip had come. Dashing, brave, exciting Phillip. He had made her laugh and cry, and infuriated her until she wanted to scream. Dear, wonderful Phillip. She loved him, too.

She loved them both.

And she had lost them both.

Tears welled up in Margaret's eyes. Why must she discover this now? What she had to do was difficult enough.

She dashed the tears away. She had to find Bernard and break the engagement. Before she lost her courage altogether.

In a dark corner of the study, Bernard sat and gazed broodingly at a smoldering log in the fireplace. After the most extraordinary night of his life, despair was now cutting him deeply, to the bone.

He had bungled everything.

Why had he pretended he didn't remember every moment of their lovemaking? The first part of the night was perhaps a bit dreamlike, but the focus had gradually sharpened, becoming more and more real as he had done everything he had longed to do for years and years. But when morning came, he had panicked, ruining everything. Margaret had obviously chosen Phillip.

Bernard pulled a packet from his vest pocket and stared at it. It had arrived today. He had meant to give it to Margaret as a surprise, but it was useless now. He had lost her.

Violently, he flung the packet away. It sailed several feet before landing on the carpet.

He was a damn fool. Phillip had been right. Even as a ghost, Phillip was more of a man than he was.

He had lost her.

What would he do now? All that was left was his work. Perhaps it was only fitting that he devote the rest of his life to studying the mating habits of the dor beetle. . . .

A glowing ember sprang out of the fire and landed on his coat sleeve. He brushed at it with his fingers, but the small spark burned through the cloth and seared his skin. A prickling pain, like pins and needles, traveled up his arm and spread throughout his body. Unconsciously he straightened his shoulders, and, with a muttered curse, inspected the small hole in his sleeve.

The door opened, sending a shaft of light across the room. A voice said, "Bernard?"

31

Margaret was confused and uncertain. She felt off-balance, as if any new shock would knock her off her feet. Almost warily, she peered around the room.

The drapes were drawn halfway, and the light was poor. She was about to leave when she caught sight of a figure seated in a shadowy corner.

"Bernard, is that you?" she asked.

He did not reply.

Margaret wasn't sure why she was so nervous. There was something in the air, a tension, but she didn't know if it was coming from Bernard or herself. Perhaps it was just that she couldn't see him clearly.

He did not move or speak, and his face remained hidden in the shadows. Her uneasiness grew. She had known him all her life, but he was a stranger. Why was he sitting there so quietly, not saying a word?

"Cecilia and Geoffrey are leaving soon for London. It's wonderful you found that post for him."

Silence.

"Geoffrey told me about your father and Jeremy. I never knew. That was very kind of you."

Silence.

"And what you did for Aunt Letty and Mr. Gillingham," she babbled. "They are already engaged!"

Silence.

She began to twist the watch in her hands. "I have your watch. I didn't realize . . . that is, Aunt Letty told me Phillip was your great-grandfather. I know you must want it back."

Why didn't he say something? Her fingers fiddled with the catch on the watch. *Click, snap. Click, snap. Click . . .*

"What do you want, Margaret?"

Even his voice sounded strange. Brusque. Quiet.

She took a deep breath.

"We made a mistake," she said in a rush. "We could never be happy because I agreed to marry you for all the wrong reasons. I thought . . . I don't know what I thought. But I know after last night we can't be married, and—" She paused to take another deep breath. Noticing the packet on the floor, she bent over and picked it up, "—and I want to break our engagement."

She looked at him, hoping he would say something. But he didn't. She wished he would speak. She was running out of breath. "After what has passed between us you will probably be relieved that I am releasing you from your promise—"

"No."

"No?" She looked at him uncertainly. "You're not relieved? Well, anyway—"

"No. I mean, no. I will not release you from our engagement."

"What?"

"Open the packet, Margaret."

Automatically, she obeyed. Inside she saw two steamer tickets booking passage to . . .

She gasped. "The Sandwich Islands? Bernard, what is this?"

He stood up and approached her, and when he moved into the light, she gasped again.

He looked three inches taller. His chin jutted out pugnaciously. His mouth was a tight, grim line. And his eyes glowered like two fiery coals.

He stopped a bare inch in front of her.

"I will not let you go. You are mine, do you hear? And whatever it takes, I will keep you. If you want to travel, then we will travel—but I go with you." His hands reached up and entwined themselves in her hair.

Speechlessly she stared up at his face.

His eyes softened to a silvery glow and his voice became a whisper. "I have loved you forever, Margaret. Ever since we were children. When my father decided to arrange our marriage, it was the happiest day of my life. And when he reneged on the agreement, it was the most miserable. But I waited, hoping that someday I would have the chance to tell you of my love."

"You never mentioned love when you proposed."

"I'm not good with words, Margaret. I doubt I ever will be. Besides, I do have my pride. You showed more enthusiasm for Jeremy's earwigs than you did for my proposal."

"That's not true!"

"It is true." He stepped forward, fitting his body against hers and tugging on her hair to tilt her face up to his. His mouth drew nearer. "I've been more than patient, but my patience is at an end. I want you to marry me, Margaret." His lips were a bare whisper away. "Marry me, and I will take you to the Sandwich Islands, or the North Pole, or the moon if that is what you want."

"But . . . but what about last night? Can you ever forgive me?"

"Dearest Margaret, I am a thousand kinds of fools.

I pretended not to remember because I was afraid I had shocked you. Now, I only want to do it again. Only this time, there will be no doubt in your mind."

His mouth closed over hers and he kissed her wildly, passionately, the skin of his jaw rasping against her cheek, his arms like a vise around her, his body hard and taut against her softer one.

She started to struggle. She broke away, staring at him. His hands were clenched on her shoulders, his face darkly flushed. They were both breathing hard.

The faint scent of vetiver and tobacco wafted upward.

She inhaled sharply and looked at him. She saw disheveled dark brown hair, and a firm but gentle mouth. She saw the slightly aquiline bent of his nose and the passionate intensity of his dark gray eyes.

Why did she feel as though she had never seen him before? No, that wasn't right, she *had* seen him like this before—he had looked exactly the same just last night.

Her heart swelled with immeasurable happiness. Flinging her arms around his neck, she cried, "Yes. Oh, yes!" And then she was kissing him back, laughing and crying at the same time.

32

They were married one week later, by special license, in the village church.

Aunt Letty smiled mistily as they recited their vows. She stroked the empty jar in her lap and whispered, "I'm so happy Bernard and Margaret are adding Eglinton to their name. The Eglinton name has not died out after all."

Next to her, Mr. Gillingham snored gently.

Jeremy was bored stiff. He wished they hadn't delayed their trip to London for this silly wedding. Mama was looking all teary-eyed and even Papa looked sort of mushy. He wished they would hurry up and finish.

Mrs. Westbourne sniffled noisily and complained to Mr. Westbourne in a low voice, "I don't know why they rushed this so. It's indecent. What will people say?"

"I don't think Margaret cares, dear," whispered Mr. Westbourne. "And perhaps she is right."

"Hmmph. I still don't like it. And why must they go to that heathenish place in China for their honeymoon? People will talk," she muttered.

"Hush, Daphne."

Bernard and Margaret turned at that moment to face the congregation. Margaret was smiling blindingly through her tears. Bernard looked as proud as if he had just discovered the mating secrets of the *Geotrupes sterocarius*.

"They make a very handsome couple, don't they?" remarked Mr. Westbourne. "Oh, look. He's kissing her."

"I can see that. He's certainly taking his time about it, too. My goodness, how long does a kiss take? For heaven's sake! What can they be thinking? Look at them! What kind of a kiss is that? Never in all my born days have I ever seen anything so . . . so improper. What will everyone think? This is too, too mortifying. Goodness gracious, aren't they *ever* going to stop? . . ."

Epilogue

On the day the wedding announcement appeared in the London Times, there was a small advertisement at the bottom of the same page:

On July 15, 1769, Roger Carew, first Earl Mortimer, testified in court that the ghost of Alicia, Lady Holwell, appeared to him. Furthermore, he claimed that the apparition spoke to him and told him that Phillip Eglinton, second Viscount Holwell, had murdered her.

One week ago, on September 1, 1847, the ghost of my grandfather, Roger, Earl Mortimer, appeared to me and told me that his entire story was a foul and accursed lie, and that Lord Holwell was innocent of any wrongdoing.

I hereby swear that the aforesaid statement is true.

—Leland Carew, second Earl Mortimer

AVAILABLE NOW

CHEYENNE AMBER by Catherine Anderson

From the bestselling author of the Comanche Trilogy and *Coming Up Roses* comes a dramatic western set in the Colorado Territory. Under normal circumstances, Laura Cheney would never have fallen in love with a rough-edged tracker. But when her infant son was kidnapped by Comancheros, she had no choice but to hire Deke Sheridan. "*Cheyenne Amber* is vivid, unforgettable, and thoroughly marvelous."—Elizabeth Lowell

MOMENTS by Georgia Bockoven

A heartwarming new novel from the author of *A Marriage of Convenience* and *The Way It Should Have Been*. Elizabeth and Amado Montoyas' happy marriage is short-lived when he inexplicably begins to pull away from her. Hurt and bewildered, she turns to Michael Logan, a man Amado thinks of as a son. Now Elizabeth is torn between two men she loves—and hiding a secret that could destroy her world forever.

TRAITOROUS HEARTS by Susan Kay Law

As the American Revolution erupted around them, Elizabeth "Bennie" Jones, the patriotic daughter of a colonial tavern owner, and Jon Leighton, a British soldier, fell desperately in love, in spite of their differences. But when Jon began to question the loyalties of her family, Bennie was torn between duty and family, honor and passion.

THE VOW by Mary Spencer

A medieval love story of a damsel in distress and her questionable knight in shining armor. Beautiful Lady Margot le Brun, the daughter of a well-landed lord, had loved Sir Eric Stavelot, a famed knight of the realm, ever since she was a child and was determined to marry him. But Eric would have none of her, fearing that secrets regarding his birth would ultimately destroy them.

MANTRAP by Louise Titchener

When Sally Dunphy's ex-boyfriend kills himself, she is convinced that there was foul play involved. She teams up with a gorgeous police detective, Duke Spikowski, and discovers suspicious goings-on surprisingly close to home. An exciting, new romantic suspense from the bestselling author of *Homebody*.

GHOSTLY ENCHANTMENT by Angie Ray

With a touch of magic, a dash of humor, and a lot of romance, an enchanting ghost story about a proper miss, her nerdy fiancé, and a debonair ghost. When Margaret Westbourne met Phillip Eglinton, she never realized a man could be so exciting, so dashing, and so . . . dead. For the first time, Margaret began to question whether she should listen to her heart and look for love instead of marrying dull, insect-loving Bernard.

COMING NEXT MONTH

THE COURT OF THREE SISTERS by Marianne William

An enthralling historical romance from the award-winning author of *Yesterday's Shadows* and *Silver Shadows*. The Court of Three Sisters was a hauntingly beautiful Italian villa where a prominent archaeologist took his three daughters: Thea, Summer, and Fanny. Into their circle came Col McCallum, who was determined to discover the real story behind the mysterious death of his mentor. Soon Col and Summer, in a race to unearth the fabulous ancient treasure that lay buried on the island, found the meaning of true love.

OUTRAGEOUS by Christina Dodd

The flamboyant Lady Marian Wenthaven, who cared nothing for the opinions of society, proudly claimed two-year-old Lionel as her illegitimate son. When she learned that Sir Griffith ap Powel, who came to visit her father's manor, was actually a spy sent by King Henry VII to watch her, she took Lionel and fled. But there was no escaping from Griffith and the powerful attraction between them.

CRAZY FOR LOVIN' YOU by Lisa G. Brown

The acclaimed author of *Billy Bob Walker Got Married* spins a tale of life and love in a small Tennessee town. After four years of exile, Terrill Carroll returns home when she learns of her mother's serious illness. Clashing with her stepfather, grieving over her mother, and trying to find a place in her family again, she turns to Jubal Kane, a man from the opposite side of the tracks who has a prison record, a bad reputation, and the face of a dark angel.

TAMING MARIAH by Lee Scofield

When Mariah kissed a stranger at the train station, everyone in the small town of Mead, Colorado, called her a hellion, but her grandfather knew she only needed to meet the right man. The black sheep son of a titled English family, Hank had come to the American West seeking adventure . . . until he kissed Mariah.

FLASH AND FIRE by Marie Ferrarella

Amanda Foster, who has learned the hard way how to make it on her own, finally lands the coveted anchor position on the five o'clock news. But when she falls for Pierce Alexander, the station's resident womanizer, is she ready to trust love again?

INDISCRETIONS by Penelope Thomas

The spellbinding story of a murder, a ghost, and a love that conquered all. During a visit to the home of enigmatic Edmund Llewelyn, Hilary Carewe uncovered a decade-old murder through rousing the spirit of Edmund's stepmother, Lily Llewelyn. As Edmund and Hilary were drawn together, the spirit grew stronger and more vindictive. No one was more affected by her presence than Hilary, whom LIly seemed determined to possess.

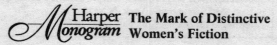 **Harper Monogram** **The Mark of Distinctive Women's Fiction**